I0636262

VEGAS WORKING GIRL

JOHN KESTNER

CITY LIGHTS
PRESS
— LAS VEGAS —

Also by John Kestner

Yesterday Rules

Vegas Working Girl is a work of fiction. Any references to historical events, real people or real places are used fictitiously. Other names, characters, places and events are products of the author's imagination, and any resemblance to actual events, places or persons, living or dead, is entirely coincidental.

Copyright © 2018 John Kestner
All rights reserved.

Published in the United States by City Lights Press, an imprint of Wolfpack Publishing, Las Vegas.

City Lights Press
An Imprint of Wolfpack Publishing
6032 Wheat Penny Avenue
Las Vegas, NV 89122

citylightspress.com

Ebook ISBN: 978-1-64119-097-8
Paperback ISBN: 978-1-64119-098-5

Library of Congress Control Number: 2018951461

For all the lost girls

The driver warned me: Be careful, scholar,
they kill in that house. I replied: If it's
for love it doesn't matter.
-Gabriel Garcia Marquez

The heart of a fool is worthless....
-Proverbs 10:19-21

VEGAS WORKING GIRL

```
┌─────────────────────────────────┐
│                1                │
│                                 │
│       Cashing Out In The Game   │
│              of Life            │
│                                 │
└─────────────────────────────────┘
```

WANT to know when I first suspected that I might be getting old?

Not adult-diaper ancient, but standing-at-the-chasm old, those first pangs of panic and fatigue that you're less than the high-living free agent you've always been. The first time an inner voice whispers, *It's over, dude.*

That moment came when I realized I was blurting out every humiliating secret I ever had. *When I was a kid, my father was an Elvis impersonator—with his own band and a stable of groupies. My hippie mother left when I was seven to find herself and, as far as I know, she's still looking. I was so clueless and paranoid at puberty that I wore two condoms for my first time, discovering that a latex tourniquet was the most effective form of birth control.* What else? I'll tell you everything! *My middle-class white guilt only goes as far as jerking off to hot black chicks on the internet during African American*

History Month. I just threw out stuff like that. Unflattering secrets, ugly memories, humiliating lessons. Just to get people laughing.

Did that make me the old dude with "nothing to prove and nothing left to lose"? Somewhere along the way, I didn't just lose my ambition and my hairline (while picking up the occasional erectile dysfunction), but did I also lose all shame? Entertaining the young-uns while inviting all ridicule as one big joke? I found myself telling everyone everything as I became the loose cannon uncle who put the whole family on edge. "Jeff's never been the same since his divorce so watch what he says around the kids." That got back to me. I heard it. Come on; I don't even drink. I've got cousins who start blurting the n-word after one beer, so let's not put me on any Child Services Watch List.

Maybe my lifelong sobriety made me even more unpredictable and embarrassing for them. I don't know. I never had the alcohol excuse.

But right now, I kept my mouth shut as I glanced around what looked like a dentist's office. Much bigger but with dull earth tones, fake plants, a framed signed photo of the Thunderbirds aerial team on the wall. Cubicles behind a reception desk. Come to think of it, my dentist's lobby was nicer than this. There weren't any issues of *Highlights for Children* here or a play area. Outside on the equally-bland exterior were the sun-bleached metal letters CLARK COUNTY CORONER'S OFFICE. I was sitting in the Las Vegas morgue. On my way in I did notice a roll-up door near the back, probably the place where the ambulances delivered the dead. If not for the letters out front and the roll-up door in the back, there was nothing to let you know that this was where they brought this city's dead. I would've designed a Transylvanian castle exterior, but my father always described me as "morbid." He knew me well enough to suggest a mortician's career because I liked to watch monster movies.

I sat silently, guarded. I didn't need anyone to tell me that when you're called to Las Vegas to identify a dead hooker, you keep your mouth shut.

———

HER BODY WAS BACK THERE SOMEWHERE. Mindy's body. She'd told me her real name a long time ago.

In the movie inside my head, she'd be under a sheet on the stainless-steel slab. Everything's in black and white, of course. If I'm going to think the word, "slab," everything turns monochromatic. Did Bogart ever play a homicide detective? I guess he can now, stepping out of the dark since there are no windows and only one naked bulb hanging over the sheet in the shape of a woman. He's smoking in here, which isn't even allowed anywhere in the building these days. Bogie snarls at me, "You got the stomach for this, kid? I've seen a hundred palookas like you go to jelly when they see someone they know on the slab." He turns to a grim-faced coroner (I'm thinking Lionel Atwill) as Lionel whips the sheet aside with a deafening blast of dramatic music—

"It's not her," I almost said aloud. I looked around with a start. I almost said that out loud! Man, what's the matter with me?

This was the reality, or at least my Vegas version of it. I

couldn't tell which was worse: my movie-fueled misconceptions of life or this crazy town's surreal realities. Yes, I was ridiculous for sitting in the lobby imagining myself in a Bogart movie, but I had just perused the gift shop in the next room. Personalized coffee mugs, souvenir scrubs, t-shirts, pens and combs. I picked out a t-shirt to buy featuring a big slot machine on the back with the words, *I CASHED OUT IN THE GAME OF LIFE – CLARK COUNTY CORONER'S OFFICE.* In this town, the city morgue had a gift shop and it was located on a street called Shadow Lane. If you don't believe me, then Google it.

How could you not picture Humphrey Bogart showing up in your life, turning everything black and white, and saying, "Let's go, kid, you're going down to Shadow Lane."

Because behind the sun-bleached sign outside and beyond the boring lobby and the delightful gift shop was a dead hooker. My life's big love story. Not the first dead hooker for this town, I was sure, but one that had a connection to me. She probably wasn't under a sheet though. I've seen enough cable TV crime shows to know that she was probably in a black plastic body bag, stored on a long sliding drawer. She would be naked, but I was sure I'd only get to see her face. God only knows how many tattoos she had by now. I got to look at her boobs once. I wondered if she still liked dark; dark red or black on her toenails.

When did I last see her? 1989? I was walking the Strip and she drove by in that piece of shit Mercedes they, Mindy and her pimp Guy Rhinehart, tried to sell me. Headlights lighted her watery blue eyes in her rearview mirror, so I didn't get a good look at her face. Just that strip of light across her frying, coked-out eyes. She didn't stop. We didn't make eye contact. I never saw her again. That was two years after we'd killed some people in the desert, but I guess that momentary passing on the Strip would've been the last actual time I saw her, which was fitting since I first met her on the Vegas Strip two years before that.

The first time I had called her up to my room like I was ordering a pizza. My topping choices were blonde, brunette or redhead. I said blonde even though I never had a preference and she showed up with hair so black that it shined like a brand-new vinyl record album. I was so touched by this girl that I pursued her for the next couple of years without ever making love to her. I didn't fuck her either. We didn't do anything. She kissed me goodbye when I first met her, but I'll get to that later. As ridiculous as it sounds, I wanted to prove that I was the Last Nice Guy on the planet; not to any showgirl or cocktail waitress but to a common Vegas whore. It wouldn't be just a very touching gesture, but it would be the Most Epic Greatest Touching Gesture of all time. A round of redemption for everyone—on me!

So, you see I am that old dude, the loose cannon uncle, just blurting out things, holding nothing back. Hoping maybe you'll see something more when you're finished laughing at me. I'd just turned forty-two, the age that Elvis Presley died and was enshrined like an entertainment god in this neon netherworld. *Bright light city gonna set my soul, Gonna set my soul on fire!* This city had it all. Tits and ass everywhere, covered in glitter and shrouded in feathers. Perfect female bodies on jumbo video screens overhead as well as cruising up and down the Strip on billboards on the back of trucks. Even the gutters had the smoldering fuck-me look from all the discarded sex ads handed out from crackhead recruits wearing orange T-shirts. The Vegas Strip was such a hot babe sanctuary that the Nevada state bird should have been a naked woman, whether she was a showgirl or a stripper or a cocktail waitress—or just the beautiful young girls who instantly look so happy to see you. The escorts, the call girls, the coke whores. It was the only place in the universe where you felt like you were walking through the opening credits of a James Bond movie and when you did walk into a casino, you *were* James Bond whether you were twenty-one or forty-two or ninety-nine. Throw in a few extra bucks and the girls will even call you Double-O Seven (they're used to numbers more than names anyway). I'd never push the fantasy that far because just being that close was exhilarating enough.

And now I was back to see another naked woman twenty years later. In the morgue. Las Vegas Jane Doe. On the Strip, she was Angelique but to me she was Mindy. Names as real as any of them, I guess. A cracked-out sex worker way past her expiration date, another dead whore but this time one with somebody willing to admit he knew her. I wondered if I was the first non-relative to show up for this sad mission. Would any relatives show up for her? What would making that call be like? How often did this happen for the bodies that turn up here?

Even though I'd been married these last few years, I'd still occasionally browse the coroner's website where discarded souls hoped for identification like a morbid Bingo game. I'd study the distorted or misshapen faces of the latest uploads and wonder if any of them could be her. Would I even be able to pick her out after all these years? Was there anything left of the girl I knew? Was it worth helping her if she was dead—

Each time I looked back on my time with her, I felt the loss and failure more deeply. Anyone can love somebody but not everyone can *save* someone. If I could slip into this town and steal one of its working girls and redeem her and fix her and love her—

I usually get that far and then I go numb with scorn and self-loathing for being so naïve to think we ever had a chance.

2

Went To Vegas

There's a thousand pretty women
waitin' out there
And they're all livin' devil-may-care
And I'm just a devil with love to spare

-Elvis Presley

JANUARY 1985

"HI," she said at the door of my hotel room and extended her hand. I clumsily gave a little shake and she held on for a moment, looking relieved. I could only imagine what she expected each time these hotel doors opened. Maybe an old, fat conventioneer who looked like J. Edgar Hoover? The bare-assed dude in a bear suit blowing that old man in *The Shining?* Jack the Ripper wearing a ball cap? There could be anything behind these doors—

"You're not a blonde," I said.

"No. Why? Is that what you asked for?"

"Yeah, come on in."

Huffing, she stomped in wearing low spike-heeled boots like the room was more hers than mine. (Now that I think about it, I guess it was). She was about as far away from a blonde as a girl could get with black jeans, a black jacket and jet-black hair. She looked like the girlfriend of a heavy metal garage band. Actually, the whole band's girlfriend. If she had been a pizza I ordered, I would've sent her back, but she was a human being and I was still in awe that I could make a phone call and conjure a real live girl into my room, so I let her in. Back in the real world, I couldn't get girls I knew to return a phone call, let alone show up at my place.

I also knew this was a mistake the moment I called because I couldn't be the kind of man I needed to be to pull off this transaction successfully. She was just as young as I was and behind that makeup and under those rocker clothes, probably a damaged soul with a hidden heart. Someone I could relate to. A victim trying to survive, a damsel who'd given up because there were only dragons now.

Seeing her as something more than just a hot young body to fuck and forget, I was already screwing up this deal.

Earlier, I'd snatched a few handbills off the Strip and smuggled them back to my room in the Stardust. These ads and business cards were everywhere as if there had been a titties-and-ass ticker tape parade every night to litter the street. My mind exploded with alarms from the moment I touched one, opening a newspaper box and snatching a selection. *WHAT ARE YOU DOING? DID ANYONE SEE YOU?* I didn't have the falsetto angel and horny devil on my shoulders from *Animal House*; I had just my own voice bawling me out, that sensible, what-shit-do-I-have-to-get-you-out-of-now speech bellowing at me all the way back to the hotel room. I think it was called my conscience.

Stepping into the Las Vegas night wasn't just entering a blinding universe of gaudy excess, it was personally connecting to a power grid that lit up every little dark corner and unspoken desire you didn't even know you had. The pulsing lights and buzzing neon were like a giant X-ray that illuminated every lust and temptation, jolting the flesh while burning away any responsibility, morality, identity. Any lofty soul was helpless at this leering circus. *Shields are down, Captain!*

I spread out the ads on the other twin bed and stared at them like the map to a bank I was casing. My sensible voice repeated over and over, *It is still against the law inside the city limits! That dumb hillbilly act won't work here, you stupid hick!* But my eyes scanned the beautiful newsprint sirens beckoning to me. These can't be the girls who would show up if I called. I recognized one of them as a *Playboy* centerfold from a few years ago, and I was relatively sure they wouldn't send her. Another red flag promptly ignored. A Chinese army parade of red flags could pass in front of me, but I'd still say, *Yep, I'm still gettin' laid.* The Boner Express ran faster and I was still going to call. I imagined a craggy old dispatcher working the switchboard as if sending a taxi cab, "Pick up at the Stardust, who wants it?"

I don't know how long I stared at the hot, sexy women gazing at me. *Hey, you'll probably get AIDS! Or rolled by her deranged black pimp who hates white boys! And then you'll get arrested—have you considered all that, Mr. Hefner?* Locked in my hotel room, the curtains all drawn, I sat there while every part of my existence argued with each other like a session of British Parliament. The brain called for order between warnings of the most severe consequences. The soul couldn't believe we were debating this. The heart didn't know what the hell it wanted, just pumping and ready to jump in any direction. But it was the southern delegation that ended up holding sway, the dishonorable John Thomas and a couple of nuts he hangs around with. Once they took the floor and made their case—

Well, I don't have to tell you who won. I made the call and she was here.

———

"I HATE it when they do that," she complained, standing between the twin beds in my hotel room. "They don't like me, so they send me when someone asks for a blonde or a redhead."

"The old lady answering the phone sounded creepy," I offered.

"She's an evil, old bitch!"

The first incredibly awkward moment passed. I wasn't J. Edgar in a fez, and I could see that she wasn't one of the air-brushed perfections from the ads either, so I wasn't reduced to basic motor skills. Since it was my first time in Vegas (twenty-one going on nine), an Ohio hick a long way from achieving double-O status, I'm sure I would have lapsed into a slack-jawed catatonic state if a Playboy centerfold showed up. I would have just blown a load at the handshake and hand over all my money. Then probably pass out. If she stuck around to go through my pockets, she wouldn't find a credit card, only a checkbook on check number four. But this was a regular girl. Dressed in cheap rocker clothes, she looked like an unskilled laborer on her way to a club on the working side of town, another pretty girl who didn't get a pretty girl's life.

I guessed late teens. Her pale skin contrasted with her bright red lipstick and those striking blue eyes. Black hair and blue eyes. I regretted saying she wasn't a blonde.

"Have a seat," I said and she sat on the other twin bed. I'd stuffed the sex ads in a drawer before she got here.

She repeated, "I hate when they do this."

"No big deal."

"You don't mind?"

"No, this is fine."

"Okay, I have to do this," she said and opened her small black purse. "Do you have a piece of paper?"

I retrieved a sheet of hotel stationary from the desk. When she took it, I noticed her red nail polish was nearly worn off. She carefully wrote, *I HEREBY RENDER THESE SERVICES—*

I craned my neck to watch her write.

"We need a contract?"

"I hate this," she muttered, concentrating on her penmanship. "Do you have the one hundred five dollars?"

I handed her five twenties and one five, the 1985 winter price for an hour with a Vegas escort.

"Okay, can you sign this here?" she handed me the pen and indicated the line she drew under our handwritten agreement.

"Sure," I said and signed *Jeffrey A. Bailey*. Yessir, my dumb ass actual name.

She stared at my scribbled handwriting with the casual concentration of a bank teller. She quickly counted the cash, then folded it in the agreement and tucked it in her purse. I did not receive a copy for my records. She turned back to me and smiled, sighing with relief, though her agitated eyes still darted around the room.

I sat down on the other bed and faced her. I couldn't believe this was happening. The thrill of kissing a beautiful stranger affected my breathing. Even my sensible voice was speechless as I trembled with anticipation.

"What do you want to do?" she asked as if the options were jigsaw puzzles, macramé or watching TV.

"What do you mean?"

"Well, do you want to walk around the casinos, do you want to talk?"

"I'm a little confused."

She took a gold case from her purse and lit up a cigarette, a practiced motion that reminded me of a thousand movies with their *Gotcha* moment. I suddenly realized that everything she said, every stage of this routine, had been a scam to get my cash—and nothing else.

"What did you think I came here for?" she asked.

Humiliated but past the point of polite society, I suggested, "To have sex?"

"That'll cost two hundred more."

"Two hundred?"

"The one hundred and five dollars went for an escort."

She tried to explain what I didn't want to hear, her eyes bouncing around the room to avoid me.

"But I don't have another two hundred dollars."

"I'm sorry," she said. "It's so misleading. I hate doing this."

I fell back on the bed and laughed, a loud, harsh, "HA!"

When I looked up at her, she was studying me through her cigarette smoke, guarded.

"I feel so stupid," I said. "I mean, this is the first time I've ever done anything like this."

"Don't feel bad. Lots of guys do the same thing."

"Yeah, but lots of guys have more money than I do."

She shrugged. "Sorry."

I laughed again, amused by my shame that I just got scammed and the weird justice that I was getting screwed without getting laid. I had a choice to make here. I could be pissed and throw her out, or I could be decent to her, which she probably wasn't used to. She'd seen a lot of drunken rages at this point but, hey, I got rooked. Why be an asshole?

I sat up. "I've paid for an hour...so tell me about yourself."

Still on guard, she gave a curt grin. At this point during our transaction, she could keep her body but her time was still mine for another fifty minutes.

"What do you want to know?" she asked, taking off her black jacket and gently folding it next to her.

"What's your name?"

"Angelique."

"That's a Kenny Loggins song."

"Who's he?"

"Did you see *Caddyshack*? He did the song the gopher danced to."

"I've seen that!"

"There's a song called 'Angelique' on one of his early albums. The name is a combination of the words 'angel' and 'devil.'"

"That's cool," she said.

"I think I read that in the liner notes."

She nodded. I doubted that she knew what liner notes were but I didn't care.

"Well, I can't get too personal because you'll either lie to me or just won't say. How long have you been doing this?"

"Two or three months."

"Do you like it?"

"It's a job."

I was certain every hooker, hitman or international drug lord said that with a shrug. *It's just a job.*

"How much of the hundred and five do you get?"

She said forty-seven dollars and change.

She didn't appear surprised by anything I asked her, and only hesitated if I queried her about her personal feelings as if nobody had ever asked her; *So, you're here to fuck me...how do you feel about that?* She said she was twenty-one and when I looked skeptical, she admitted to nineteen, which I didn't believe either. She was from Kansas City, her parents were dead, and the relatives she'd rebelled against kicked her to the streets. She had come to Vegas to become a dancer. Didn't drink or do drugs. I had no idea how much to believe.

"Don't you worry about getting hurt?" I asked.

"Sometimes."

"I mean, this is pretty dangerous. You're taking some guy's money and leaving him with an unresolved hard-on. Horny and ripped off can bring out the worst, especially if he's drunk or something." (Yes, the twenty-year-old me actually said things like "unresolved hard-on").

She smiled, but couldn't mask her worry. "I know."

"You're so young, but you sound like you've seen a lot."

She laughed, "Yeah, well, I've been through the shit!"

If I'd had the extra two hundred dollars, I'm sure I would've handed it over, so I wasn't kidding myself that I was such a nice guy. Her black hair and black clothes struck an alluring contrast between a tough street uniform with a face that looked self-conscious and even vulnerable. Of course, I'd fuck that! So, please, no nice guy points here because nice guys weren't supposed to be in these situations.

"What do you do?" she asked as she crossed her legs.

"I'm a writer."

Her darting eyes locked onto me and she stared harder at me through the cigarette smoke.

"I'm not a working writer, so it's not like I'm rich and famous," I added. "Not yet, anyway."

"I like to write poems," she sheepishly said.

"That's great. You write too."

The ice broke and the masks slipped aside. It didn't take long to go from skittish escort and jittery john to a sweet, friendly date between two kids barely out of their teens. She relaxed and I wondered how long it had been since she felt that, but she always kept an eye on the door. She said her real name was Mindy. Mindy Spires. Now that we were business partners, I told her I was really Jeffrey A. Bailey. As my dizzying lust and anxiousness abated, I was pleasantly surprised to drop some role I was supposed to play and see her now as simply a normal girl in a bad situation. If that was what she really was, and not some crazy nymphomaniac who chose this vocation, maybe she needed someone to care. Someone to rescue her and give her a way out. Maybe she needed me.

The phone rang, a loud clanging that made us both jump. I looked at it, incredulous. Between rings, I said, "Nobody knows where I am." As strange as it was to say that, something a character in a spy novel or a movie would say, it was also oddly liberating.

I was living a story now! I was one of them.

"I know who it is," she snapped and stomped over to answer it. She snatched it up.

"Hello? Yeah, I'm alright." She listened for a moment, said, "Okay," hung up.

"I have to go."

"Oh, well."

We stood and she turned to pick up her jacket.

"As an escort," I clumsily said, "do you, like, say this stuff all the time, like it's part of the job to open up like this?"

She said with emphasis, "No."

"Okay, so, what do you say about having dinner tomorrow night? Anywhere in town."

"Is tomorrow Sunday?"

"I don't know. What's today?"

"Saturday, I think."

"When the sun rises, it'll be Saturday, right?" I asked, enjoying this confusion. I was even disconnected from time and space here! I didn't know what day it was!

"The sun'll be up in a couple of hours."

"Yeah. So, tonight then. Saturday."

"I don't know. Saturday's kind of busy," she said as she slipped into her black jacket.

"Afterward, we can go to the MGM Grand and dress up like a cowboy and saloon girl for an old-time picture." I wasn't sure where that came from, or why I suddenly remembered seeing that during my earlier wanderings.

She thought about it and smiled. "I've always wanted to do that with someone."

"I like you," I blurted. "And, from the past hour, I'm tempted to say even more— "

"You don't know me."

"Do I get points for wanting to?"

She blushed.

"I can see it in your eyes," I told her. "I can see the look of someone who's...been through the shit."

"I hear what you're sayin'." She grinned.

"You look like you could tell me something."

She jotted a phone number on the napkin on the nightstand. "Gimme a call," she said. "I have one of those speakerphones."

She put her arms around me and kissed me on the lips, holding on tightly. A firm grasp with a gentle kiss, like a lover. Like someone who cared. This was not how these scenes were supposed to play. I was seriously screwing up everything.

"You take care of yourself," she whispered.

Coming from a girl whose future was so bleak and uncertain, whose life knew so much more danger and degradation than I'd ever know, it just broke my heart. *You are really screwing this up—*

Standing in the open door, I watched her disappear

into the darkness behind the hotel, her spiked heels clicking on the pavement. Wearing all that black, she vanished. I looked back at the Strip. Snowflakes drifted through the cold neon night and hit the pavement, melting instantly.

I would spend so many years trying to understand what happened that night, wondering how one spark connects a boy to a girl to the point of completely wrecking their lives. Mindy would be dead before I could even grasp the damage of my own grandiose naïveté, but at that time I thought maybe I'd find both a great love and a great story in this town. All those high hopes and crazy risks drifted down like those weird desert snowflakes disappearing into the puddles and gutters.

I watched her disappear into the darkness behind the hotel and mouthed the words, *I love you.*

This was how I chose to enter adulthood.

———

OTHER THAN BEING a complete dumb ass, what else do you need to know about me at this point?

Tall, lanky. Thin brown hair that just hangs. Several friends have told me I look like John Ritter from "Three's Company." From small-town Ohio, which should help you imagine what a sheltered innocent I was at the time. No suspenders or John Deere ball cap. Go ahead and imagine those if that helps you see me as a hopeless bumpkin. My dad really was an Elvis impersonator after my mom left on her identity quest. With no mother around, there was a complete absence of maternal influence, except for the weekend girlfriends—my dad's groupies. I'd tell a childhood friend that I thought his sister was cute and he would respond with disgust and horror. I never understood that. Every single one of these creatures was alien, unrelated and firmly sexual from day one. Any one of them could be a groupie, right?

With a father as Elvis *sans* Gladys and Priscilla, we had the Friday afternoon briefings from him to me and my little brother (fourteen months younger). The Southern drawl always got thicker as the weekend got closer: "M'kay, boys, this weekend, we're gonna have a house guest. Her name is Gloria. An' we don't need to mention Linda or Edna or Laura or the other Gloria to her."

"Why not? Don't they know each other?"

(Give me a break for asking: I was seven).

Years later I always chuckled to myself that 'house guest' was his euphemism for 'groupie.'

The facade where I grew up on Beaver Street (real name, believe it or not) looked like the other hundred-year-old homes in that town, but there was a little bit of Vegas going on in our house, right there in the cornfields of Ohio. Elvis' Vegas albums played on the hi-fi stereo, Dean Martin was on TV, and there were the house guests: sassy groupies with big boobies in halter tops and bell-bottom polyester pants wandering from the king's chamber upstairs. Sometimes smacking chewing gum and jiggling by as they strutted between me and the TV, once in a while winking. *You're gonna dig this, baby,* they appeared to be saying. Alone with the TV and stereo, I caught glimpses of the neon kingdom while my dad enjoyed the spoils of impersonating its most glittering sovereign. He even had his own band and his own fan club. I told myself that I would grow up and go there someday, and I left Beaver Street, taking my rich fantasy with me.

I wanted to be a screenwriter and write the movies that distracted me from my weird, lonely upbringing. I dropped out of college to head west in hopes of making it to Hollywood one day, ending up in Phoenix, Arizona instead. My mother and her second husband had moved there, but they soon divorced. I kept in touch with him and he invited me to Las Vegas. That's how I landed in the Stardust Hotel, amicably talking to a young escort named Mindy Spires, the girl whose street name combined angel and devil.

That was why I never judged or condemned Mindy for what she was doing in Vegas. My childhood had been a blur of groupies, Bond Girls, and *Playboy* centerfolds in the sock drawer. Who was I to judge? Everywhere else looked like Squaresville, baby, Loser Town, Clydesburg—

But now I was in the town, on that stage, part of the show. Of legal age and a free agent, a cub reporter looking for the scoop in a city that had *everything*. Love, high stakes drama, excitement, danger—I wanted my story! But, unfortunately, real life never let me create or shape or even suggest notes on it and there was no second draft.

I got what I got and I was lucky just to survive.

———

THERE WAS a glimpse of the man I should have been—but I missed it and lived to regret it.

"How was the hooker, man?" Kevin asked when I found him at a blackjack table in the casino.

"Don't waste your money," I told him. Even in Las

Vegas, it felt a little weird to hear my ex-stepfather ask me about my session with a prostitute.

Like most people in the ever-shifting hierarchy of my early life, the first "stepfather" hardly fit as a responsible parental figure. That wasn't a bad thing. Kevin Daugherty was only about twelve years older than me, but he'd been my mother's second husband. "Your mom likes 'em young," he leered at me once, long before I understood what that meant.

He was a Vietnam veteran who came back to be a mailman in West Virginia. They settled down and Mom appeared back in my life on weekends, holidays and summers. When I was in my early teens, the other mailmen who came to Mom and Kevin's house were also former military, some serving in Nam, too. They were rowdy and loved smoking weed, drinking and laughing. It was there I first heard the F-word. I heard them use it so many times in so many ways; I wondered how I got to twelve years old without having heard anyone else say this strange limitless new word. So, I grew up in two houses, one where they said that word all the time and the other where they did it.

One time the mailmen watched Super 8mm porn on the living room wall while my mother rolled her eyes and retreated to the dining room to read a book. She never said, "Jeff, come with me." No one ever said, "Hey, there's a kid here," which I thought, as the kid, was completely awesome.

Later on, in the 1980s, I was the only person who wasn't surprised when the term "going postal" was added to the lexicon after a rash of mailmen went nuts and shot up their workplace. In my part of the world, I thought everyone who came back from combat started delivering the mail. I saw the parties ramping up to that, remembering the moments when flashbacks from the bush floated to the surface and they had the thousand-yard stare that went back to Nam. But I never thought these guys were dangerous. It helped that Kevin looked like George Carlin with long thin hair and a beard, but the seeds of Going Postal had been sown in the 1970s. If it hadn't been for weed, I was sure Going Postal would've started much earlier.

Even though Kevin had always spoken to me like a fellow adult while never acting like a full-grown square himself, I still felt odd discussing hookers in Vegas with him.

"I want to hear about it," he said as he lit a cigarette, turning his attention back to the cards.

"Okay, something to talk about on the way home."

He politely blew his smoke straight up at the lights and video cameras overhead and tapped the stack of chips on the green felt table next to his ashtray.

"I'm gonna pay for this entire trip with a couple hundred left over," he said.

My mother and Kevin had a bitter, contentious divorce but I remained an aloof and isolated bystander, as I had for most of my life when it came to family, so I kept in touch with Kevin. He was one of my characters so how could I let him go? The old folks from the hills used terms like "our people" and "you're blood" but the generation that spawned me, the Boomers, laid waste to the institutions and sentiments in the 1960s, turning their attention on themselves in the 1970s. By the time I came of age in the early 80s, the concept of "family" had been completely fragmented by self-involved grown-ups, step-people, and the music of Elvis Presley. (Maybe it was the devil's music after all).

I don't personally blame Elvis. I'm actually a big fan myself. I didn't turn into him, but I could see the benefits if I ever decided to take that route.

So, since my actual kin never wasted any time moving on to new marriages and somebody else's kids, I kept in touch with my pot-smoking ex-stepfather and, in the winter of 1985, he took me to Las Vegas.

We rode in his brown, sun-faded Mercedes Benz, snaking north out of Phoenix on US 93 through the Joshua Tree Forest. I didn't ask how he got a Mercedes since I remembered that Kevin always had a cool set of wheels. When I was a kid, he usually had muscle cars like a Camaro or a GTO. He'd made the jump to a Mercedes and it was a smooth ride, even though the seats were frayed and the interior reeked of cigarettes.

At that time, US 93 consisted of two lanes winding through the mountains with dangerous curves and roller-coaster drops. Little white crosses sprouted up to signify fatalities but I never noticed any of the other batshit crazy drivers paying any heed, even with horrible skid marks to underscore the biggest clusters of crosses. I even saw a cross or two on the open stretches of that road, wondering how those people died. US 93 during that time was known as Blood Alley.

Passing all those morbid memorials and getting stuck behind lumbering semi-trucks, I was still excited about going to Vegas.

"I work with a lot of older guys at the plant," I told Kevin during the ride up (I'd just started the security gig at the nuclear power plant). "Retirees from the military and police. One of them said he worked as a cop in Vegas. He told me about a casino burning down in '58 or '59, the El Rancho or something. He told me you should've seen the people running into the burning ruins to pick through the hot coals for silver dollars. He said, 'Those sons-a-bitches were *burning* themselves to get that money!'"

After we drove over Hoover Dam, we cruised into Nevada under a flat ceiling of gray winter clouds. We crested an overpass and saw dozens of casino billboards and stoplights that stretched through a city called Henderson. Farther in the distance I saw the other city below on the desert floor. "Is that it?"

It seemed like a cluster of dreary, ordinary structures. Was reality about to rob me of my dreams of Las Vegas?

We checked into the Stardust Hotel, which I thought looked like an oversized bowling alley in the dull winter daylight. The dinging and clanging of slot machines and the metallic splashes of coins didn't completely fill the stale casino air. Not like I figured it would.

"It'll look different at night," Kevin assured me. "It turns into Vegas in the dark, just like an old whore."

Kevin took a nap but I was too wired to be there, on the dazzling Strip, the Pleasure Capital of the World, so I headed out. The sidewalk had cracks, stains and bubblegum splotches like any other city, and I buttoned my coat in the cold wind, but I was in Vegas!

I stopped to study the massive sign for the Stardust that towered over me. The lights weren't on yet; the yellow metal surface was faded and peeling. Barber poles were more dynamic. I breathed in car fumes from the slow, honking traffic and saw telephone poles and convenience stores, webs of electric wires overhead. I walked past a long row of dirty, battered newspaper boxes. Littered all around them were the thin newspapers inside each box: handbills for escorts. The only flashing lights I saw were *DON'T WALK* on the corner. I didn't have to leave Ohio to see that.

I could live without Santa, a flat tax rate or a normal family, but there better be a Las Vegas. I wanted the vibrant, surreal fantasy I'd seen in movies and on TV, and it wasn't here.

As I stood on the corner, waiting at the light, I didn't know which way to go to escape this buzzkill Clydesburg. A sleek new Jaguar slid to a stop in front of me with a stunningly-beautiful woman at the wheel. She was alone. She was everything this city wasn't. Bright red lipstick, big blonde curls, the best cleavage money could buy, and sunglasses on an overcast day. I couldn't help but gawk. She looked back at me without seeing me, her eyes hidden and her smooth face devoid of expression, like a finely-sculpted statue of perfect, indifferent beauty. Every cliché about a goddess driving a luxury car came to mind but I wondered what her real story was. She didn't wake up one day in that car.

The light changed and the Jaguar sped away. Its license plate read WINNING. Someone won that car; someone won her. Probably in that order. I looked at the loose handbills littering the ground and flapping in the cold wind, then back at the receding Jag disappearing into traffic.

For just one second in broad daylight, I felt the familiar surge of lust but also saw a selfish shadow that saw that blonde the same or less as that car. Something to be purchased, used and discarded, fucked and flung away. I was the guy who understood the score and could see what needed to be done. I almost said aloud, *I could buy you if I had the money, Ms. Jag Bait.*

But that wasn't me. I wasn't that hardened and cynical. I wasn't that selfish. I always chose to do the right thing by others. Empathize with each of those sexy little creatures I had no history or connection with. Forever the nice guy. It took me ten minutes in Las Vegas to see the man I needed to be for this whole transaction to work and to realize that man wasn't me.

Later that night I met Angelique/Mindy Spires and our twisted little love story was set in motion, but that afternoon, even before I saw it in all its nocturnal glory, I was also falling in love with a city. Surely, I didn't have to be that guy to be here. I didn't expect a Jaguar with a WINNING license plate but I didn't have to hand over my soul to enjoy this swingin' town, did I?

But a part of me still thought as I watched the blonde drive away, *I could buy you.* I shivered and looked up at the desert sky.

It was spitting snow.

```
┌─────────────────────────────────────┐
│                  3                  │
│                                     │
│        There Were Other Names       │
└─────────────────────────────────────┘
```

SOMEBODY CALLED.

That was how things hit me these days. All CAPS, like a status board in some bus terminal. This is what's going on in my life. YOU'RE GOING NOWHERE. YOU ARE ALONE. YOU HAVEN'T SPOKEN TO ANOTHER HUMAN BEING FOR TWO DAYS. GO TO WORK.

As I walked through my front door and saw the Caller ID flashing across the room, I stopped in my tracks. Maybe I would be lucky and the call would be a telemarketer. I closed and locked the door behind me before staring down at the pulsating red light as if it signaled the blinking countdown of an atomic bomb. No one in my family knew of the months of turmoil and damage going on in my household so it wouldn't be them. No news is good news to my clan. So that left either the estranged wife or even the police. How bad did my life have to get that I welcomed telemarketing hassles over the voice of the light of my life?

I pushed the Caller ID button and the number appeared.

SOMEBODY CALLED FROM LAS VEGAS.

I knew that area code. Seven-oh-two. And I knew the only person in Las Vegas with my number was Danny Olsen. We had worked security at the Los Arcos Nuclear Power Plant back in the 1980's. I was a college dropout who wanted to read and write, so I was perfectly content to sit along fences and shake door knobs all night for a living. Danny had been a Marine and moved up fast, but the blowhard corruption and mind-numbing boredom drove him to the Vegas PD.

A POLICEMAN CALLED ME FROM VEGAS.

His voice was friendly enough. Normal. "Hey, buddy, this is Danny up in Vegas. Gimme a call. Anytime tonight, no matter how late. I need to talk to you about somebody."

Unless Elvis came out of hiding, I had a pretty good idea who his "somebody" was going to be. I returned the call.

"That girl you had me look up when I first moved here," he asked, "her name was Melinda Spires, wasn't it?"

When he'd first joined the PD in the early 1990's, I'd asked him to run Mindy's name on his police computer. She had a couple of warrants for drug charges and prostitution, but nothing too serious. I remember thinking: Thank God, she wasn't connected to anything else we did!

"Sure, Mindy."

"She went by Mindy?"

"Not on the street. To me, she was Mindy. Way back when there were other names. She had several."

She's been busted. She hit bottom, she asked for me. I had a long history of relationships where I was the last call before professional help or a suicide attempt. Every damaged woman remembers the last nice-guy sap they could call after they've irretrievably fucked everything up. I had to reconcile myself to the fact that the great loves of my life were emotional saboteurs looking for a lifeboat from their latest maritime disaster, not princesses looking for a trusty white steed for a happily-ever-after. I was never the prince. I was the captain who appeared to steer for the iceberg every voyage.

"When was the last time you saw her?" he asked.

"Over fifteen years ago. In 1987."

As anxiously as I wanted to hear about her, I also quickly realized that this was a policeman calling me, not just a good friend who had been my best man at my Vegas wedding.

He said quietly, "I thought it was Mindy Spires."

Was he pausing out of consideration or was he taking notes?

"She's dead, isn't she?" I asked.

"I'm sorry, man, but we've got a Jane Doe up here, an unidentified deceased female. I hope it's not her, but maybe you can help us."

I closed my eyes and lowered my head. When I opened my eyes, I was suddenly aware of the heavy silence I'd been living with for the past few months. My marriage was in shambles. My house had been solitary confinement. On the other end of the phone line, Danny waited.

"Do you think it's her?" I finally asked.

"Well, we ran a Social on one of her IDs and the name came up Melinda Spires. That wasn't the name she was using when she died."

"What happened to her?"

"It was a homicide."

"Somebody killed her?"

"Oh, yeah."

"And you can't find anyone else? Next of kin? I mean, the last time I saw her was 1987."

She drove by me on the Strip in 1989 without seeing me, but I didn't think it was a good idea to have any association with her after 1987.

"No one can help us."

I bit my lip. I wondered if these past few months of other turmoil would leave a permanent groove in my lip from all the frustrated biting. When I tasted blood, I felt like a wild animal gnawing at his own leg in a trap.

"Wow, you remembered her name," I said.

"Well, you'd mentioned her a few times and I remember when you asked me to do a search on her back when I started."

I drew a breath, held it.

"I'll come up. I could use a road trip right now."

"That would be great," he said. "It would only take a second and we'd get a chance to visit."

"I've got the next four days off so I'll drive up."

"You guys can stay at our house," he said.

He didn't know I wasn't part of the regular married world anymore. He had no idea everything had fallen apart on my end. No one did but myself and my little fractured step-family.

"Does Allison know...about the Vegas thing?" he ventured. "About this girl?"

"She knew Mindy was one of my writing projects."

He couldn't help but emit a single laugh.

"That's what you called it?"

"That's the only thing Mindy ended up being to me," I said evenly.

"I'm sorry, man," he said.

After I hung up, I stood in the unearthly silence as if noticing it for the first time. I could see and hear and think again. The numbing, settling descent stopped and I was alive again. If I had been paralyzed by my dying marriage, then I was now returning to another love story from my past. It had ended, but it wasn't over. Not until the other survivors were dead, including Mindy. Was it her? Was it really over? Surprise, confusion. Memories flashing like lightning. I was rejoining the living again because someone was murdered.

A VEGAS POLICEMAN CALLED TODAY ABOUT A DEAD HOOKER.

I said aloud to the empty room, "The end."

———

WHAT ELSE DO you need to know about me this time? Twenty years after meeting her. The present.

Still tall. "Lanky" left when the paunch arrived after years of pizza and hot wings and anything else I felt like eating. Somehow, I still had hair, still thin but enough to keep getting a full haircut every few months. No drinking, no drugs, no kids of my own, so my hair was still brown.

There might be some gray hairs arriving if I follow through with the divorce once I get back from Vegas. *If I came back from Vegas,* I should say.

This Mindy thing could blow up into so much more. A simple divorce that wrecked me was now the least of my worries.

After throwing together a weekend suitcase, I unlocked my desk drawer and dug down for the RADIOACTIVE notebook. I'd swiped a RADIOACTIVE sticker from the nuke plant and affixed it to its cover, mostly as a joke, but now it was a very valid warning. There were no statutes of limitations for some of the crimes in my Vegas story, and what was in this notebook was ready to contaminate everything.

I had done so much stupid shit in Vegas in my search for a story and in the end, I had to hide everything. A writer with a story he could never tell.

At least until now.

———

I STOOD in the doorway of my house and wondered how many more months or years I would have hidden here from the world. I had learned nothing. With all the strangers and step-people in my life, I still ended up as a hapless stepfather who was made to feel like an alien in his own home. In my own bed, in my own skin.

Fuck it; I'm going to Vegas, baby. I thought of all the athletes who loved to cry out during their greatest victories, "I'M GOING TO DISNEYLAND!" Down here on my end of existence, we say, *Fuck it, I'm going to Vegas, baby.*

Carrying a notebook filled with incriminating confessions, leaving a home that wouldn't miss me, stepping into a homicide investigation that has a higher body count than they know about, I defiantly hit the road and sped into the desert. Let's go see Mindy.

Let it all come out now.

4

Met Some People

JANUARY 1985

JANUARY 1985

"AND, dude, I think I'm falling in love with a hooker out here," I blurted into a free phone in the Frontier Casino.

I hadn't slept. I lost all sense of time and space. I had to hang on to hygiene and motor skills in case I got a hold of her. I was running balls to the wall at full retard but I didn't care.

Kevin, my stepfather, had stumbled in around dawn, said he broke even at the tables (so much for taking home any extra money) and fell into a deep snoring sleep. He didn't even roll a doob before crashing, which was his routine. I headed out to the Strip again and lost myself in the holiday-like bustle of a Super Bowl weekend in Vegas. It certainly felt like a holiday, except the widespread cheer and goodwill to all men had more to do with nonstop partying by drunken heathens. It was all fueled by godless betting of ungodly amounts of money on a football game but I saw that every weekend could be like this, a neon blur of money, booze, sex, and fun. It was like the first Christmas after the abolition of the Naughty List as I wandered through a sea of sports jerseys and ball caps for each side in the big game.

In Caesar's Palace, a towering black football player, all muscle, jewelry and money, strutted around the casino floor wearing a suit, sunglasses, and an NFL ball cap bearing two gorgeous white girls on each arm and, no kidding, a football in one hand. He broadly smiled at any attention. I never cared about sports, so I didn't know who he was.

From the other direction, an oiled muscle man dressed like Hercules paraded with two raven-haired girls dolled up as stripper versions of Cleopatra. The toothy football player and his trophy girls passed the muscle man and his trophy queens with mutual respect, gladiators nodding and smiling at each other. Good gigs if you can get them.

Where else could you see something like that? On a Hollywood studio lot, they're just actors passing each other between sound stages. In Times Square, anyone in costume was probably homeless, crazy and smelled like piss. But in Vegas, nobody bats nor rolls an eye at anything because this could be the first city in human history to operate on the level of your craziest dream.

As I stood in Circus Circus watching frowning old people feed their retirement money into slot machines, I looked up at scantily-clad female acrobats slowly spinning upside down, hanging by their ankles and smiling seductively as they drifted by overhead. Cocktail waitresses strode by with giraffe-like grace, all cleavage and fishnet stockings and balanced drink trays. Titties getting drinks, titties orbiting overhead—it was my craziest dream, a titty world! From the moment I pulled the curtain back that first night in the Stardust, I wasn't in a real world anymore. I was someplace better.

After I inspected the peeling Stardust sign and saw the incredibly-hot Jaguar chick, I went back to the room and found Kevin still sleeping with the curtains closed. Underwhelmed by my first ten minutes in day-lit Vegas, I lay down on the other twin bed and dozed off. I woke up sometime after dark and couldn't find the light. I could see a dim glow around the closed curtains but knew it had to be after dark. Whatever it was, it was as bright as daylight seeping through the heavy curtains. Kevin was gone. Groggy, I walked to the window, sharply pulling the curtain back.

"Oh, my God," I said.

Outside, it looked like an invasion of UFO's landing on a carnival midway. The dull, ordinary city I'd seen earlier had, like some magic trick, transformed into the bright light city Elvis sang about. There you are! Viva Las Vegas! Kevin had been right: the old whore was awake and she looked spectacular.

I brushed my teeth, wetted and combed my hair and put my shoes on to dive in. The next day, I was still going. I didn't even think about getting tired. Now that I had seen Vegas at night, another cloudy winter day couldn't take me back to the drab, disappointing city of yesterday. I met Mindy and now saw this town for what it should have been to me: the location for my first real story! I felt plugged into a weird energy that overrode physical and mental fatigue. I could sleep when I left, or if I eventually died. I wasn't just another clueless tourist struck dumb in the big town. I was the lead character trying to save a damsel-in-distress. She gave me her real name and I had her personal phone number. I didn't have to deal with that gravelly-voiced old lady at escort dispatch. I wasn't one of those saps who busts a nut in some hot young girl and falls in love—we hadn't even done it yet! *I was in the spot-light, baby!*

I couldn't figure out when to call her. There were no clocks in Vegas casinos. Did Mindy have a clock in her life? When was a good time to chat with someone who was on call all the time? Someone who lived her life in increments of hours or even minutes at a time, and she probably didn't want to remember most of them.

Wandering through the Frontier Casino, I spotted a line made up of mostly elderly gamblers waiting for a complimentary phone call to anyone in the USA. As I progressed through the line, I wondered who I could call and what would I tell them? This wasn't anything I could share with anyone who cared about me since they would immediately and correctly conclude that I'd lost my mind.

When I got to the next open white phone, I called my best friend back in Ohio, Pat McCracken. I wasted no time telling him that I was falling in love with a hooker.

His lowered voice asked, "What?"

I laughed. "I know, I know—I'm cracking up in Vegas! You should see this place."

I don't think he knew what to say and I couldn't artic-ulate much with my frazzled senses and scrambled emotions. It would've been the snickering cliché to fall in love after having sex with her, but that hadn't happened and somehow, in the tits-and-ass landscape of Vegas, it made this more real.

I'd heard about the spark, the click, the fire that ignites when two lovers meet for the first time. Eyes light up, butterflies in the stomach, breath taken. Something unforeseen, uncontrolled, and usually unquestioned. Something meant to be. Was this that feeling? I knew I could be this stupid, but could my whole life suddenly take a turn into Dipshit City Limits after one meeting?

I could usually rely on my buddy Pat for at least a laugh or some incredulous mockery, but he sounded subdued and guarded as we spoke, like a friend phoning in to cheer up a hostage.

"Dude...watch what you're doing, man," he quietly said.

The last time we hung out was just before we quit college (he went back for his Ph.D., I took off out west) and suddenly I remembered a poster that hung in my dorm room: Joan Jett. The bad-ass girl rocker. Black hair, black leather clothes. Defiant, alluring, someone who couldn't be hurt anymore, someone who could hurt you back. I was so hot for her. Waking up to that poster on my wall every day in college, had I conditioned myself to fall for the first girl who showed up looking like Joan?

"Be careful, man," Pat told me.

I told him I'd call back later and hung up. I caught a few grins from the old folks in line who heard me.

In the early afternoon, the day after I arrived in town I decided to try Mindy's number. No answer. No answering service. I wandered around, jingling the change in my pocket, ready to feed it all into the pay phones like a slot machine. When would be too soon to try again? I waited a couple of hours—or what felt like a couple of hours. I got something to eat, rerunning the night before and my hour with Angelique. Those eyes. They were so blue against that pale skin, framed with that black hair.

She said she'd only been doing this for a couple of months. What kind of life could that be? What would she need to do to get out of it? When had I last slept? Unable to remember, buzzing on energy I didn't understand, I sat in a casino restaurant and considered plotting an escape for a girl I'd just met. I'd have to get an apartment for us. I was living with my mother and her third husband (he was younger too). I could only imagine how this was going to go over.

The sun was setting behind another cloudy day when I tried the number for a third or fourth time. The Vegas lights were coming on, and the weird little universe was coming back—

"Hello?"

It was a man's gruff voice, deep and croaking, the male equivalent of the frog-voiced old woman working the escort number.

"Is Angelique there?"

"She's not in. I'm taking messages for her."

"How about Mindy? Is Mindy Spires there?"

There was a long pause. Was it a mistake to use her real name? If this was her pimp, what would he do to her if he found out she was using her real name on the Strip?

"No, she's not here either. Who are you?"

"I'm Jeff. A friend."

He said he'd give her the message and asked where I was staying. When I told him, he said that if she didn't want to call me back, he'd leave a message for me himself at the front desk.

"Fair enough," I said.

"Is this about a date?"

"No, I just wanted to talk to her."

"You're the one that's leaving tomorrow."

He knew about me.

"Yes."

"Yeah, she mentioned something about you. You're twenty-one?"

"Yeah."

"She said you were really intelligent."

"Oh. She did?"

I may need her as a personal reference after this weekend.

"I'll give her the message."

"Thank you."

He hung up.

———

"YOU LOOK like the one who's been up all-night gambling," Kevin chuckled when I returned to the room after dawn.

I had actually been up for two nights, wide awake from the moment I threw open the curtains and saw the Strip in all its luminous glory. I'd spent most of the previous evening in the room at the Stardust, too excited to sleep and too dumb to question the insanity. I had a chance to see her again and I didn't want to waste that opportunity on sleep.

I would've felt more ridiculous anywhere else, but I

found it hard to be rational in a city where I could step outside and see an eighty-foot clown adorned with hundreds of thousands of lights smiling down at me. How could I know what was real at this point? *She saw that I cared since she told her pimp about me! She kissed me for free, right on the lips.* I couldn't bring myself down or turn away from the first real excitement in my life. Every night ended everywhere else except in Vegas where it was now early Sunday afternoon. I realized I couldn't last much longer.

Standing at the pay phone, my legs trembled, a completely involuntary response. Mindy answered but slurred her voice, exhausted.

"Can we meet somewhere?" I asked.

"Where do you live?"

"Phoenix, Arizona."

"Do you know where Fremont Street is?"

"No, I'm still learning the town," I said, thinking she meant a Fremont Street in Phoenix. I didn't know there was a Fremont Street in Vegas either.

She said they had kept her busy the night before and, if she had had one more job, she would've made over a thousand dollars. She apologized and then fell asleep. I could hear her breathing until someone snatched up the phone. It was the gruff voice from before: "Who is this?"

"This is Jeff. I talked to you earlier."

"Look, pal, we've been out all night and we just got in. Do you know what she's doing right now?" His voice was hostile now.

My chest sank, everything felt suddenly heavy. "No."

"She's stretched out fast asleep on the couch. What do you want? Do you want a relationship?" he asked harshly.

"Well, she doesn't want that hearts and flowers shit, do you know what I'm sayin'?"

"Yes," I said, my jaw aching.

"She's a working girl, do you understand me?"

"Yes."

"Do you know what she *does* for a living?"

The energy was gone. I was suddenly so exhausted that I thought I was going to break down and start crying as the voice angrily scolded me.

"I'm sorry," I managed to say. "I just wanted to talk to her before I left. I'm sorry I just didn't catch on to all this."

There was another long pause as I hunched into the booth.

"Where are you?" the croaking voice asked.

"I'm at the Stardust."

"Do you know where the Palm Room is?"

"No."

"Hell, ask anybody. Go there, get yourself a cup of coffee, and I'll be down to talk to you in fifteen minutes."

"Why do you want to talk to me?" I asked.

"I want to see the look in your eyes. I want to see you. Get a cup of coffee and wait."

"I don't drink coffee."

"Then get yourself some tea."

———

WHEN I TOLD Kevin that I was going to meet the hooker's pimp in the coffee shop, the amused, slightly stoned expression he'd had since hitting Vegas disappeared.

"You're *what?*"

"I know it sounds kind of crazy," I told him, "but he wants to meet me."

"What did you do? Pop her legs out of their sockets? Tell him to file for workman's comp."

"No, we didn't do anything at all."

He did an exaggerated double take.

"What?"

We checked out of our room and were planning on hanging around for the Superbowl before driving back to Phoenix that night. When I told Kevin about meeting Mindy's pimp, he turned very serious and I wondered if he was angry with me. His eyes darted around the casino as we stood in front of the Palm Room.

"Alright, look," he said. "I'll be sitting out here at a slot machine to keep an eye on him. If anything goes south, just give me a signal."

"A signal to what?"

He opened his sports coat and grabbed the handle under his arm. He drew one of the biggest, scariest-looking knives I'd ever seen.

"I'll gut the fucker before he gets the chance to do anything," Kevin said.

I was stunned. The most threatening person in Las Vegas was suddenly my ex-stepfather.

"Well...he just wants to talk."

"About what?"

"About her."

I didn't look concerned until I saw Kevin's knife. He laughed and said, "You get into the craziest shit, Jeff."

The raspy voice of Mindy's keeper had said I would know who he was: a "big ole friendly bear" wearing a fedora. There was no missing him. He came lumbering up to the entrance of the Palm Room, three-hundred and fifty pounds, older than I expected, dressed in a gray suit with a dark gray fedora on his head. I waved him over and stood to shake his hand.

"Call me Guy," he said.

He hefted himself into the booth across from me and turned both cups up to be filled with coffee. The only things small about him were his mustache and his gray eyes, which appeared to be perpetually narrowed with suspicion. The waitress filled both cups with coffee and Guy started to dump sugar into them.

"She's unique, isn't she?" he said.

I nodded, watching him empty the sugar dispenser into the coffee.

"She's prime rib for breakfast. But you can see that. I taught that girl everything she knows. I gave her that look. I had her dye her hair black to show off those blue eyes. I've got eleven thousand dollars wrapped up in her."

Although his stare was severe and sometimes hostile, the two hours we spent talking felt like a father-suitor dialogue instead of a pimp-john deal. He referred to himself as her bodyguard, chauffeur, business partner—everything but her pimp. When he praised her, he called her Angelique, and if he mentioned any personal affection, she was Mindy. I kept smiling and nodding so Kevin wouldn't barge in and slit Guy's throat.

"I fell for a hooker when I was fourteen," he told me. "I know what you're going through. Mindy's one of a kind."

"I can see that."

"When Mindy came to me, she was starving to death on the streets—her arm was this big around," he said, holding up his fingers as if holding a twig. He pointed to a plain-looking waitress nearby, "See that little gal there? I can take her and give me one month and I'll have her looking so fucking great you wouldn't believe it. And, hey, Jeff, I'll tell you this: do you know what makes the best wives?"

"Hookers?" I asked, cringing since I realized I hadn't used that word yet.

"*Ex*-hookers."

"Well, that's what I meant to say," I said, embarrassed.

"They know so many things. And, if I was twenty years younger, I'd go after Mindy. Now I'd be lying if I said I've never checked her out, but I don't sleep with her. Do you know how much money she made last night?"

"She told me over the phone nearly a thousand."

"Almost a thousand dollars in one night."

In adjusted box office receipts, that made her 1985's *Gone With The Wind.* Or *Jaws.*

The steam from both coffees rose into his face and curled up the brim of his fedora, mixing with his cigarette smoke. He looked like he was on fire as he glared at me, daring me to be impressed by her income.

"That's a lot of money."

"But I don't go for just money. Hell, I had some guy from India offer me ten thousand dollars to take her back to India and be his *Maha Rishi* or whatever the hell they have. One sociologist out of New Mexico wanted to buy a house for her, give her the title, and then he'd come and see her all the time. No, I don't go for just money. I care for Mindy."

I flashed on the scene from *Sunset Boulevard* where Max the Butler recounts all of Norma Desmond's hysterical fans to Joe Gillis that were either long gone or didn't exist.

He stared at me through narrowed eyes. "Mindy told me you wanted to be a writer, right?"

He told me several stories, most bragging about Mob connections or his own ability to make things happen. He was once arrested on six felonies and told a lawyer that he'd give his wife a fur coat if he got him out. Mindy nearly cried when Guy took her coat, but he was a free man.

"What are you really doing here?" he asked. "Jeff? That's your real name?"

"Yes, it's Jeff."

He stared, waiting.

"I'm a nice guy," I told him, "and I want to give her a nice life. I want her to be safe and happy and whole. And I want her kids to be safe and happy because they'll never know where I found her."

I wasn't sure what else to say, so I just sat there while he studied me.

"Here's what I'll do for you," he finally said. "Five hundred dollars and you've got two days with her. When she gets a call to go out, she's got to go, and she'll be gone for about an hour and a half. Now, do you want to fuck her?"

"I'm not sure how to answer that."

"Well, are you paying to fuck her or be with her? What's so hard about answering that?"

I stared back at his patient but probing eyes.

"I'm not here as a customer. I want to be someone who cares for her. If anything happens between us, I would want it to be because she wanted to."

"What if she doesn't want anything?" he asked.

"You mean if she doesn't want me?"

He shrugged.

"Then I move on. It wasn't meant to be. But that's up to her."

"It's up to *us*," he said. "Up to me first, Jeff."

I nodded.

He gave me an impressed smirk through the coffee steam and cigarette smoke.

"It may take me a while to get the money together," I said. "I'm just a security guard at a nuclear power plant."

"She told me that."

"I want to have money to do things with her. Nice things."

"Don't worry about that," he said, waving a hand. "You'll be eating steak in the Imperial Palace on Guy when you come up."

"You'd do that for me?"

"I'll tell you something, Jeff. I approve of you. That may not mean shit to you, but Mindy does what I approve of. If I don't approve of something, she don't do it. So, here's what you do: you go home and think it over. Then you write me a letter and tell me you're willing to go along with my terms. Then I'll have Mindy write you."

"Okay."

"You don't smoke?"

"No."

"No drinking and no drugs. If she tells me there's been drugs, I'll kill you."

I glanced at Kevin outside at his slot machine, staring like a patient predator. I'd never seen him like that before. Vietnam did, but I didn't.

"All right."

He smirked at me again; his eyes narrowed to slits. He pulled a pen from his jacket and wrote an address on a napkin.

"Why are you doing this for me?" I asked.

He stopped and looked at me. "When I was young, I knew a girl named Jody Spinner and I was in love with her."

He reached across the table and touched my hand.

"I didn't even do that to her and I went through hell for five years because of her. I know what you're going through. I never went after Jody. If Mindy means that much to you, then go after her, Jeff."

I wondered if he knew what that really meant. There was no role for a pimp in Happily Ever After. He would be out of a job.

"There ain't no hell like not knowing," he said. "You're a polite young man. Nice-looking too. And, if you think Mindy's the one, then don't let her go."

As we walked out of the Palm Room, I nodded to Kevin and he waved. I told Guy, "That's my stepfather."

"Hell, I'll meet him," Guy said and lumbered toward Kevin.

I introduced them. Kevin smiled guardedly. Guy pointed at Kevin and then at me, saying in his grave, dramatic way, "I want to tell you something. This guy is the first guy I've ever approved of here and that means something."

I flushed with embarrassment and glanced at the floor. Guy turned and handed me the napkin with his name and address written on it.

"Don't give this to anyone," he said.

"I won't."

Kevin stayed at the slot machine as I walked Guy to the casino exit. He turned to me at the door and held out his hand. I shook it.

"You write," he said.

"Well, sir, it's been a—-"

"Don't call me Sir, call me Guy."

He shook my hand, winked, and opened the glass doors.

"Write," he said.

I watched him walk away knowing that going after Mindy meant getting her away from him.

———

AS WE HEADED BACK to Phoenix, Kevin was silent until we made it to the state line and across Hoover Dam, our return to the real world.

"What exactly do you plan on doing up here in Vegas, Jeff?" he asked.

The Mercedes wound up past the observational parking lots over the Dam and Lake Mead. I was thinking about that large knife in Kevin's jacket. Had that always been there?

"I'm going to save someone."

We cruised into Arizona as I plotted my next visit to Las Vegas.

"What do you think he's going to say about it?"

I thought it about for a few miles.

"I don't know."

5

Radioactive Waste

APRIL 2005

THERE WAS a lot of new four-lane highway for the drive
from Phoenix to Vegas. It wasn't quite the Mad Max
mixture between a two-lane rollercoaster and a meat
grinder anymore. There were still appalling crashes and
fresh fatalities because people still drove like demented
assholes but the new wider berms were wiped clean of all
those little white crosses dotting the way twenty years
ago. Anyone wishing to designate the point of departure
for a loved one had to put up their own roadside shrine,
which they did with bigger crosses, fake flowers, candles,
and sometimes even fading photos.

I wondered if the previous little crosses were removed
by hand or just bulldozed over in the interest of progress
and expediency. Either way, I said, So long, Blood Alley.

You had your chance.

———

STANDING in the registration line at the Stardust Hotel, I stared into the casino where Guy had walked away from me after our first meeting in the Palm Room all those years ago, although it wasn't called the Palm Room anymore.

For this trip, I tried to stay at the Tropicana since the current rumors were that the Trop would be the next original casino set for demolition, but a convention on that end of the Strip jacked up the rates, so I drove to the older northern end. When I saw the Stardust, I knew I had to stay there. I was certain the hotel would be around since they'd recently added two new towers of rooms to avoid becoming the next big show of dynamite and destruction. Their rooms were eighty dollars cheaper than the Trop so I decided to stay here, the first scene of my crimes. This hotel was where I'd met Mindy, although those rooms along the Stardust's original wing had been replaced by truck bays, and this casino was where I'd first sat down with Guy, although the café had been renamed and remodeled a few times since then. Later I stopped by the café's podium and asked the older Asian man if this used to be the Palm Room. He said he hadn't been here long enough to know, but he would get his supervisor.

"How long has your supervisor been here?" I asked.

"Oh, long time. Three years."

"Nevermind."

As I stood in the slow-moving line for a room, I stared at the casino and mentally squinted into the past at the huge man in the fedora who had met me here. I was still trying to figure out why he'd let me into their lives. I was only a customer, but since I had to work overtime to come up with what he asked, I could hardly be considered a spineless sugar daddy to exploit ruthlessly. Five hundred dollars for two days with them. If he'd used Mindy's hourly rate at that time, I could have been charged a little over five thousand dollars! But there was no guarantee of sex, which was his business. Factoring in any emotions probably screwed up his billing system. I knew I was sincere about Mindy. Behind all his sales bluster and the way he referred to her as a product, his sex creation, he didn't allow me into their lives because I was seeking the greatest fuck of my life. And he couldn't possibly believe that this bumpkin kid was going to write his best-selling story—-or was he just that naïve about the business of writing?

There was also his story about Jody Spinner. Was it real or just bullshit? Did he see a reflection of his younger self in my earnest pursuit of Mindy? Was he reminded of the same illusions before this world turned him into a morbidly obese hustler on the Strip? What could happen that might lead me to such ruin as well? How does someone end up here, like *that*?

No, I think he liked me. A nice guy had wandered into their street-hustling lives of cold cash, bail bonds, and heartless hand jobs. I had been the wide-eyed rube for his swaggering underworld stories but the only time I thought he was going to turn that criminal ruthlessness on me was when he thought I was going to take her away from him. Other than that, he treated me like a friend or someone close. I thought about his life of sleazy johns and cynical cops and I knew that none of them treated anyone like him with respect. No one ever called him "sir." Maybe

Danny would back when he was a street cop, but he'd still arrest him.

When I checked in, I got a room on the thirteenth floor of one of the newer towers.

"You guys have a thirteenth floor?" I asked.

The prissy and well-groomed clerk looked like he wanted to offer me a twig of hay to chew on as I took in life in the big town.

"Yes, you're in thirteen-o-sixty-nine," he said and slid the card keys toward me. Since I planned on calling Danny from a pay phone before heading up to my room, I was also looking for quarters. I happened to be looking at the date on a quarter when I got my room key. The date on the coin was 1969.

"I'm sorry, what was that?" I asked the clerk.

"You're in room thirteen-oh-sixty-nine. Thirteenth floor, room sixty-nine."

The moment called for some Beavis and Butthead snickering—-ha! sixty-nine, twice! --but I knew what I was here to do so the coincidence of that smutty number instead felt creepy and mocking.

My room was very nice. I threw open the curtains and saw the new Wynn Hotel and Casino under construction down the Strip, rising where the Desert Inn once stood.

I dug out the RADIOACTIVE WASTE notebook (leaving the divorce packet in my bag), flopped on the big double bed, and leafed through the pages. I glanced at an old Strip handbill and tucked it back in the cover pocket. I skimmed the notes from my first trip. I used carbon paper for letter writing back then, mostly to track what I'd written to keep from repeating myself to different friends.

The letter I'd written to Guy upon returning to

Phoenix after that first trip to Vegas was dated February 6, 1985. The address was to their townhouse on Twain Avenue. I laughed several times reading it, shaking my head at its solemn and respectful tone. I wasn't writing a small-town judge for the hand of his blushing virgin daughter, I was writing a pimp about one of his whores on the Vegas Strip but you wouldn't see that from what I'd written. The one consistent passion of my life had always been writing, and it was my writing that consistently recorded just what a complete dumb ass I'd been for most of it.

P.S. Should you ever call, my mother or her live-in will take any messages if I'm not home.

I was living with my mother in '85 after following her from Ohio to Arizona. Kevin and his gutting knife split almost immediately and, just as I was a shielded child with my mother's first divorce from my father, I was kept in the dark about her divorce from my stepfather. So much of their lives never included me. All their consideration and mercy about sparing me any pain or involvement instead made me incurious and detached from the activities of my own blood relation. *That's their business.* It's not that I didn't care, I just didn't know how. *I wonder what's on TV.* I knew my apathy wasn't right (or normal), I just never knew how to feel anything else. You could get more out of a Ouija board than me. In fact, I may have been the first human being in history to say, "Sucks to be you."

Which was almost how my mother reacted when I told her about Mindy after returning from Vegas as we sat at her kitchen table. She stared through her cigarette smoke, more annoyed than angry.

"You get yourself into more shit, Jeff," she said, testy.

"That's what Kevin said."

She mashed out her cigarette. "Don't feel like you have to save this girl."

That's the line I remember the most because I *had* felt like I needed to save this girl. I yearned to prove I was worth something, that I was someone valuable who'd never made it off the bench. Here was my chance to show a heroic level of selflessness and forgiveness. There was also the love story between an exile from reality and a hooker from Las Vegas, a story of redemption that everyone could get behind. Who *wouldn't* want to see this couple succeed?

"If she's who I think she is, then she'll be worth saving."

Mom said nothing for a few moments. "I just hate to see you take such a dangerous risk."

I shrugged. "It's only for two days."

She drew in her lips and narrowed her eyes.

"Mom, I work at a nuclear power plant. I might actually be *safer* in Vegas for a couple of days."

She smirked through a pinched look of anxiety. All our bad or difficult choices hadn't made us any less of a family, they just kept us from ever having any say in each other's lives. She could have ordered me to stay away from Vegas but nobody had ever ordered her to do anything and, if they did, she didn't do it. The Sixties kids thought their rebellions were new and subversive—-until they had kids.

"By the way...did Kevin always carry a big hunting knife on him?" I casually asked.

She rolled her eyes as if I'd asked if he had some annoying habit like chewing his nails or sucking his teeth.

"He's always had that damn knife," she said. "They really needed help when they got back from Nam. I figured he would've snapped long before now." She sighed and blew smoke aside, adding, "Always ready to gut somebody."

Several questions came to mind but my expression remained impassive. He always had that knife and was always ready to "gut somebody"? Did I ever really know him? A couple of years later, Kevin met a New Age hippie chick, married her, had a kid, and moved back to West Virginia. I never saw him again, and if he ever gutted somebody, it never made the news.

After that first weekend in Vegas, I called Mindy but she said she couldn't talk long. I heard Guy cough in the background.

A few hours later, the phone rang. "This is Guy," the grating voice said. "This call is on me."

He handed the phone to Mindy and we spoke for a couple of hours.

She playfully asked, "Did you write a book about me yet?"

I wondered if she had any idea how long it took to write a book.

After a while, Guy got on the line and reiterated the terms: five hundred dollars. I would stay at their town-house; I would eat like a king. I heard her voice across the room but couldn't make it out.

Guy relayed her message, "Oh, and she wants you up here."

When I hung up, I couldn't believe how happy this

made me feel for the rest of the night. I listened to the radio and only thought about writing without actually writing a word. Anything I pecked out at this stage would be too ridiculous for even me to stomach. Phil Collins' latest song, "One More Night," was getting a lot of airplay then. It became the haunting song that made me think of her. In an instant, music meant something to me again.

When she called at the end of the week, Guy got on to offer a new deal: if I sent two hundred dollars to him, I only had to bring two hundred with me—-knocking a hundred off the original price.

"And I'll tell you something else, Jeff," he croaked in his melodramatic way of issuing a pronouncement, "I might even retire her, do you know what I mean?"

"I think so."

I rushed out the door in my uniform, running late for my evening shift at the nuke plant, but I wasn't excited, I was now suspicious. Why was Guy so good to me? Retire her? Even in my naïve euphoria, the "hearts and flowers shit" phase of this venture, I wondered how he could make such an offer, how could he give up what made him his money?

Unless he loved her too. Unless he knew what that life would do to her, and probably quickly.

I sent her a Valentine's Day card. The phone calls back and forth continued, my mother shaking her head as she handed me the phone.

Once when I called, she asked, "Jeff? Jeff who?"

"You know—-"

"Oh, Jeff in Arizona! How ya doin'?"

She said she hadn't heard from me in a while. It had only been three days, but I remembered that in that town days and nights were confusing and irrelevant, that it could feel like a week passed before someone got a decent nap—-and it didn't have to be at night. She thanked me for the Valentine's card and told me it stood on her TV.

She told me, "This makes me feel like a kid again."

It was funny to remember that now, lying on a bed in the Stardust all these years later and reading my Radioactive Waste journal: she *was* a kid then.

Mindy and Guy switched off quite a bit during our calls. Guy told me about being a fighter pilot in his younger days, but he mostly talked about his life with Mindy. "I took her to a Korean job, and there were two more of 'em hiding in the bathroom, thinkin' they only had to pay for one. I told 'em, I don't know any of your karate shit but I'll take one of you slant-eyed mother-fuckers with me. They each ended up paying and they each got a turn with her. See, I look out for her, I take care of her, but business is business."

Of the night I met Mindy, he'd said, "She never gives her personal telephone number out."

After I met Guy, she'd said, "I was so shocked, I couldn't believe it. He never gives out our address, let alone let someone come here!"

On another call, she mentioned that Cowboys, Inc., a company that ran horse-drawn carriages up and down Las Vegas Boulevard, closed down after a horse went berserk, overturned a carriage, and put a female tourist in the hospital.

"I love riding horses," she said. "That happened to me last time I was on a horse. It freaked out on me. The horse was called Rocket, and he was a rocket! Man, I thought I saw that guy in the black robe and no face and the the—"

"The sickle."

"Yeah."

"The Grim Reaper."

"Yeah. Him."

A pause. Her voice lowered. "He's gone now so I can say what I want. You know, I'll be sitting here talking and Guy'll be telling me what to say."

"Really?"

Now I wondered what was coming from her —-or him.

"I really like you, Jeff," she said quietly.

I wanted to ask; Is he still gone?

She went on, "If I didn't want to talk to you, believe me, I wouldn't be talking to you."

"I appreciate that more than you know."

"You're the first young guy I've ever met who seemed to have his head together."

I wanted to tell her that everyone I knew thought that of me as well until I'd met her. Anyone I'd confided in about her thought I'd lost my mind.

She whispered, "It's like we were supposed to meet."

We listened to the silence. How far should I go in expressing myself? Would *I love you, Mindy* be the stupidest thing in the world to say?

"Guy's thinking of opening a male escort service too," she said briskly. "But there'd be a lot of weirdos and guys calling up for guys. There's a lot of those around. What do you think?"

I got the message: Guy was back.

In the next call, I told them I had the money and we set the date. I also made the flight arrangements.

"I can't wait for you to get here," she said. "I want to have a good time. I want to laugh."

She told me they had five different phones and that she needed to switch me to another line so Guy could take a call.

"Sure."

The line clicked, but I heard her on another phone: "Hello, Donna, this is Angelique. Hello? Is anyone there?"

She returned and said, "Okay."

I heard buttons clicking and then Guy's furious voice in the background, "There's so much goddam confusion around here!"

Mindy quickly said, "Well, I gotta go."

Guy's voice was loud and livid: "*Get him off!* We just lost a date!"

I said, "I'll see you Wednesday."

"Bye-bye."

I hung up and stared at the phone. Guy sounded completely enraged, over the loss of one "date." How could he encourage something between Mindy and me? He had to know there wouldn't be any more "dates" if Mindy and I became a couple. Or did he? Could he possibly think I'd always look away as long as she brought home the cash?

My mother sat smoking at her kitchen table. I told her about the general arrangement but I didn't tell her about my own misgivings. As foolhardy as I may have been, I knew I was trying to do something good and that would be enough, that would somehow *protect* me.

After Mom and Kevin's divorce, just before my first trip to Vegas, she met an Arizona cowboy named Daryl and he soon moved in with us. A one-man Amish barn-raising crew, Daryl could use any tool, operate any machinery, and drive every type of equipment. He was always saying things that sounded like a foreign language to me--"That's the intake manifold" or "You're gonna need a twelve-volt for that." He shot any type of gun and loaded his own bullets, held fierce opinions after a few beers but always maintained a polite and humble attitude. In the Sixties, Mom's first husband, my father, became an Elvis Presley impersonator and in the Seventies, she married Kevin, the hippie-dippy mailman. In the Eighties, she fell in love with the Marlboro Man. The only pattern here was that there was no pattern. She was still looking for herself.

After that last phone call to Mindy and Guy before my flight to Vegas, I wandered outside where Daryl worked on the barn he was single-handedly building on Mom's property.

"What they have to say?" He was repairing a sander. "Your friends up north?"

"I told them I'd be up Wednesday."

I was the naïve and crazy stepson, a young writer too young to write about anything while working at an old man's security job, running off to Vegas like some misguided knight trying to rescue a hooker. Daryl had too much common sense to tolerate my idiocy for long.

He turned and said directly to me, "Look at it this way. You'll meet her for dinner somewhere and kiss her and she just got done giving some old fat guy upstairs a head job. I mean, that's blunt, but that's what she does for a living." He glared at me, defied me to be insulted or outraged.

I thought about telling him about the cheating girl-friends I'd known since moving out west, damaged single moms who'd played out that same scenario (without exchanging money, as far as I knew). Were they that much different?

"I know," I said, scolded. "But I've got to find out. I can't stop now."

I started to the house but then turned back to say, "I appreciate your honesty."

———

TWENTY YEARS LATER, I sat on the bed in the Stardust, staring at the RADIOACTIVE WASTE sticker on the journal. If I got through this trip and was allowed to leave, I vowed to burn this binder on my way back to Phoenix. Cutting all ties and destroying the evidence. The road looked darker and the future foggier now that I knew about Mindy's dead body and wondered what others they'd found to connect us. I thought of a roadside rest north of Wickenburg where I could consign this radioactive material to the flames on an outdoor grill.

The sun was sinking. I felt hungry. Danny hadn't called back so I called his cell number.

"Hey, where are you two?" he asked immediately.

I could hear other voices and police radios in the background.

"I'm at the Stardust."

"Why aren't you staying with us? You're more than welcome."

"I know, dude. I'm sorry. I just...I'm here by myself."

"Where's Allison? Couldn't she come?"

I swallowed.

"It's over. We've been separated since December."

"*What?*"

"I'm sorry I didn't tell you any earlier."

"What happened?"

"I can fill you in later. Where are you?"

"Possible crime scene. We've got a deceased person in the desert."

"It's not related to the Mindy thing, is it?"

"No, it may not even be a homicide. We find a lot of homeless out here. Alcoholics, drug addicts. They just die out here but we still have to determine if it's natural or not."

"Wow. Uhm, there's a name I can give you. I don't know if it'll help, but it was someone who had a pretty strong bond with Mindy."

He asked, "Her pimp?"

"Yeah, her business manager. Guy Reinhart."

I spelled it.

"Got it. Give me your cell phone number."

"I don't have a cell phone."

He sounded incredulous. "What?"

"I know. I'm the last man on the planet without one."

"They're hard to live without anymore."

"Unless you don't want to be found," I said.

He gave a short laugh and asked, "Why wouldn't you want to be found?"

"'Cuz I don't know who's lookin' for me. It'll be good to see you. It's been too long."

"Yeah, definitely," he said. "I'll stop by when I'm done here."

I told him my room number, then asked, "So when do you want to do this ID thing?"

"Tomorrow. I'm jammed in the morning but we can get to it in the afternoon if you're up for it."

"That's what I'm here for."

"You okay?"

"I'm okay. If it's her—-I want to see her again."

———

WAITING FOR DANNY, I stood at the window as the sun sank behind the mountains. The construction lights at the Wynn across the Strip flashed to life. The rest of the casinos were coming to life as well and the crowded street looked like a slow-moving river of white headlights next to a river of braking red tail lights. Further down, plumes of smoke rolled into the sky, signaling the first pirate show had ended at Treasure Island.

So much had changed. Construction cranes were now a permanent part of the city skyline.

When I came to town with friends in the late Eighties, when I didn't care whether it was safe for me to show my face or not, I would drive them around and give them my own personal tour.

"You see the top floor of the Desert Inn? That's where Howard Hughes lived behind heavy curtains and aluminum foil and plotted to buy all of Las Vegas."

The Desert Inn was the most recent casino to be blown off the face of the earth, detonating on October 23, 2001. Before it was obliterated, the once classy casino was dressed up for the movie *Rush Hour 2*, a lame sequel to a Jackie Chan movie that turned a few bucks. "So, they had to rape the Desert Inn before they killed it," I said when Danny told me about it.

"There's the Sands! That's where the Rat Pack held court. I've heard that it wasn't unusual for Dean Martin to come off stage between shows and deal Blackjack at one of the tables."

Blown to rubble two days before Thanksgiving, 1996, almost a year after ole Dino passed away himself. Throughout the decade, earthshaking explosions that obliterated the old Vegas hotels were just part of the show. The Dunes in '93, the Landmark in '95, the Hacienda with the Sands in '96. The Aladdin, where Elvis married Priscilla, went in '98 to make room for a bigger Aladdin.

The 1990's brought explosions and destruction right onto the Strip but that wasn't the first decade to offer such high-powered pyrotechnics. News stories, photos and postcards documented the 120 atomic bombs that blasted the desert floor about 75 miles outside of Vegas throughout the Fifties. Mushroom clouds as entertainment. Only in Vegas.

"And behind the Flamingo is Bugsy Siegel's house. The mobster credited for starting Las Vegas. Warren Beatty played him in the movie version. Bugsy had an escape tunnel built under the house just in case he needed to make a speedy getaway."

The last of the Flamingo's original buildings were razed in December of 1993. Bugsy's house was demolished to make room for another friggin' wedding chapel. At least there's a plaque acknowledging what was there, something you didn't see around town very much. I always believed that Bugsy's house should've been a museum for the Mob in Las Vegas but nobody asked me. It wasn't on that plaque but I read in an unflinching encyclopedia that "'The Flamingo' was (Bugsy's) pet name for (lover) Virginia Hill, because of her expertise at deep throat oral sex." They can dynamite every original hotel and casino on the Strip but they will never completely bury Vegas' colorful past. Nor should they.

I took one friend of mine, another Elvis fan like me, into the Hilton in the mid-Nineties to show him the grand showroom, a venue built especially for Elvis in the late Sixties. At the entrance, Plexi-glass cylinders contained a bronze statue of the fallen idol, his guitar, and one of his rhinestone jumpsuits and boots. A shrine fit for a king.

Even they were gone. At the front desk, no one could tell me what they'd done with that stuff. The casino needed to make room for another row of slot machines. The Elvis statue eventually turned up in the lobby where it stands today. If you look in the showroom, all the tables and booths have been removed and replaced with rows of movie theatre seats. You might as well be sitting in a high school auditorium.

I know, I know, the bottom line of Las Vegas is the money. Nobody cared about the history. *What happens in Vegas, stays in Vegas* was the latest tourism campaign as the city celebrated its centennial in 2005. As long as a big chunk of your cash remains inside the city limits, Vegas does just fine. If they have to bulldoze over the rest of its significant landmarks—*let it roll, baby.*

A quick rap at the door and I didn't feel so adrift and alone.

"Hey, man, how ya doin'?" Danny asked as he marched into the room.

Even dressed in T-shirt and blue jeans, Danny looked

pressed and meticulous, a toned photogenic athlete with every hair in place and a direct laser beam stare. His intensity could be intimidating and his energy exhausting but his desire to please God, along with a sharp sense of humor, gave him a genuinely humble spirit. If Danny didn't have Jesus in his heart, he probably would have been a Terminator. The only part of Danny's faith that he wasn't anxious to share was that he was a Mormon, but we never talked about that. I saw his name spelled DannyL Olsen on a work schedule once and asked him about it. He shook it off and I found out later that DannyL meant something in the Mormon faith, but I never brought it up again.

He firmly shook my hand and slapped my back with a quick hug.

With emphasis he asked again, "I mean, how are *you*?"

"I hope it's not her."

He looked the room over.

"These tower rooms are nice," he said.

We both looked at the binder on the bed and he laughed, "Radioactive Waste?"

"A sticker from the plant," I explained and felt a twinge of anxiety.

It's all going to come out now.

"Do they make you wear suits or anything?" I asked.

"For court, formal interviews, otherwise I just wear what I want."

"Cool."

He walked to the window and scanned the Strip. Danny was still in great physical shape. His hair was shorter and the goatee from his days on the Vegas P.D.'s gang unit was gone. When he turned back to me, his eyes fell on the journal.

"I don't have much time tonight," he said. "I still gotta stop by the office before I go home. I figured you guys would stay with us."

"A lot's happened this past year. It's not that I didn't want to stay at your place." I added, "I just really need to be alone right now."

I couldn't tell him that a part of me felt like radioactive waste, contaminated. I didn't want the suspicious person I felt I was—-for knowing Mindy, for knowing more--in his home, near his family. If everything went south, if the investigation dug up too much, I didn't want Danny to have to explain to the Vegas Police Department why he had me in his house. Being led out his front door in hand-cuffs would be humiliating enough.

He sat down at the table next to the windows and asked, "So... what can you tell me about Melinda and these people you knew?"

6

Carnal Etiquette

MARCH 1985

I LOST my fear somewhere over Hoover Dam.

As flight time approached for my second meeting with Mindy, I kept telling myself, *you're not going to get murdered*. I didn't know if I would board the plane or not.

Who was I kidding? Life was throwing me a bone right of the gate, giving me a story, a transaction, a mission. James Bond would do this, so stop being a pussy.

In the Bond movies, 007 always ended up with the hottest girl. In the novels, he actually fell in love with Pussy Galore or Tiffany Case but they never worked out. He rescued them from master villains, menacing hench-men, a giant octopus, whatever, but they couldn't settle down for love and domesticity.

Even as I fantasized about out-Bonding 007 by saving Angelique in real life, I also had to consider that a normal life might not be enough for her after Vegas.

After landing at McCarran Airport, I walked through the terminal with my bag, feeling like a scruffy under-dressed hick in jeans, a corduroy jacket and black biker boots. A woman behind a charity table waved a moose puppet at me and said in a silly voice, "Enjoy your stay in Las Vegas!" I bought a cloth rose at a cart selling fake flowers and called Mindy's private number from a payphone.

A half-hour later, I spotted Guy huffing through the terminal toward me, his arms swinging like boneless tentacles on each side of his massive bulk. He looked like he'd been up for a week, and spending all that in the same jacket. He had the gray fedora on his head and his eyes were completely bloodshot. He reminded me of Jackie Gleason as Minnesota Fats in *The Hustler*, except Guy played him as a pasty, gasping fat man. I wondered if I was being hustled.

"Hey," he gasped, "I told her you inherited five hundred thousand dollars and you were coming to Vegas to marry her." He winked at me.

He drove his Town car like a drunk, weaving and wandering all over the street, saying he had to wake himself up. He pulled into a Carrow's on Tropicana. "I want to talk to you before we get to the townhouse."

I thanked him for letting me come up to stay with them. He waved it off. "She made a thousand dollars last night in two and a half hours," he explained, although I had no idea what that explained.

"It takes me a month to make that much," I muttered.

"Don't worry about it."

At a booth he could fit in, he slammed cup after cup of coffee with sugar and woke himself up.

"Eat," he said.

"Flying kills my appetite," I said. So did stressful situations.

He ordered a monstrous breakfast, extra everything. They should've just pulled our table out and slid in the buffet itself.

"Let's get one thing straight," he said. "Do you remember what we agreed on?"

"Yes."

"Have you got the two hundred?"

I slipped ten folded twenty dollar bills out of my left jean pocket and slid them under my hand across the table.

"Give it to me outside," he said, lowering his voice.

I pulled the money back, my mind flashing on James Bond drawing cards from a baccarat shoe with his fingertips.

"And no sex," Guy added.

"I said, 'Only if she wants to.'"

"That's right," he nodded, "but I'm gonna tell you something, Jeff, and I ain't bullshittin' you either. What's the one thing you've got that's one step ahead of every other guy in this town?"

I shrugged.

"You haven't fucked her yet," he supplied. "Is anyone sitting behind me?"

"No."

"Okay. Mindy, on the whole, hates guys. Do you know why?"

"Because they only want her for one thing?"

"That's right! Now if you really wanna get close to her, don't fuck her. Even if she wants to."

"Even if she wants to? How do I pull that one off?"

He poured sugar into his coffees, taking my unused cup to have two at all times. "She may try and test you. She may try to find out what it is you really want from her."

"Well, I'll do my best."

I resisted the urge to salute—

"No pun intended, but don't fuck it up by fucking her. Now if you want some fucky-sucky, I can set you with someone else for that."

"Come on, Guy, that's not the point here."

He sat back, grinning and narrowing his eyes with approval.

"Tell her you said that," he told me.

I would have to wait for the proper romantic moment to say to her, *Guy offered to get me some fucky-sucky, but I said no.*

Outside our window, a Chevy convertible that had seen better days pulled up and parked with a FOR SALE sign in the window.

"Call that guy over when he comes in," Guy said, shoveling in his extra-everything breakfast. I watched the driver enter and waved him over.

He was tall, nervous, his eyes were watery and frantic, and he towered over our booth. The driver and Guy talked about the car, but the driver kept looking at me. The last time I'd seen this kind of raw desperation was from an alcoholic panhandler who broke down in front of me on a street back east when I was in college. I took pity on him and gave him a twenty-dollar bill. He tried to kiss my hand and I fled. But this guy said he could sell the car for three grand, easy, but he would take two thousand dollars cash on the spot.

"How are you going to get around?" I asked.

"I'm livin' out of my truck camper out behind the Circus Circus."

I wanted to tell him to go home before he pawns off too much to ever make it out of town, which was *right now*.

Guy ended the negotiations by shaking his head and waving his cigarette. The driver slinked off and sat at the counter.

"There's two things that I don't know if you're man enough to hear."

"Try me."

The driver came back for another deal. Eighteen hundred dollars. He and Guy bartered until Guy waved him off again.

Guy stared at me and sighed.

"Do you know why she doesn't do blacks?"

"No."

"She didn't tell you anything about it?"

"No."

"Back in Kansas City, she was raped by one when she was sixteen. *Brutally*. Tore her open, do you know what I'm saying?"

I looked outside in disgust, my eyes landing on the Chevy's FOR SALE sign. "Yes," I said.

"She spent three months in the hospital over that. And when she got out, her mother would call her a 'nigger whore' and tell her to go up to North St. Louis where she belonged. In front of nine people she called her that. She might tell you about it."

I thought, I don't want to know about this.

"I picked her up off the streets when she was on

crutches. That crazy old bitch threw Mindy out on the streets when she was on crutches with no place to go."

So, he was the one who brought her to Vegas.

Guy casually filled me in on the sad details of her life: she was born in the backseat of a car to an insane mother and alcoholic father in Missouri, that's why her birthday was in November and her birth certificate puts it in December. They went without electricity quite a bit.

"So, to her, for all purposes," he said between bites, "they are dead."

Up to this point, I felt like Mindy had sunk to the level of selling herself on the Vegas Strip. After hearing about her life before, maybe selling herself on the Strip was a step up for her.

The driver came over with another deal, which Guy shot down, and we got up to leave. I didn't find out what the other thing I wasn't "man enough" to hear was, but after hearing the first one, I decided I could go without hearing the second.

Guy stopped at a pay phone and, for a joke, called Mindy back at the townhouse and said my plane had crashed in the Rocky Mountains. Never mind that my flight was closer to Mexico than the Rockies. He said he was sorry and hung up, chuckling. "She'll probably be cryin' when we get back."

I didn't believe that. He was tipping her off, telling her we were on our way. He would be trying to orchestrate everything this visit but I'd watch her. She'd determine how I would feel.

I handed him the money in the car, low and across the seat. This time he took it.

I had officially paid my toll to the Las Vegas under-world. Hmm. I should write that down.

———

GUY WAS STILL in a joking mood when we got to the townhouse on Twain Avenue. I had been too close at the pay phone, so he couldn't openly talk to her. At their townhouse door, he grinned and asked me to wait outside for two minutes because he wanted to play the plane crash joke a step further. I'm sure he wanted to tell her that I wasn't to be just another paying customer—-or that she needed to keep stringing me along. I counted off two minutes and rapped on the door.

She was in a black swimsuit, a high-riding one that exposed her pale hips and ass.

"Hi," she smiled.

"Hey."

To this day, I remain amazed at the strength and power of desire. I had been told the worst things possible about this girl—she was a Vegas whore, for God's sake—and yet I wanted her more than my money, my future, my safety.

I handed her the cloth rose. All the crazy thoughts I had for her came flooding back. All I had to do was see her to know why I was doing this.

"Thanks." She walked over to the TV and placed it next to the Valentine's card I'd sent her. So, it was there. She said she wanted to change her clothes and padded up the stairs.

Guy draped his sports coat over a dining chair. Something in the coat clanked against the chair, metal to metal, like a gun.

"You can put your bag there," Guy said, pointing at the corner next to the sofa.

I dropped my bag and sat on the sofa. The furniture looked bland and overstuffed, exactly what I expected to belong to an obese smoker. The carpet was a dull gold shag. Thick curtains covered the windows and a cheap chandelier hung from a black chain over the black wrought-iron dining table. A monochromatic painting over the sofa looked like it had been discarded from an office waiting room.

Guy sat at the dining room table, staring at me, smoking another cigarette. After a moment, Mindy appeared at the top of the stairs. She'd changed into black jeans and a black blouse with flashy silver stripes. Our eyes locked as she came down the stairs. I stood. I've been told I'm an easy guy to read when I do show any type of thought or emotion, which doesn't happen very often. If she had doubts before, she probably knew she had me then. *Here I am, Mindy. I came for you.* She smiled.

"So," Guy said. "Our writer's here."

I couldn't take my eyes off Mindy. I could think of no words. I sat down on the sofa again.

"What have you written?" he asked.

"God, Guy," Mindy laughed. "He just got here!"

I glanced at Guy but kept staring at Mindy. She stood on the other side of the coffee table and looked happy to see me. She blushed. I didn't feel so ridiculous.

"I started writing screenplays in high school."

Guy's brow creased. "Screenplays?"

"Movie scripts. I want to be a film director one day."

"Movies?"

"I did write a novel while I was in college."

"Did you get it published?"

"I'm having a retired secretary in Phoenix help me type it up."

"What's it about?"

Mindy rolled her eyes, shook her head.

"Guy," she repeated, exasperated. "He just got here!"

I shrugged and told her, "It's okay." I turned to him. "It's a coming-of-age story about growing up in the Midwest. First love, first heartbreak."

He looked as unimpressed as I felt inadequate. Trying to explain my novel of first love in the safe small towns of Ohio to a Las Vegas pimp made it feel hokey and irrelevant. *You* are going to be my first *real* story—

Guy said, "I'd like to see it. Just to see a sample of your style."

I felt a twinge of panic and dread. It would be the same panic I'd have showing Ernest Hemingway or Norman Mailer my first Harlequin Romance novel.

"Okay. I'll see about sending you a copy when it's ready."

"First love?" Mindy asked.

"Didn't work out," I said.

"They never do," Guy grumbled with satisfaction. "Not your first ones."

Mindy asked with sarcasm, "Do any?"

"Well, since we've got company, somebody needs to go to the grocery store," Guy said, abruptly changing topics.

He didn't feel like going. He was going to send Mindy. When she asked if I could go along, there were a couple of sharp looks between them. She waved him off. His eyes narrowed.

"He can carry the beeper," Guy finally said.

As Mindy put on her spike-heeled boots, Guy explained to me that she needed to carry a beeper. In 1985 Las Vegas, a woman with a beeper meant one thing so I had to carry it.

We stopped by a shopping mall to return a tie Mindy had bought for Guy. It was only a few years after my teenage dates at Eastland Mall in Columbus, Ohio. I kept reminding myself where I was and who I was with, suppressing a bemused grin. I was a long way away from the malls of my youth.

On that first visit with them, one hour at the mall and at the grocery store was my only time alone with her. After the mall, I pushed the cart at the grocery and Mindy picked out food. I wish I had a picture of us doing this mundane chore. It represented what was supposed to come afterward: our happy ending, our life after surviving a Vegas courtship, which we never had. As she frowned at packaged meat, I fought the desire to reach out and touch her hand. Or her jet-black hair.

"Hey, this is the meaning of being Middle America here, you know?" I said. "Out doing the shopping. The normal stuff. A normal life."

She turned and smiled. Only a couple of hours into this trip and the words bellowed inside me, *Run away with me!*

We tossed food to each other, and weighed apples. I plucked one apple from the bottom and then had to jump against the display to keep them from spilling onto the floor. She laughed and fled with the cart.

In a boisterous mood, she said in the checkout line, "God, do you think that woman's wearing enough gold chains?"

I turned. That woman was standing right behind me. Older and with more gold chains than Sammy Davis Jr. and Mr. T combined, she glared at us, her mouth drawn tight.

As she drove back, I asked, "Why me, Mindy?"

She glanced at me.

"Why would you allow me into your townhouse with all the other guys you must meet, the ones with good looks and rich guys and all that. Why have anything to do with me?"

Her expression clouded over with anger as if I'd insulted her, then she looked withdrawn.

"Those guys...aren't guys," she coolly explained. "They're just customers. I only see their money. If I do see past them, I only see jerks and assholes."

"I'm sorry," I said. "This is all just really new to me." *Please run away with me.* "Okay?" I asked.

A smile flickered back onto her face. "Okay."

Back at the townhouse, things continued to go well until Guy commented, "I've got her programmed."

He was sitting at the dining table where we'd left him, smoking another cigarette as we carried in the groceries. Suddenly self-conscious about doing too much with her in front of Guy, I sat on the couch as Mindy put the groceries away in the kitchen. Guy was explaining how Mindy's thought processes worked when he said, "I've got her programmed."

She charged out of the small kitchen and cuffed Guy, smacking him up side his head. Hard.

"*I hate that word!*" she yelled.

I froze. This little teenage girl just smacked a three-hundred and fifty-pound man as hard as she could. I wondered if he was going to snap her in half. But he didn't move. He only opened his eyes and continued after she stomped back into the kitchen, slamming the refrigerator door and cabinets.

"She doesn't like that word, but that's what it means," he said. "I know everything she's going to say and I tell her what she says to people."

I could see her in the kitchen. She turned to me and rolled her eyes.

Guy raised his voice as he called out to her, "What do you see when you see a john? Not Jeff, but a john."

"His money," she answered.

"Do you feel anything?"

"No," she said, her eyes locked on me.

"What do you try and do?"

"I try to get his money without doing anything."

She deliberately kept her voice at a robotic monotone, all the while mischievously grinning at me.

"That's right," Guy said, grinning too. "That's programming."

"I hate that word!" she yelled again.

As we hung out for the rest of the afternoon, I noticed that it wasn't unusual for her to suddenly attack Guy and they would wrestle like a couple of kids. While he was piled on the couch on his side, she would walk in and suddenly lunge at him, landing on top to smack, pinch, pull hair and pound on him. Most of which he took. If he retaliated, he would lock on to her ankle and tickle her feet. I was sitting in the chair across the coffee table the second or third time this happened and decided to cover the event for the World Wrestling Federation.

In an announcer's impassioned voice, I said, "She's not trying to win, she's just trying to hurt...this...man! Why doesn't the ref stop this match!"

They both stopped and looked over at me with curious expressions.

"I went to a couple of wrestling matches once," I said, shrugging.

They laughed.

————

BEFORE IT GOT MUCH LATER–-AND before the evening would really start—-Guy wanted something to eat, so we went to a Sizzlers steakhouse nearby. We had shrimp and steak. Guy sent his steak back when it wasn't big enough and ordered more. He also ate what Mindy didn't eat of hers.

A van filled with sorority girls from the University of Nevada Las Vegas unloaded outside and they put tables together to accommodate them nearby. Mindy glared at them as they chattered and giggled. She eventually said, "I hate girls like that."

As someone who quit college because he was having too much fun, I was wondering how in the world someone could remain a college student with decent grades in Las Vegas. It was like trying to solve Algebra problems in the Playboy Mansion.

I leaned toward Mindy to say, "Hey, Life never asked them to be any more than what they are." I glanced at them and shrugged, "They don't know any better."

Mindy looked at me as if those clueless coeds weren't so much better than her now, as if something that bothered her now made sense.

"Right," she said, her mood improving.

I glanced at Guy. He was watching me, too.

Back at the townhouse, we digested our meals in front of the TV. As Guy flipped through channels, he landed on *Last Tango in Paris* on the Playboy Channel.

"Hey, this is one of my favorite movies," I said. "Brando's awesome in this."

Guy left it there. Upon seeing the first subtitles, Mindy said she had to get ready for her evening and headed upstairs. I could tell they weren't into it. Mindy returned in a robe after a shower. We were all talking when they noticed the scene where Maria Schneider masturbates on a mattress while Brando breaks down and cries in the next room over his dead wife, a suicide. I grimaced. Great timing. Our conversation stopped dead.

Guy finally said, "Favorite movie? This boy's some kind of pervert."

But it was mostly meant as a joke. I generally impressed them with my comments and answers. When I did, either one of them would say, "There's another one," and make an imaginary mark with their finger. Mindy headed back upstairs. I felt like they were studying me as much as I was observing them.

I was still explaining what it was I liked about the movie when I noticed Guy looking up the stairs. I stopped talking and looked up too. I know my mouth was open.

She stood at the top of the stairs and stared down at us. She wore a silver dress that glittered with each move. Her silky legs, shining in sheer black hose, stepped out of the slits in the dress as she descended. She had a boa of black and white feathers around her shoulders. The blue of her mascara and the bright red lipstick made her skin look like a pale marble. This was Angelique. This was the woman who pulled down thousands of dollars a night.

"Wow," I said quietly.

"Look at him," I heard Guy saying. "All moon eyes."

I glanced at him. He'd been watching me the whole time.

———

THEY LET me ride around with them that first night, cruising from casino to casino in the big Town car. Mindy changed out of the dress—she just wanted me to see her as Angelique—and she put on a dark blue top, black jeans, and a black jacket. Her real working clothes. They complained about the escort service they worked through. At one point, they had me call the service on a pay phone for a price check just to hear that gravelly old voice again. They called her Gravel Gerty. I hung up and turned to them in the car.

"Am I supposed to get turned on by that voice?" I asked. "That's the voice you hear through the door when you're trying to rub one out in your grandmother's bathroom."

"This boy is a pervert," Guy said, nodding.

The service didn't like Mindy and they hated Guy for having so much control over her.

While Mindy was on a job, I sat with Guy in a casino parking lot. I felt like a spy, a deep cover agent, studying some nefarious operation from the inside to find the right moment to strike, to pull her out of here, and the man I was to betray was sitting right next to me.

"I don't let her talk to the other whores. Because if she's around them, eventually she'll be one of those bitches."

"And they don't like you?"

"They hate my guts! Just to get back at me, they'll send Mindy over to a nigger's room. You watch. It'll happen."

I winced, as I always did when I heard that slur. That was a dirty word in my house, growing up, as bad as any other. Within fifteen minutes, the time it took for Mindy to walk up to the room and back, she returned: that's exactly what they had done. If a black guy opened the door, she turned and walked away.

As we drove off, Guy said, "Three of the girls she works with lives with niggers. Nothing else fits anymore, and they're the only thing that can satisfy them."

I said, "I thought that was a myth."

"Oh, no," Guy said.

I looked at Mindy between us. She was shaking her head and staring straight ahead.

Guy added, "And Orientals don't have any dick at all. I just love Koreans. They just line up and giggle and hand over their money."

He laughed. And I forced a laugh.

They needed to go by the escort service office, and they decided to drop me off at the townhouse until they got back. They gave me a key, and I headed in. I stretched out on the couch and, ten minutes later, the phone rang. I forgot to ask what to do about the phone. I closed my eyes and counted seven rings before it stopped.

Guy stopped back alone to pick me up. We cruised

around until Mindy's voice came over the beeper: "Guy, pick me up now, pick me up *now*, pick me up now."

We swung by the Dunes. I got out, allowed her in between us, and we took off. She said she had another call with another girl downtown on Fremont Street at the Golden Nugget. Guy drove the big Town car down Las Vegas Boulevard. I kept thinking to myself, *This is crazy.*

When I'd been there with Kevin, we had never made it down to Fremont Street. I'd missed seeing Vegas Vic, the famous cowboy sign I'd seen in so many movies. I had looked for it on the Strip and had left wondering about Vic and the other landmark casinos. I'd walked from one end of the Strip to the other. Was the cowboy sign gone?

The Town car turned the corner onto Fremont Street and

I was stunned into saying, "There it is." I'd never seen so many lights in my life. It was like gliding into another universe of blinding colors and pure energy. Almost sci-fi. I thought of the line I could never hear from *2001: A Space Odyssey* (even though all my Kubrick lit says is there): "My God, it's full of stars." You could still drive right into them then, before they closed the street to cars and built the canopy that added twelve million more lights to that galaxy. It just doesn't have the same effect walking into it than driving into it. Mindy and Guy were oblivious as we dropped her off at the Golden Nugget, but I will never forget that moment for the rest of my life.

On the way back to the townhouse, Guy explained to me the difference between a working girl and a whore. A working girl will do what she must for the money and put out the least amount of effort.

"Isn't that all women in general?" I asked, deadpan.

Guy's flabby jowls flapped slightly, confused.

"That's a joke," I muttered.

"A whore will fuck anything for a buck." Mindy was a working girl.

He added, "Now don't ever call her a whore."

"I wouldn't do that, Guy," I said, shocked that he felt the need to warn me.

We had just walked into the townhouse when the phone rang. It was Mindy. Something had gone wrong and he was trying to calm her down. He told her to get out of the Nugget immediately. Guy hung up, fuming. The other girl had botched the deal and taken off with all the money.

We hurried out to the car and Guy squealed the tires out of the parking lot.

"*That cunt!*" he roared, sailing through traffic. "She's the biggest fucking whore in Vegas! She's been eighty-six'd from every hotel on the Strip—-and the cops know her and her car!"

I held on to the door handle, watching cars whizzing past us and lots of yellow lights changing overhead.

"She drives a white Camaro with spoked wheels and sticks out like a goddam thumb! And she fucks *everything!*"

We pulled up to the curb, I jumped out, Mindy stepped in, and I got back in before Guy sped us out of there.

"What happened?" Guy snapped at her.

"Well, I went up to the room—-"

Guy raised a hand to cut her off and leaned forward to bark at me, "I don't allow this whore to be seen with Mindy so Mindy always meets her at the room!"

Annoyed by Guy's interruption, Mindy glared at me. "So, I get up there and there's only one guy inside. He wanted two girls. She was there," Mindy said evenly. "So, she picks up the money and goes into the bathroom and stuffs it somewhere. Then she walks out."

"No more doubles!" Guy raged.

Mindy shook her head.

They went directly to the escort service and had me wait outside. It was just a business park, not too far from a busy boulevard. I leaned against the Town car and watched the traffic go by. I had left Ohio to write movies in Hollywood, and made it as far as this. There were a lot less interesting places to be than this, I guess. *Get me back to those lights—*

"Women can't show other women what pleases a man," Guy pontificated while cruising around during another job. "A man has to do that. The only thing a woman knows how to do is lay down and spread her legs. Have you ever heard of a 'snapping pussy'?"

Before I could answer, he went into a racking cough, and I wondered if he was going to crash into another car or a telephone pole.

"That's a pretty bad cough you've got there," I noted.

"Yeah."

"Maybe you should do something to get better."

I was referring to his nonstop chain smoking.

"Ah! Some doctor said I ain't got too much longer to live."

I was stunned. He was obviously in terrible shape, morbidly obese and huffing and wheezing after any minimal movements but it was the first he'd said anything about his own health.

We picked her up and it was another no-go. When the customer found out that he would not be getting anything but time with her for one hundred and five, he refused to pay even that. For whatever reason, she'd let that out before collecting the cash.

We went to a coffee shop a few blocks from the Strip. As the waitress led us to a table, Guy charged past her and went to the booth he wanted, where the windows ended. Mindy shrugged at the outraged waitress and said, "He sits where he wants to."

Chatting over our drinks, we spotted a police cruiser outside pulling in. I was sitting against the wall with Mindy next to me. Guy sat across from us next to the last window. As the cruiser passed behind the wall next to me, I did a silly wave. Both Guy and Mindy winced. It freaked them out.

"You can get arrested for *nothing*," Guy hissed. "Let alone pulling stupid shit like that!"

I told them and then demonstrated that the cruiser was behind the wall next to me when I waved, so the cops never saw a thing. Eventually they relaxed, and we were back to talking about movies or telling jokes.

She got a call at the Hilton, and we headed over.

"That's where Elvis performed," I said.

"Elvis was a punk," Guy muttered.

I let it go.

Security was tighter there, they told me, so they wanted me to walk in with Mindy. Like we were a couple. "They know what girls by themselves comin' in at this hour are there for," Guy grumbled.

Guy dropped us off and we walked in. As we approached the entrance, she said, "Will you hold my hand?"

I smiled at her. "I thought you'd never ask."

So, we walked through the casino, heading for the elevators, holding hands. Like a couple. Not just an escort and her—

Was there some derogatory name for a sap like me? A guy who covers for a girl who hustles in their hotels? It wouldn't be a cuckold because they at least sampled the goods at some point, right?

"Wait for me," she said.

I glanced around and said, "Kiss me. Let's really look like a couple."

Her eyes looked across the casino.

"He's with the car," I whispered.

"Don't be so sure."

She grinned, stepped forward, and kissed me. I reached for her arms but she stepped back and walked toward the elevators. Still grinning. As far as I knew, she hadn't kissed anyone else that night. This was long before I learned that most escorts never did kiss. Not the safe ones, anyway.

I sat at a slot machine where I could see the elevators. After a cocktail waitress asked me if I was okay or if I needed a drink, I declined but fished around in my pockets for change. Three quarters. I waited ten to fifteen minutes to feed each one into the machine, so it looked like I was actually doing something.

I thought about what my mother's boyfriend said, "She'll be up there giving some fat old man a head job--"

She came out of the elevator. I jumped up to join her.

"Asshole," she said, referring to the guy she just left. "They're crazy if they think I'm gonna do anything for a hundred dollars!"

I remembered that I wanted to do more for a hundred

dollars when I met her. As I thought about what Daryl had said ("head job!"), I wasn't bothered by kissing her tonight: I kissed the lips of a little hustler who ran off with the cash, not a whore who'd earned it.

We saw the Town car in the parking lot and started toward it. Guy's window went down and he said, "Hurry up!"

We jumped in the car and he threw it in drive.

"Security's on to us!" he said.

I glanced back and saw a Security car coming up the aisle with its lights off. Guy swung the Town car around and gassed it down the aisle next to it. He careened us over a curb and out onto the entrance road. I saw another Security car with its headlights on racing to catch up. We squealed tires turning out onto the boulevard and zoomed away.

But I was thinking, "At least I got to hold her hand and kiss her."

We were back at the townhouse when she took another call. A guy at the Tropicana. She called him back and asked him to meet her in the lobby. He didn't want to. She insisted on meeting him first, so they settled on the café. She told him to look for a girl with black hair, blue shirt, black jacket. She hung up and distastefully said to us, "I think he's black."

Guy and I went into the café first and took seats at a table. He ordered coffee and then said to me, "Don't even look at her." I drank a Coke and watched over his shoulder. This felt like being a spy. I remembered Sean Connery as James Bond saying in *Diamonds Are Forever*, "I understand the Hotel Tropicana is quite comfortable...."

Then I spied another woman sitting near the entrance.

Black hair and blue shirt. Mindy entered the café and took a seat across the room from us away from the other girl dressed like her. My eyes met Mindy's and I made a subtle gesture to the other girl. She looked at her but didn't see the connection.

A nervous, lanky black guy came bounding into the café wearing sweat pants and a red and white sports jersey. He eagerly went straight to the wrong girl and plopped down right next to her. They talked for a few moments. I would've paid one hundred dollars to hear that conversation, which appeared light and amiable. After a few moments, he got up and bounded back out. I tried not to laugh out loud. Mindy shrugged. She still hadn't noticed that a description of her matched the other woman.

We finished our drinks and, as we were all leaving, I noticed another black man, sharply-dressed in a suit, had joined that other girl.

Mindy called him back from a pay phone and said there had been a mix-up, but he still wanted to see her. She said she was going off duty, and he should call for another girl.

The sun was coming up. Back at the townhouse Guy dropped on creaking dining table chair, his back to the wall, smoking a cigarette. Watching. Mindy got a blanket for me and asked if I needed sheets for sleeping on the couch. Blanket would be fine. I was exhausted, but her eyes were bright, alert, tense. She was trying to communicate something to me. I was too tired to decipher it. She knew Guy was watching her too.

"Good night," I said.

She smiled and went upstairs. What had been left

unsaid? Did she just want to be held? The second-floor bathroom light turned on and, from where I slumped on the couch, I could see her shadow undressing on the wall high above me. Guy finished his cigarette but didn't go up until the bathroom light turned off. I could hear them talking but couldn't make any of it out.

Earlier that night she'd said, "Shit," and he'd told her to watch her mouth. As they grew more comfortable around me, he didn't mention anything more about her language. He certainly didn't hold back his own. When she answered the phone in front of me and openly discussed prices, she hung up and was promptly berated by an irritated Guy: "From now on, you take your calls upstairs!"

I butted in and said, "Hey, that's okay. I want to get to know you. You don't have to hide anything from me."

––––––––––

THEY DIDN'T HIDE anything from me.

Mindy was an escort, a Vegas sex worker, a young hustler who went alone to hotel rooms and came back with the cash, no questions asked unless by Guy, who wanted to know everything. She did what she had to do to get the money and then get the hell out. If a john who otherwise repulsed her called her bluff by bellying up her spontaneously exorbitant price—-well, she ended up with the money. Overtime, hazard pay, whatever you want to call it. The IRS wasn't going to hear about it.

How did that make me feel? Did I have the right to feel pangs of jealousy for these desperate strangers in hotel rooms, the "old fat guy upstairs who's getting a head job"?

I shrugged it off. I knew how she felt about those

people in the rooms. They were suckers, assholes, lonely strangers who would never get close to her. She had nothing but contempt and disgust for those who could afford her and she laughed while escaping with what she took from those who couldn't pay for more than one hour of her company. None of them were ever getting *her*. Mindy's body might be for sale but that was it. Although her heart and soul might be eroding and crumbling like a sand castle in the evening tide, I doubt that anybody came to Vegas looking for those parts of her anyway. In fact, I doubted if her customers could've even picked her out of a crowd after blowing their nut in one of the condoms from her purse—-they got what they wanted and sent her away.

But I had a chance to save all of her. I was willing to overlook so much just to be near her. I was hopeful enough to wait patiently to make love to her someday, even as she sold her ass all over the city of sin. Of course, I didn't delude myself. I knew she was a whore. I also never forgot that no matter how much I wrapped myself in the lofty robes of a long-suffering martyr for true love, if I had had the two hundred more she wanted that first night, I would've been one of those suckers, those assholes, another lonely stranger, and I would've lost her forever.

———

I WOKE up four hours later. I tried to go back to sleep but couldn't. They left their bedroom door open so I listened to Guy loudly snore for over an hour. Once in a while, Mindy would blurt out something. She even swore in her sleep. She sounded like she was frequently jolted from nightmares. I wondered if her nightmares would go away if I took her away from Vegas, from Guy.

I smiled as I thought of how Guy dispensed his wisdom upon me no matter how laughably simple it often sounded. With only some high school fumbling and reckless college humping under my belt, I probably did look like a small-town bumpkin who knew nothing, but it was funny how Guy made selling a girl's ass sound as complex and ambitious as splitting an atom or running a corporation. My small-town manners forced me to try to appear as the grateful pupil at all times. I even tried to keep a straight face.

The phone rang and woke them both up. I could hear Mindy, groggy, tell the caller, "Well, it's one hundred and five for an hour and whatever we decide on...."

Guy dropped down each step like a hulking Sumo wrestler in a muscle T and striped boxers. At the bottom of the stairs, he put his back to a wooden post under the loft and rubbed back and forth, reminding me of how he called himself a "big, ole friendly bear" when we first met.

I quickly showered and sat on the couch. Guy sat at the table, drinking coffee and trying to rouse himself. Mindy appeared at the top of the stairs and said she wanted to go horseback riding.

"I've never done it," I said, "but I'll try it."

She showered and came down, wearing a white blouse pulled down off her shoulders. She looked better than she had going out to her jobs the night before. Guy's eyes narrowed as she walked around him and into the kitchen.

"You're not wearing that like that," he told her.

"Like what?"

"Like that. Down over your shoulders."

She snapped from the kitchen, "I always wear it like that."

"Melinda," Guy said, gritting his teeth. "I never let you wear that blouse like that."

"Bullshit!" she yelled and charged out of the kitchen and up the stairs.

He looked to me. "I never let her wear that like that...never."

Her voice was furious from the bedroom upstairs, "Fuck you, Guy! I don't want to hear that shit!"

She came back down the stairs with her black boots and stood at the bottom of the steps.

"You let me wear this like this in broad daylight," she shouted, to the point of tears. "When we went to the grocery store, and I had it like that and you said it looked nice that way."

Guy turned to her and, with as much cruelty as he could muster, said, "You look like a Mexican *whore*."

Silence. He'd told me to never, *ever* call her that. My eyes moved to her. She dropped the boots and sprang at Guy. She smacked him across the face with a sound as loud as their shouting. I was stunned, immobilized. She really clocked him.

"Don't you say that to me!" she shrieked, completely hysterical. *"You don't say that to me!"*

Standing next to him, she smacked him across the top of his head several more times. And he took it. He only put his arms up to deflect her, but never retaliated, never struck back. She turned her face away from me and rushed back upstairs. I stood up.

Guy kept his eyes closed and sighed. Smoldering but

controlled, he said evenly, "I never let her wear it like that."

She screamed from upstairs, *"Fuck your shit, Guy!"*

"Our neighbors are faggots," Guy said to me. "Do you know how we know? Because we can hear them through the walls when they just talk normal."

"Fuck them!"

I was at the top of the stairs when Guy probably opened his eyes and noticed I was gone. I got to the bedroom door and saw Mindy standing in the dark bedroom on the other side of the bed. She looked frazzled, wiping away tears. She saw me and looked surprised. I just wanted to go to her—-

"Get down here, Jeff," Guy's voice boomed through the townhouse. I was sure the gay neighbors heard him, too.

Mindy and I stared at each other. I started to say something—-

"Now," Guy said from below.

I turned. At the top of the stairs, I stopped and looked down at him at the table. His jacket was still draped over the chair behind him but a German Luger handgun was on the table in front of him. I knew he carried something when I'd heard it clink against the chair earlier. I went downstairs because I didn't want the neighbors to hear it fire a shot. Especially at me.

APRIL 2005

DANNY SAT up in the chair, thought about how to react, then laughed.

"So, you were *staying* with these people?" he asked. "For their *story?*"

"I know it sounds crazy but I wanted to write, so I had to find something to write about."

Danny laughed again and said, "You're a dork!"

"Yeah. Pretty much."

"You could've gotten yourself killed."

"I'm not the reckless dork I used to be," I told him.

He stood up and glanced at the night outside.

"I need to get going," he said.

"Do you want to get something to eat?"

"I can't. I've got to stop by my office before I can go home. We can do this ID tomorrow."

"I'll follow you down."

Danny's eyes held on the RADIOACTIVE WASTE sticker as he walked toward the door. I grabbed my denim jacket on my way out.

As we walked toward the elevators, he asked, "Did you ever write about it? About her?"

"I haven't yet."

"That's funny. You risked your life to get a hooker's story and never wrote about it."

"I will. Someday."

I didn't believe he was pulling a Columbo on me but I tried to keep from looking shifty. The pings of the elevator rose in the shaft as it approached.

"I did care for her," I said. "It wasn't all about writing, no matter what our agreement was or what was said."

The elevator opened and we stepped in. Surrounded by mirrors, we rode down without saying a word. Before the doors opened, I said, "I loved her, Danny."

He didn't laugh.

"Even knowing what she was?"

We stepped out and maneuvered around a cart piled high with luggage. I slowed to a stop as Danny turned to me.

"She was thrown out on the streets for getting raped by a black guy. Maybe her family would've been a little more understanding if she'd been gang-raped by white boys, I don't know. She was a beautiful young girl who'd been screwed over by everyone in her life before she landed here. Abandoned by her family, scooped up by some pimp...I wanted to give her another chance."

I glanced at the slot machines clanging and ringing in the casino. I added, "The girl I met was worth the risk."

"You've got a good heart, buddy. I don't doubt that. But you're still a dork."

We walked past the shops to the rear entrance.

Danny said, "See if you can remember any names they mentioned, people they knew. Go through your journal. It's worth a shot."

"Okay."

"Maybe it's not her," he said. "People go through names like crazy here. It's sad a lot of them end up this way but maybe it's not her."

We stepped into a chilly night wind outside. For the first time perhaps, I was certain Jane Doe was her. I didn't know why but I knew. Maybe because this was the first time in decades I was talking about her with somebody else face to face.

"Do you want me to call you tomorrow?" I asked.

"I can call you," he replied, whipping out his cell.

"I don't have a cell phone," I reminded him.

He looked at me as if I didn't have my driver's license or proof of insurance and US citizenship.

"I'll stay in my room until I hear from you."

He headed out to his vehicle, saying over his shoulder, "You need to get a cell phone."

I wandered to the Strip and walked all the way to Tropicana Avenue. The night was mine and I felt like checking out the changes and losing myself in the crowd. But no matter how anonymous and invisible I felt in the churning tourists under the flashing lights, I kept thinking about the murder investigation going on beyond the glow. I kept hoping it wouldn't be Mindy in that drawer out there in the dark. Did she die alone?

The ghost of Dean Martin said, *Of course not, pallie, the*

guy who killed her was there too! My imagination even provided a rim shot from the band and I wanted to cry.

The indifferent crowd just flowed around me like I was a rock in a stream. *Don't crack up out here*, I told myself. Then I realized how thoroughly ridiculous I looked. How stupid I felt. Yes, my nerves had been worn down by the upcoming divorce. Yes, I was nearly breaking down for a lost hooker I never had sex with—

But you left her.

That stopped me dead in my tracks. Up to this point, I'd only remembered Mindy as I first met her, when everything clicked for me with her. But I did leave her. For all the crazy, foolhardy bullshit I jumped into for her, I left her behind in the end.

For the rest of the night, YOU LEFT HER flashed in my mind like the gigantic marquees above that read TOM JONES or FOLIES BERGERE.

Behind the Tropicana, I spotted the San Remo's sign that advertised a five ninety-five prime rib dinner. I decided to distract myself with what used to be one of my favorite Vegas rituals: the incredibly cheap prime rib dinner, about three dollars and ninety-five cents or four ninety-five when I first came to Vegas. Prime rib at fast food prices. I ate five to six times a day back then.

"I asked to sit in the non-smoking section," I told the waitress.

"This is the non-smoking section," she told me.

The man at the table next to me was smoking. A couple across from me was smoking so much that their table looked like it was about to burst into flames.

I tried not to sound like a complete smartass. "How

can this be the non-smoking section if everyone else is smoking?"

"You're at the edge of the non-smoking section," she explained, showing her first signs of irritation.

"Can I get a little further into the non-smoking section? You know, *away* from the smoke?"

"It's all the same room," she grumbled as she snatched up the laminated menu and took me to one of the many empty tables we'd passed moments before. She was right. It was all the same room, but I preferred the stale smoky air near the back wall instead of the fresh plumes blown in my face. I decided to withhold a portion of my tip to benefit research into service industry attitudes in relation to smoking and non-smoking seating. Tonight, that felt like a worthy cause. If anyone asked for that donation, I wanted to be sure I had it. Bitch.

Although I didn't remember any worn vinyl seats or the carpet looking faded, this coffee shop had an atmosphere of decay and decline. It didn't feel like Vegas, it felt like a Denny's in a bad part of town.

The food didn't help and my mood darkened. The salad was suspiciously pale, the baked potato dry, the vegetables soggy. The prime rib was a chewy imitation of the succulent cuts I remembered. It was crappy fast food at fast food prices.

I sat staring at the Strip outside.

Hello, Vegas. Promise me everything--pleasure, greed, desire, addiction, (it's all in the presentation!) but take it all. Never have so many had so much fun losing everything they have. Every decadent empire would've lasted another thousand years if its capitol had been Las Vegas.

If Mindy was dead, then Guy had to be dead. Vegas

had too many hooks in him; the remnant of an under-world that kept him posing, all that reckless Eighties cocaine cash for every indulgence, buffet lines to take a break from the danger and pile on the pounds. The blizzard was coming.

I sat in the aging San Remo with my half-eaten dinner, feeling morbid and paranoid in the craziest, happiest place on earth. Forget Disneyland, even though this Fun Capital of the world had a death toll. Three people can keep a secret if two of them were dead and the survivor remains exiled to his dull, distant life elsewhere. But now the exile was back and the bright lights of the Strip that used to dazzle me now made me feel exposed and undone.

And, you prick, you left her.

SOMETHING WASN'T DIGESTING RIGHT.

I only walked a short distance from the San Remo when the first cramp kicked me right in the stomach. It was such a quick and sharp pain so soon after my meal that I doubted it could have been anything I ate. I limped across Tropicana's walkway to the MGM and decided to take the monorail back toward the Stardust. The last time I was up, the monorail that ran from the MGM down to Bally's (the old MGM) was free. Now it cost money, but it ran all the way down to the end of the Strip and, of course, I had to eat at nearly the opposite end.

Another cramp hit and I nearly doubled over in pain on the monorail. Hanging on to the rail, it made its stops as I tried to figure out which station would put me closest to the Stardust—-or a restroom. Man, where did this come from? Could stress cause this?

I probably should've exited at the Venetian and started making my way back to the Stardust, but I ended up riding out to the Hilton. Since the next stop was the Sahara, I limped off and made my way down the escalator. Now I was sweating. Are you happy? You got a cheap prime rib dinner—-and some crippling food poisoning along with it. *You deserve to shit yourself!*

I needed a bathroom. Now. I ended up in the Star Trek Experience restroom, feeling as if I was giving birth to some frightening alien creature. Something with tentacles and eyeballs. It hit me just that fast. I was surprised the polluted cut of prime rib didn't tear its way out of my belly like the chest-bursting little monster from *Alien,* and I would've tipped the little fucker a twenty spot to be on its way. This wasn't a shit. This was a NASA booster rocket test. Hey, Ghost Dino, are you laughing? Where's my rim shots?

I won't even tell you what he joked at that last line.

I slumped in a stall for a while, catching my breath, hoping that was it. Nothing like a violent stomach illness in a town that had no day or night to stick me firmly in the moment, removed from my own life, my own identity.

All right. I was at the Hilton. I thought about the open stretches between me and my Stardust room. There was the Hilton parking lot, the intersection, then the longest space past luxury condos going up where the Landmark Casino once stood to the rear entrance of the Riviera.

I left the Star Trek Experience bathroom and headed for the front entrance. I stopped to look at Elvis merchandise in a shop to give myself a few moments to make sure another attack didn't hit. The cramps were enough to almost knock me down and deliver a dire warning: you've got seconds to find a bathroom or risk detonation. How I could evacuate anything more was beyond me since I felt like I'd left my entire digestive tract in a stainless-steel Star Trek toilet.

Out on the casino floor, making a run for it, I felt it again and fled to the restroom in the back of the Hilton casino. Just as bad, and just as much, as the first time. I tried to distract myself by wondering who was president the last time I soiled a perfectly good pair of pants. I put my money on Nixon. Johnson for sure, but I wasn't *that* old.

Okay. I had to make it to the Riviera. Easily the longest stretch of this journey back to my room.

The next cramp punched me as I approached the crosswalk next to the Hilton sign. The traffic light changed and I struggled across the crosswalk as others casually strolled. I focused on the back of the Riviera across a very wide and very empty parking lot. I saw bushes ahead and wondered if I was going to have to make the terrible choice between shitting in them or in my pants. Vegas should be used to seeing some crazy shit, I thought ruefully, perhaps even mine.

I wished I'd stayed back in the coffee shop and polluted every toilet stall. I could limp out and tell the waitress, "Sorry about the stench but, hey, it's all the same building!"

I started laughing out loud, walking like the gimpy sidekick from a million Western movies.

When I was twenty-one years old, I had come to Las Vegas seeking excitement and adventure—-and found some weird version of it for me. Now, twenty years later, returning to experience a new drama, I was starring in a cliffhanger where life and humiliating death depended on the distance between public toilets. *Viva Las Vegas!*

Fortunately, the convention center doors were unlocked and I made it into the restrooms inside. The building looked completely empty, so I didn't hold back on groaning with pain and exhaustion. Now I was dizzy. I had to be losing vital organs. Maybe a rib or two, perhaps some teeth. This was my third restroom visit. Had I even eaten that much in a week?

Steadying my breathing, I made my way through the Riviera Casino, which was celebrating its fiftieth anniversary. One of Liberace's pianos and one of his cars were displayed, along with photo panels of famous celebrities who performed there over the years. After stopping in the casino restroom, I felt a little better or maybe just more comfortable since there were no more long sprints between restrooms.

I wandered through the fiftieth anniversary exhibit, looking at the photos and skimming the captions. They had all played here. Frank Sinatra, Wayne Newton, Liberace, Ann Margaret, Bob Newhart, everyone but Elvis, who exclusively played the Hilton when he came back in 1969. I tried to grin at photos of Dean Martin, decked out in a dashing tux and smooth smile for every shot, a drink in one hand and a cigarette in the other. I wondered if he knew he'd been crowned the King of Cool in the Nineties before he passed away. I wondered if he was so cool that he didn't even care.

He made everything look so light and easy. I had played my father's record albums of Dino when I was growing up in my little Midwestern hometown. My favorite was "I'm Not the Marryin' Kind," a clinking two-minute melody of fluff he'd crooned in a Sixties spy spoof. I lived for those swingin' spy movies on late night TV. The Guys, the boys I grew up with, and I used to listen to that song, sipping Pepsi like it was a martini and marveling at the breezy voice.

> *It's always been my plan*
> *To stay single any way I can*
> *I'm just a happy man*
> *I'm not the marryin' kind*

WE WERE JUST kids and we didn't understand much but I knew there was something incredibly cool about a guy who wasn't a total fool for love. Puberty hit us like a smoking shot of Kryptonite, baby, and the dames had our number, but not ole Dino's. He even *sang* about his cheerful indifference and we'd listen to that record, knowing that we were hearing the hippest thing in the world—-the sound of a happy loner, somebody in control. A little piece of Vegas took root in me—

At that moment, I realized that none of the Guys came around on weekends. They never saw my dad's entourage or the groupies. Maybe their parents had warned them to stay away from the Bailey house on weekends. Something dark and dangerous went on inside that house, something so terrifyingly *grown up*. Little towns saw everything. I grinned at the photos of Dino and thought, *I grew up in the coolest house on Beaver Street and never even knew it.*

I left the Riviera and made it back to my room. I took a hot shower and flopped on the bed, putting the journal aside.

The next day would be difficult. My imagination was already playing it out like a film noir nightmare, entering a dark room to see a body under a sheet starkly-lit by a bright bare light bulb. (Come on, nobody remembers Lionel Atwill? He would've been a perfect coroner). How long had she been dead before they found her? If it was Mindy, how did she look in death? How bad would this scene play tomorrow?

I should've watched more Court TV.

I turned off the light and stared at the glow under the curtains, drifting off into a dream of Vegas showrooms that still lived in my fantasies where Frank and Dean frolicked and crooned in spotlights, stunning beauties in glittering dresses lounged at all the tables, no kids to spoil everything, everyone smoking and drinking, and a huge man in a fedora presiding from a back booth. He looks like a mobster and reminds everyone of Brando in *The Godfather*. Everyone in my dreams knows who I am but they don't know the fat man in the booth. The pimp.

I'm uneasy as our eyes meet because I knew him, and I'm afraid because I also knew how much he had on me.

8

Carnal Etiquette, Part Two

THE GUN on the table in front of Guy made him look like a real gangster.

The fedora, the oversized suits, the tiny moustache and smoldering stares had been props and poses but the German Luger handgun before him was real. I'd never seen a real Luger before and wanted to ask about it, but I knew why it was out so I said nothing.

As I stood on the stairs in their townhouse, my eyes darted between the gun and his steady gaze. His eyes never left me.

I descended the stairs and sat down on the sofa. Guy, facing the loft, now stared up at the bedroom door. After a few tense moments, he picked up the gun and slipped it into his sports coat on the back of his chair. Did he now realize who I was? Was my cover blown? As long as I stayed under his control, his programming, did he see me as a threat to his hold on Mindy?

We sat in silence, watching the bedroom door.

"Turn on the TV," Guy grunted.

Commercials played on the screen, their jingles smothered in the tension.

A short time later, Mindy appeared and came down the stairs. She'd recovered. Brittle politeness gave way to relief. We went on as normal, whatever that was.

In one of our phone conversations before I flew to Vegas, Mindy had said she wanted to cook for me. At the time, I thought it was one of the things Guy coached her to say. "Reel him in, girl, he might be a rich writer someday." As I thought about it, I remembered another call when she'd blurted out, "Shut up, Guy, this is my conversation!"

She burned the bacon. She burned Guy's eggs. She put the smoldering plate down in front of him and went back into the kitchen. Guy held the plate up for me to see and said, "See this? This is what you're getting yourself in for."

She appeared in the kitchen doorway. Smiling.

We'd had fun picking out apples at the store, but I couldn't recall anyone eating one.

While Guy was eating, I flipped through channels on the TV. When *The Flintstones* cartoon appeared on the screen, Guy bellowed out, "Ah, now you've done it! That'll be on all day."

"What?" I asked.

"All she watches is cartoons—-"

She called out from the kitchen, "Not all the time!"

"What do you watch all day?" he asked.

"I don't watch much TV," she replied.

"But what do you watch when you do?" he asked, then turned to me to say, "Cartoons."

I left the channel on *The Flintstones*. Maybe she watched cartoons because they were her only happy childhood memories. I could relate to that sanctuary, losing myself in a TV screen. I'd done it all my life.

By the time we were in the car, cruising down the Strip, we knew there wasn't enough time to get to the stable and arrange a horseback ride. When we got in the car, Mindy kissed Guy on both cheeks and apologized for rattling his teeth. I was looking out the window of the Town car at the casinos in daylight, watching the newspaper boxes of sex ads going by, and Guy was singing "Everybody Loves Somebody Sometime." I wondered if he thought Dino was a punk, too.

At the original MGM Grand on Flamingo, just before it became Bally's that year, we did have time to go into the old-time photographer in the back shops while Guy went to the coffee shop. I dressed up like a gunslinger with Mindy as a saloon girl decked out in red. I gave her the color photo and I kept the sepia-tone antique one.

We were walking back to Guy in the coffee shop when I blurted out, "I'm trying so hard to be different, Mindy. Not to be one of *them*. You know, the jerks and assholes."

"You're not," she assured me. "If I didn't like you, you wouldn't be here."

Guy was drawing biplanes on his place mat when we found him.

Back at the townhouse, Guy wanted to play another prank on Mindy. Since my arrival, he'd told her that my plane had crashed, then that I'd inherited a half-million dollars and was coming to marry her, then some blonde hit on me on my flight, then when she came out of the MGM Grand restroom and didn't see me, he said I ran away. Now he wanted to fool her into believing I was half-black.

"No, sorry," I said. "I can't go along with that. Plane wrecks and blondes, maybe, but I will not go along with that."

I didn't particularly care about my racial background —-it was her response that kept me from going along. If she'd been traumatized as badly as Guy said, this wasn't anything to joke about. But the fact that he wanted to joke about it made me wonder: was everything bullshit with him?

I was sitting on the couch when Guy pulled some Polaroids out of his jacket pocket. She jumped up.

"No, don't!" she cried.

Guy casually tossed one of them to me.

I caught it. She lunged at me and we wrestled back onto the couch. She straddled me and fought for the Polaroid, laughing. With her legs around me and her body rubbing down onto me, I was instantly hard. A fire started and we could see it in our eyes.

"All right, that's enough," Guy sternly said, his eyes closed and his face scowling with anger.

She lifted off me and I sat up. As I walked the Polaroid over to him, I noticed it was of her. She had her tongue out and her eyes crossed in a goofy expression. Written under her was, *"That's right, sir, $105 for everything!"*

———

SHE WORE the silver dress that night, the one that glittered. The one that transformed her into Angelique, the goddess of the Strip.

"We're having prime rib for dinner tonight at the Aladdin," Guy announced at the townhouse.

Behind the wheel of the Town car, he said, "I'm gonna give you both some time together. I'll either sit at another table or stay in the casino."

I smiled as he winked and added, "On me."

"He sits where he wants to," Mindy told the flustered waitress as Guy stalked into the restaurant.

Or should I refer to her as Angelique? The makeup, the black hair, the pale skin, the dress—-she really did look like another person. She was glamorous and self-assured, and I was in blue jeans, a blue work shirt, and a corduroy jacket. John Boy Walton escorting the She-Goddess of Lust.

Someone was sitting at their regular table so we waited until they left. Their favorite waiter had the night off. Guy sat down with us but said he would leave after we ordered.

Mindy excused herself and went to the restroom.

I turned to Guy and said, "I'm thinking of asking her to come to Arizona on my days off. They're during the week, and it would only be for a couple of days."

He said abruptly, "No way."

"What?" I asked, surprised. I thought things were going better than this.

"No way," he repeated. "Do you know how much we can lose in two days? She's got to be here when the calls come in."

I felt crushed. I was expecting too much. *He showed you his gun, stupid—*

Guy said with a grin, "But I want you to ask her. Because I want you to hear *her* say that."

Right. She's "programmed." That carefully orchestrated production that she was completely programmed by him, which I felt was a house of cards, was about to be put to the test.

Angelique returned, striding in high heels as her shimmering legs stepped out of the slits in her dress. This Vegas façade completely hid the teenager in black jeans who liked to watch cartoons. I stood. She slid in between us, and I sat down, swallowing.

"Jeff here's got something big to ask you," Guy said.

She turned to me and smiled. Her bright blue eyes looked happy and hopeful.

As much as I wanted to get her away from Vegas, at that moment, I really wanted her to say precisely what Guy predicted—-no, programmed her—-to say. But, for some reason, even knowing that there was a German Luger under the table across from me, I made a long, impassioned plea to her. She could come to Phoenix; I'd pay for the flights, all the arrangements. We could ride horses, whatever she wanted to do. I wanted her to come. I wanted her out of Vegas.

She thought for a moment, her blue eyes locked on me.

Then she said, "I don't know."

"No way," Guy said, not just raspy but menacing.

She whirled at him and viciously said, *"I said, I don't know!"*

"Melinda, you can't leave until we get these deals made! Do you know how much we could lose in two days?"

"You can't expect me to work every single day of the year!" she hissed at him.

"When these deals are made, you can retire and take off for two weeks if you want to!"

The waiter brought our salads. Guy didn't leave. I didn't expect him to at this point. If she had answered like she was programmed to, he would've wandered out to the casino and left us alone, secure in knowing that she was under his complete control. But she wasn't. I had over-played my hand and he now knew he could lose her.

I ate my salad and glanced at Guy. He was so furious that he wouldn't look at me. I saw that both of his hands were still above the table, away from the gun.

"What's wrong, Guy?" I casually asked.

He narrowed his eyes at me and fumed, "We are so close to the end of the tunnel. She doesn't need this hearts and flowers shit; do you know what I'm saying?"

"Yes."

"We could lose maybe three thousand dollars if she's gone for two days while she's riding off into the sunset with you!"

He kept his voice low, ranting at both of us in a tone more threatening than his bellowing. He had all the authority of a furious parent along with the frantic anger of a betrayed lover. He only paused to order dinner for himself.

"Hey, look, I'm sorry," I said, putting my hands up. "I'm just a shit-kicker from Ohio. I don't know anything about your business plans. The question was asked and the answer was given. So, let's just drop it."

Guy and I stared at each other across the table. I don't know if he saw past my nervous expression to realize that

I knew his hold on her wasn't as tight as he believed. Did he see that I could actually start plotting to get her away from him, from this town? But I also knew he had a gun under that table and that I was the worst poker player to ever hit town.

If I had a cigarette I would have lit it because this was definitely one of my life's movie scenes. And I didn't even smoke. I was across the table from a hulking caricature of a villain, engaged in a high stakes game for a beautiful woman, for her heart and soul, while facing down the barrel of a hidden gun. I would spark the lighter, inhale the first drag, and work in the line every man on the planet dreams of saying when asked *who the fuck are you*: "The name's Bond, James Bond...and the lady will be leaving with me."

Instead, we ate our prime rib dinners in silence.

Did he take this enormous risk because he believed I was a good guy and that I truly loved her, that I would be better for her? That I was too good to ever steal her from him?

After dinner, I babbled about how ridiculous it was for me to even ask Mindy such a question. I even reached across the table and took her hand, mocking myself by saying, "Yes, come away with me to Arizona with the scorpions and the cactus and the nuclear plant—-we'll be very happy together!" Guy looked amused, but the undercurrent of suspicion would not go away. When I glanced at Mindy, she wasn't laughing. She looked like she was still considering it.

You're not helping me, baby—

"Yeah, right, Guy," I said, turning back to my plate. "I ain't got anything to offer her now."

The thrill and pressure of my movie scene gave way to the inert and tedious awkwardness of our reality.

"Well, Mindy, what do you think?" I asked after our plates were cleared.

"I don't know," she said.

"What he means when he says that is, 'Mindy, what do you think of me so far?'" Guy threw in.

Angelique turned and stared at me.

"Something like that," I grinned.

"Look," Guy chuckled. "He's actually blushing."

Mindy said, "I like you."

"Look at him! All moon-eyed over there."

I went to the restroom and slumped against the wall next to the sinks. I splashed water in my face and dried off. James Bond? You idiot!

Bond would've known not to play his hand this early. Guy let me in because he believed his bond with her, her obligation to him, couldn't be endangered by anyone. If I hadn't been such an immature, easy-to-read rube, I might have slipped around his pride to really connect with her, to plan her escape. The game had commenced but I had too much in the open now.

When I got back, she drummed her fingernails on the table at me until I would look at her. She smiled. They were talking about hotels, and I asked them details about how they operated.

Guy chuckled and said to Mindy, "Usually it's 'come away with me into the sunset,' but we're dragging him down into it. Can you see him as a runner?"

They laughed.

"Why, do you have an opening for a runner?" I asked, a little too loud.

Guy hushed me and looked down. Mindy laughed out loud. Our waiter was standing right next to me. After our waiter left, Guy quietly told me that a runner was a whorehouse employee who supplied fresh towels and linens for the girls. Guy also informed me that the black man in the suit sitting in the booth next to us within earshot was Head of Security for the Aladdin Hotel. You picked up little things like that as a local.

As we escorted Angelique through the casino, she happily took both our arms. Until Guy told her to knock it off. She was never to appear in public as if she was with anyone, especially in a casino, especially as Angelique.

As we waited for the valet, the Head of Security appeared. He greeted us like we were high rollers, asking, "How are you folks all doing tonight?"

"Doin' fine," I said.

He briskly continued his rounds.

———

WE'D LEFT the Aladdin and were in a bookstore. They said it was a bookstore, and it had BOOKSTORE in giant block letters on the marquee outside. What it left off the building, located at the corner of the Strip and Sahara, was ADULT bookstore. It was more of a department store for sex.

"What...what is *this*?" I asked.

I hesitated to pick it up. Just the look of it alone, brand new and for sale, appeared sordid and dirty. It was some type of harness. I could see the pouch where the genitals were supposed to go—-

"Hey, Mindy," I heard Guy say behind me. "Look at him!"

Dressed as Angelique, Mindy scouted the Sado-masochism section and closely checked out the absurd merchandise. Nothing was packaged with illustrations to explain their kinky uses so I was left with my imagination. The most difficult part was figuring out what parts of the apparatus went inside the human body and which parts stayed out.

"A lot of freaks come to Vegas," she said, picking up something made of leather with a lot of shiny buckles. "Most carry their own equipment. Sometimes an entire suitcase full."

I stood next to her, looking around. I noticed that there were only guys in the store, all of them alone.

"There was a guy who paid good money just to kiss and play with my feet for an hour," she said quietly. "There are just a lot of freaks in this world. I hear about what some of the other girls deal with—-and I absolutely hate golden showers."

"Do you know what that means?" Guy asked from behind me.

"Yes, unfortunately."

I saw a monstrous two-foot dildo on the shelf in front of us. I pointed at it and asked, "Does that thing talk?"

Guy's loud cackle filled our end of the store and he repeated that for the rest of the night. He got such a kick out of it that I didn't have the heart to tell him I quoted it from my favorite comedy movie, *Animal House*.

"Hey, Mindy," Guy said from the next aisle. "You ought to tie him up with some of that stuff."

It didn't sound like he was kidding. Bound and help-less at the mercy of Guy didn't sound fun.

"Not for me, I don't think," I said.

Looking over the devices, attachments, enhancements, and the vast array of baffling tools around me, I finally found some evidence for human evolution, not in phys-ical or intellectual development but in what it takes to get mankind to the bone zone. I felt like a Cro-Magnon tugging at my hairy club in an alien lab of sex.

They didn't buy anything. As we walked out to the car, she suddenly stopped and faced me.

"Okay, some guy pays you a thousand dollars to lead him around on a leash and make him lick your boots. Would you do it?"

I thought about it. "A thousand dollars?"

"Sometimes."

"And that's all you do?"

"Sometimes."

———

AS PUNISHMENT for messing with Mindy's programming, I wasn't allowed to ride around with them that night. When we were walking through the Tropicana casino, I was in the middle when Guy said, "Mindy, you walk between us. You can't look like a couple out here."

"Business is business, and pleasure comes second," he'd said back in the Aladdin. I got dropped off at the townhouse.

So much for our dinner alone.

I answered the phone the first time it rang. The guy on the other end asked for Angelique. I said she wasn't in.

Then he asked for Guy. I said he wasn't in and could I take a message—-

He hung up.

The second call asked for L'Oreal.

"Uhm. No, she isn't."

"Tania?"

How many names did she go by?

"No."

"All right. Thank you," he said and hung up.

Well. At least he said Thank You.

They had the Playboy Channel on their cable TV, but I quickly bored of the tanned nude girls playing volleyball on a beach, which seemed to go on for hours.

I wondered what Guy and Mindy were talking about as they made their rounds out there. Was this just a big scam on me? Could they be in on it together, working out their next strategy to sucker me in? For what? I had nothing. Mindy made in a couple of hours what I made in a month.

When we'd been hanging out at the townhouse earlier, I'd come down the stairs to find Mindy reading aloud a poem she'd written to Guy. She stopped reading and asked me if I wanted to read her poems. She handed me the notebook and I opened it to find a letter she'd written to Angelique.

"What's this?" I asked.

"That's personal," she said, making no move to take it. "Please don't read it."

I ended up putting the notebook down and we talked before the evening got started.

Now, banished to the townhouse, I read through the whole thing. Mindy was writing to Angelique, the cold, conniving woman she needed to be. She was admitting to her alter-ego that she was lonely deep inside, that she's waiting for, in all caps, her TRUE LOVE. *I love you* appears in almost every other line of her poetry.

When I finally find the one I love,
The one we both wait for day and night,
He'll kiss us both and then you will go
We'll kiss you goodbye into our lost blinding night.

THEY WERE simple rhymes for the most part, but they bared her soul. It was on these pages where her hopes stayed hidden and protected. How could I reach this girl? How long would it take to prove I wasn't one of the guys who called her—

There was also a letter Guy was writing. I guessed to an ex-wife, perhaps the one whose picture he flashed at me in his wallet during our talk at Carrow's. The photo featured a younger woman, late twenties, kind of pudgy. In the letter, he wrote that he didn't want to kill her because of their baby. He couldn't tolerate LIARS, written in large caps the way Mindy had written TRUE LOVE. I skimmed the rest of Guy's letter and I found the reason he wanted to kill this woman: she had slept with his nephew and the nephew had told Guy. The wannabe-mobster pimp of Vegas also left behind a messy real-life out there in the hinterland.

Under the notebook, I found a ledger that kept track of all of Angelique's "dates." The amount of money earned was listed with the date. Next to each one was either a checkmark ("perfect gentleman"), a T ("Talk"), or a checkmark with a line making an X ("perfect gentleman but turned into an asshole"). I knew this because there was even a guide explaining the system on the first page.

I did some quick calculating and found my entry. T, for Talk. But there was an asterisk next to my T. Or a star, I couldn't tell. I looked through everything else to see that no one else earned one. This was in Guy's handwriting. What did that mean?

They got back around five that morning. Mindy changed out of the silver dress and into some shorts and a T-shirt. Guy snatched up the phone and called around town: a friend had been busted by the cops last night. It was on the eleven o'clock news and everything. If I hadn't left the TV on the Playboy Channel and then old movie channels all night, I might have seen it.

I was under a blanket on the couch when Mindy got another blanket and sat back next to me, stretching her legs out on the coffee table. Still on the phone, Guy immediately began snapping his fingers at us. We looked at him as he angrily shook his head. He couldn't see under our blankets. I took one of the pillows and wedged it between Mindy and me. She giggled. He appeared satisfied.

I changed the TV to MTV and landed on Phil Collins' music video for "One More Night." I turned to Mindy and said, "I'd ask you to dance but I don't think he'd like it."

She made a face and whispered, "He's a pain in the ass."

Guy hung up and then called his bondsman to explain the situation to him. The guy in jail said he was going to have another friend of theirs killed. Guy muttered, "That guy's so fucking stupid, I'll have to pull the trigger for him."

Listening to the Phil Collins song, I sat next to the girl

I loved and plotted her escape to a Happily Ever After as street hits were being discussed across the room.

"Who was that?" I asked.

"That was a hitman, and he's one of the dumbest son of a bitches you'll ever meet," he told me. "I paid him three thousand seven hundred and twelve dollars once to have someone hurt."

"What had they done to you?" I asked.

His eyes focused on me.

"They called me a pimp."

They went to bed around sunrise. I was afraid to go to sleep because my flight was in three hours. I thought a lot, but not clearly. Watching TV couldn't keep me awake so I sketched a drawing of Mindy in her notebook from our Old West photo. I should've thrown the sketch away. It wasn't very good but it would remind her of me. She would see that I wanted to commit her to paper in any way I could, either through writing or drawing.

I picked up the phone downstairs at nine o'clock and dialed their number. Mindy, groggy and incoherent, answered and I said I had an hour to get to the airport. When I went up to take a shower, I saw Mindy sprawled out across the bed in a long black T-shirt, trying to wake herself up. Guy sat on the floor, his arms thrown back on the bed, a line of saliva drooling from his mouth onto his massive belly. Wearing only baggy boxer shorts, he drew labored breaths in and out. I noticed his nightstand was crowded with prescription bottles. He sat cross-legged, like a heaving Buddha.

But he did make it up. He dressed and lumbered down the stairs.

I stood with my back against the front door with my

bag at my feet. The Valentine's Day card still stood on the TV. Next to it was the Old West photo. The cloth rose was stuck in a black chain where a light hung next to the kitchen. She would find my sketch later. Hopefully I left enough reminders and made some mark on her life. Maybe she would write a poem about me.

"Hey, Mindy," I called up to the loft. "Maybe I'll see you again. What do you think?"

Her thin voice came from the bedroom: "Okay. I'd like that. I'm sorry about this."

Guy picked up the car keys from the dining table and looked at me, mouthing, What?

I shrugged and said upstairs, "Go back to sleep."

I wanted to hug her, maybe even kiss her goodbye.

Guy asked if I wanted anything to eat on the way to the airport, but I wasn't sure if I was going to make my flight or not.

"How do you think it all went?" I asked.

"It went all right," he slurred, as reckless and depleted as when he picked me up. He coughed miserably, hanging on to the wheel as much to remain conscious as he did to stay on the road.

"You gotta go slow, Jeff," he said. "Three months ago, we didn't have a dime to our names. We had just got busted and we were out on our own. Now we got a place, a car and she just spent seven hundred dollars in Frederick's of Hollywood last week. I want to retire her ass. I don't want her to end up like those other whores that are fucked out and old before their time...but you gotta go slow."

"Well, if I'm welcome, I'll be back."

"You're welcome."

"But...I can't...pay anymore."

"I don't want your damn money," he snapped.

We got to the airport and he stopped in front of the terminal. I got out and looked back in at him. He was looking away and held out his hand. I reached in and shook it. He grinned at me.

"She likes ya," he said.

"Well, that's what I came here to find out."

"But go slow. Slow."

"I will."

"Write us a letter."

"You take care of yourself, Guy," I said. "And thank you."

I was surprised I didn't hear a swell of violins to sweeten the sendoff from a Vegas pimp. Welcome to my life.

On the plane, I watched Las Vegas drop away under me. I became aware that it was morning, that time already started to have meaning again. Until I was ready to leave, I rarely saw a clock.

Three frat boys near me anxiously looked out the windows of the plane. The stewardess brought them Budweiser's. One of them turned to me.

"Hey, is that the Grand Canyon down there?" he asked.

I looked out and saw the winding canyons below Hoover Dam.

"No," I told him. "But you'll know it when you see it."

———

WELL, I didn't get murdered.

I stepped into their world without getting arrested,

getting shot or getting anything on me (take that however you like) but I also found out that bringing her back to my normal world wasn't going to be so easy.

If we were in a 1940s movie, Guy the Pimp's conscience would eventually overtake him and he would angrily point at the door and yell, "Go! Get her out of here, away from this degrading life!" It wasn't that hard to imagine him in black and white since he already dressed like a *film noir* hoodlum.

But unfortunately, we were not working from a script where studio committees agreed on a basic morality and common decency for each plot development, where everyone agreed that true love triumphs, and even the pimp character's heart is softened to the point of sending his lady of ill-repute away to save her. We were in the 1980s, in living color and harsh reality, and nobody followed any script, adhered to any notion of decency, or even acted like God was even looking, let alone an approving audience seeking vicarious thrills and easy answers. The test audience was turning on our movie characters and wanted to see them suffer.

Harsh reality number one: Guy owned Mindy. He brought her to Vegas, created Angelique and she had to earn. Harsh reality number two: any interference with Number One made me a rival for her heart against the rightful owner of her body.

I still had to navigate the moods and contradictions of Guy, the "big ole friendly bear," but it wasn't only his appearance that resembled a huge, unpredictable predator. His boasting, his temper, his appetites were all volatile and impulsive. He was who he had to be at any given moment. Fueled by his pride, he was either the biggest, baddest motherfucker one moment, the devious master manipulator the next, or finally the most generous surrogate father figure another moment later. Even blundering through my void and formless youth, I never knew anyone as precisely engaged in the present moment as Guy Reinhart. No matter if his various guises conflicted, he was what he needed to be at the time and I needed to act accordingly. Impressed, intimidated, or touched.

When I first met him, I believed he accepted my naïve sincerity to reclaim Mindy from her past (also her present), and that I cared more about her than her body. Behind all his street posturing, Guy didn't want this life for her and I bought his first love story about Jody Spinner. I treated him with respect, like a human being, I shared emotions for her too, I cared for them both—-I must have seemed like an alien from another planet when I thought about the people they knew personally, if anyone.

He also had to be Guy the business manager to survive, to make it from night to night. (I still hesitate to refer to him as a "pimp" to this day). Because I claimed to be a writer, he had to play his character with even more presence and conviction, his vanity egging on each performance, or maybe he was just full of bullshit because he was afraid to lose her to a younger guy. I never knew. As long as I didn't push any confrontations or ultimatums, I was welcome to stay with them, waiting them out.

I just didn't see the storm that was coming.

If I had, I should've tried to get them out, tried to spare them both from the descending blizzard rolling over Vegas. If I got them back to Phoenix, I could've explained to everyone that this was my fiancé Mindy's uncle and he would be staying with us for a while. Did I mind supporting a new wife and her chain-smoking, overeating uncle? No. You gotta make the little woman happy.

We could've left Vegas as human beings, all of us, if I had only known.

After that first weekend, I never saw them again without the suspicion that they were on some substance, some interference diffusing their thoughts and disrupting their emotions in an already baffling hall of mirrors. If Guy's attitude had been difficult to read for my first visit, he became impossible to discern afterward.

I had been so naïve about everything else that their new addiction wouldn't become clear to me until it was far too late. I worked in a strict environment that only allowed alcoholics to slip between the narrow cracks of Human Resource Departments and Employee Assistance Programs so I wasn't as educated for the signs of hardcore drug addiction as I should have been.

It snowed when I first met Mindy so long ago at the Stardust, just a brief dusting that melted instantly, but that was nothing compared to the avalanche of white powder about to blow into Sin City. I ended up knowing the two noses that could clear the Strip faster than a Buffalo street crew in a New York winter.

Snow in Vegas. An avalanche of cocaine. Cool visual motif.

I should write that down.

APRIL 2005

I WOKE up on my own after a fitful night of weird dreams with strange memories. Maybe they were the aftereffects of the food poisoning. When I turned on the TV while shaking off my grogginess, I saw the huge black numbers of 69 fill the screen and thought I was still dreaming until I realized it was the hotel's video Keno game. Why did I wake up on that number? Was this town mocking me? *Sixty-nine again—HA! Get it?*

Danny wanted names. I didn't hold out much hope of finding any in my journal. My times with Mindy and Guy were insulated and very controlled. I never saw her johns and I was left outside wherever they went. There had been a car dealer, a friend of Guy's, but I was only introduced to him because Guy wanted to impress me with a relic in the car dealer's possession. I'd also thought Guy wanted to use me to impress the dealer by bragging that a writer was chronicling the life and times of Guy Reinhart. I doubted if I wrote down the car dealer's name.

I showered and dressed so I would be ready when the phone rang. I knew Danny was busy with his wife, getting his kids ready for school, heading into the office, reviewing files and cases and dealing with any new homicides that happened overnight. I paced alone in my hotel room, thinking, *I'm going to see a dead body today.*

Sitting at the window, I opened my journal to look for names. 1985, following my first weekend with Mindy and Guy.

Called Mindy last night. She kept saying "Jesus Christ" a lot, and I think I frowned every time.

I had two pet peeves: taking the Lord's name in vain and the N word, both from my Midwestern Methodist upbringing. I've winced at both my entire life. I never called her on either. I figured we could exorcize her later. Her deprogramming from Las Vegas to real life would probably require holy water, cattle prods and a ball gag.

I'd written, I see us doing things together, being very intensely private, being happy. We can look at each other and smile at what we'd been through and no one has to know. It would be our secret, our bond. I wonder if she can have kids.

"Do you know what you get when you cross a prostitute with a Chinaman?" she asked.

"No."

"Someone who sucks your laundry clean."

She said she liked that one. I'm still trying to figure out what's funny about it.

Guy got on and kept in character, talking about money, money, money. They're going to California in the next couple of days to see about getting some money to start their own business. Mindy spoke of a millionaire who liked her and may open up a cathouse and let them run it for him.

We'll just have to see how all of this turns out. I know what I want for Mindy but it doesn't have anything to do with a cathouse. Whatever. I'm in for the long haul.

No name for the millionaire anywhere in my journal. Did he even exist?

I keep thinking of a line from *Jaws:* "Well, why don't we start leading the shark into shore instead of him leading us out to sea?"

The rest of my journal for 1985 was filled with exhaustive speculations and detailed desires for what I hoped my life with Mindy would be like. I continued working at the nuclear plant, furiously reading and writing. I didn't have much contact with her after the first weekend with them, just phone calls and unanswered letters, so she became more of a symbol or a prize, a quest instead of a real person. I wasn't silly enough to blurt out "I love you" at the end of our phone calls but I spent countless hours thinking of her and dreaming of our hard-won marriage, our beautiful reward for not giving up on love.

My transformation from free-floating college dropout to wise-ass working stiff continued throughout that year and I ended up having sex with the bitter divorcees I worked with. They all fit the same profile: mid-twenties, angry single mothers, horny for a boy toy; too far into their own pain and rage at their children's fathers to pay much attention to me. Standing naked in an unfamiliar bathroom in the middle of the night, hoping their bratty, insolent kids didn't wake up, I realized that most of these women were willing to give their bodies just to find an ear to vent about their broken families, not find another soulmate. The sex wasn't bad if I didn't mind the bitching. Staring at the dark hickeys on my shoulders or under my collarbone (the MILFs were very careful not to feed workplace rumors), I realized that these single moms who said, "Fuck me, Jeff" could've just as easily cried out, "Fuck you, (insert ex's name here)." It'd been more fun in college since everyone knew everything was temporary and half of my hook-ups openly spoke of steady boyfriends back home. Either way, I was made to feel like I would never be a coed's first choice or a single mom's next option, which probably said as much about me as them, but at least I got laid.

When you're in your early twenties, a hook-up and the revenge or grudge fucks were all still checks in the win column. *Pow!*

At first, I felt a ridiculous pang of guilt that I was cheating on Mindy—-until I considered what she was doing at that moment up in Vegas. I figured my casual humping and polite listening paled in comparison to Mindy's life as Angelique. If these women had made more money than me, who knows, maybe I could've even earned a little something myself. Kevin Daugherty, my ex-stepfather and postal transplant to AZ, told me about all the senior gals who looked like the horny old lady cartoon from *Playboy* on his mail route, standing every afternoon at their front doors in see-through nightgowns, soaked in gin and perfume. Now there was a new love story for the Eighties: a Sin City escort in love with a Sun City gigolo. If an opening for a mail carrier ever came up, maybe I should apply. Why not? I was working at a nuclear power plant just to see what went on inside for something to write about. It was all material.

No, Mindy and I were just doing what we had to do while waiting for our time together, for our real life to begin.

I wrote Mindy a few letters but she never answered me. It made sense to me. After seeing their world, I understood how anyplace else didn't matter and you didn't leave any evidence anywhere, especially with a stamp on it. Guy would've never allowed a piece of mail that could be connected to them out of his grasp anyway.

I moved out of my mother's home and shared an apartment with Gil Rozell, a hard-drinking nuke officer who, like me, was too young for "gate gazing," the older guys' term for security at the nuke plant. He was probably the funniest guy I've ever met and our humor got us further with the female employees than the ridiculous bragging and posturing of the gruff Alpha Assholes we worked with.

Before I knew it, a year had flown by as the planet whirled on. The Challenger space shuttle exploded and then the Russian nuke plant Chernobyl blew up. For months after a visit to New York City, Rozell repeated something he'd heard the newspaper vendors bawling out on the street corners: "R-R-R-ROCK'S GOT AIDS!" Sex, drugs and rock-n-roll were being replaced by AIDS, space debris and radiation clouds. During my off time, I banged out screenplay pages on an IBM Selectric and occasionally banged the bitter divorcees while their kids (if I was lucky) were with "the piece-uh-shit father" for the weekend.

In May of '86, I called Mindy again and wrote in my journal:

They want to see me. Mindy talked to me most of the call and even impressed me by remembering different things from our time together over a year ago.

Then Guy got on the phone.

"Have you got anything about us yet?" he asked.

"What do you mean?"

"The book you're writing. About us."

He first dangled Mindy in front of me as the love of my life, securing a future for her when he died. Now he knew about my other desire. The one for her story.

"Well, I'm working on it. I mostly write screenplays."

"Hell, then write it as a movie, I don't care."

"Okay."

"I'll give you what you want," he almost growled. "Shit, I'll help you take Hollywood the same way I helped Mindy take Vegas."

But Guy hadn't died. During my first visit, he gave me the impression that he was gravely ill and wanted Mindy taken care of should something happen to him. "I want to retire her ass," he'd said. But he'd also made sure I'd seen that German Luger when he thought he might lose her sooner than he'd planned. We couldn't consult the grim reaper—-that sickle guy with the black robe and no face, as Mindy thought of him—-but it was his timing we needed for Mindy to be able to leave with me. Death's lack of participation in our story wasn't helping me out.

I should've used the months following my visit to allow myself to cool down, to think about everything and see how lucky I'd been to walk away unscratched, but I was too far in. This wasn't just a romance, it was so much more. A mission, a rescue, a high-concept project.

If Guy thought I was losing interest in her then he would need to find another hook to lure me to Vegas. *Shit, I'll help you take Hollywood the same way I helped Mindy take Vegas.* He wanted me back in their world. Guy, like the devil, had figured it out. That's how he got me to go back, that's how the devil gets you.

He offers you what you really want.

———

I COULD HEAR the maids working their carts from room to room outside until they reached the Do Not Disturb sign on my door.

Danny, the only person in the world who knew where I was, hadn't called. I opened my address book and dialed his cell number.

"This is Olsen," he said, stern, all-business.

"Hey, I just wanted to let you know I'm up and around."

"How are you, brother?" he asked, his voice relaxing into a friend's.

"I'm good."

"I'm dealing with something right now so it's gonna be maybe a couple of hours--"

"Okay. I'm here. Just say when."

I hung up and went to the window to stare at the Strip. Although I felt nervous about today, I liked being here. At least I wasn't home.

I set up my portable DVD player and dug out my Vegas viewing discs I'd brought along. *Viva Las Vegas* and the special edition of *Elvis: That's The Way It Is*, of course. The original *Ocean's Eleven* with Frank and the boys. I also included two James Bond films: *On Her Majesty's Secret Service*, because it was a favorite, and *Diamonds Are Forever*, which was filmed in Vegas in 1971.

I played *Diamonds* while I waited for Danny. It was the first campy Bond film and everyone in it, especially Sean Connery, looked like they were having fun. The movie had dazzled me as a kid but quite a bit of it—-from the prissy gay hit men to the joke names like "Plenty O'Toole"- went right over my head. I knew nothing about sex but even my little kid brain understood that the pinnacle of success meant wrapping me in white mink with a naked Jill St. John on a bed-shaped aquarium somewhere over the Las Vegas Strip. You know you've made it when that happens. I never recorded that goal on any grade school documents but it was always there.

A depressing thought hit me: Great, all these years later I ended up still watching that movie on the Strip, not living it. No aquarium water bed, no mink cover, no Jill St. John.

Fortunately, I imagined the ghost of Dean Martin standing at the window at that moment, saying after blowing out some cigarette smoke and taking a sip from his drink, "Hey, neighbor kid, don't sweat that spy scene you're always dreamin' about. You gotta remember there was twenty guys with tool belts standing behind some hot, bright lights and everybody there is waiting for somebody else to tell 'em what to do. You gotta remember that none of that really happened in the first place. It's just dah movies."

I'm not expecting anybody to believe that the ghost of

Dean Martin visited me in a Stardust hotel room but I do know that whether it was some residual Vegas spirit or my own subconscious desperately trying to get me to grow up, I knew that was something too smart for me to say, a revelation I was too dense to make on my own.

"Thank you, Ghost Dino," I said to the empty window.

Danny rapped on the door during the scene where Bond gets knocked on his ass by the gymnast chicks, Bambi and Thumper.

"Hey, man, how ya doin'?" he asked as he marched into the room. "You ready to get this done?"

"All set."

He looked sympathetic. "Once we get a more definite ID on her, we'll be able to get moving faster on the investigation."

His eyes scanned the room, again stopping on the RADIOACTIVE WASTE sticker on my journal. I grabbed my jacket and left the Do Not Disturb sign on the door. We rode down the elevator. We got into his SUV and headed out of the Stardust parking lot.

"Did you find anything on Guy Reinhart?" I asked.

"Nothing. Not one thing on him."

I turned. "How can that be?"

Danny shrugged. "Different names. Aliases. Happens all the time."

"But I saw mail. Bills and stuff with his name on them."

"That doesn't necessarily make it *his* name."

The Stardust wasn't far from the coroner's office. We drove under the freeway and cut into some side streets, heading toward a hospital building.

"Is it in a hospital?" I asked.

"No, they're in offices across the street."

I glanced at the street sign.

"The coroner's office is on Shadow Lane?" I asked.

"Yeah."

"Wow, that is actually pretty cool."

He pulled into a parking lot next to a one-story building that reminded me of my dentist's office in north Phoenix, except it was marked Clark County Coroner's Office. There were two windows on the side of the building in the parking lot that looked like bank teller windows, and next to those were two roll-up doors for vehicles.

"Am I going to see her body in there?" I asked.

He shut the SUV off and we sat for a moment.

"No, they don't do it that way anymore."

"Would you think I was a complete wussy if I asked how they do it?" I asked. "So I'll know what to expect."

He grinned. "No. It's not like the movies where they take you back in a room and whip some sheet away." He got out of the vehicle. "They're just gonna show you a picture."

"Oh."

I followed him around to the front entrance in the bright desert sun, glancing at the building, thinking she was in there somewhere, what was left of her. Maybe it was her, maybe not.

We walked into the lobby. A receptionist sat behind the counter. I could see a maze of office cubicles behind her and heard voices and phones ringing, although I felt a respective hush throughout the entire building. People are so quiet and respectful around those the least aware or capable of appreciating it. A sign next to a door read, *Funeral Home Personnel Only*. In the lobby, there were state flags in one corner, a plant in another, and a framed auto-graphed photo of the Thunderbirds flying stunt team mounted on the wall.

Danny told the receptionist who we were, his succinct detective voice kicking in. I didn't really listen to what he said. I started feeling nervous and uncomfortable. I was about to become an official witness in a murder investiga-tion. I signed in on a clipboard and followed Danny into a hallway. On the right, two doors were closed. I could see a lecture room through the open door on my left. Danny turned and walked back to reception. "Which room are we in?" I heard him ask as I stepped into the empty lecture room and spotted a glass case along the side wall.

Inside the case were hats, mugs and T-shirts for the coroner's office. One of the shirts had a slot machine with the words stenciled on the back, *I CASHED OUT IN THE GAME OF LIFE! Clark County Coroner's Office*. The Vegas coroner's office had a gift shop.

"We're in here," I heard Danny say from the hall.

We stepped into the first small conference room. Danny had been here before.

"Have a seat, if you want," he said.

I sat down next to a small table. In the corner was a TV monitor with a hand control. The monitor was dark.

"You okay?" he asked.

I allowed a laugh. "I like the souvenirs out there."

He grinned and remained standing. "It's for charity," he told me. "The proceeds go to education for the coro-ner's office."

"It's been over fifteen years," I said. "What if I can't tell who she is."

"Just do the best you can. That's all we can ask."

"Is that what they'll show her on? That TV?"

"If it works. It hasn't worked for a while."

The door opened and two men entered. One wore a suit, the other a tie and shirt under a white lab coat. The guy in the lab coat held a manila folder. Neither looked like the great character actor Lionel Atwell. You need to Google him for an image as a mad scientist to really appreciate this—

They spoke with Danny and then introduced themselves to me. I couldn't really concentrate on what they were saying. I kept looking at the folder. It was, after all, what I was here for. To identify a murdered woman, to see if I knew her.

If only these guys knew how we got here, both her and I.

They all stood across the table from me as the lab coat guy opened the folder and handed me a photo. I reached for it, held it in front of me.

At first, I thought I was looking at an unwrapped Egyptian mummy. The skin was drawn tight and etched with wrinkles around her mouth, dried out like parchment. Her hair looked like black straw but there were other colors, lighter, separate tones. Her bangs were uneven. Her nose, her cheekbones, they were what clicked. If they ever found Queen Nefertiti in a Saharan tomb, she would look like this by now. Mindy obviously got into more than cocaine after the blizzard of 1987.

I don't know how many times I blinked. They said nothing.

"Her eyes are blue, aren't they?" I whispered.

They were closed in the photo in a lifeless sleep.

The lab coat guy said, "Yes."

I hesitated one more second because it wouldn't be true until I said it out loud.

"That's her."

Detective Olsen turned to the others and said, "Melinda Spires. I've got her file."

I put the photo on the table and took another folded photo from my back pocket. I showed it to them.

"I don't know if this will help but...this is what she used to look like."

At first, they only stared at the copy of the sepia-toned photo of Mindy and me from twenty years before. I'm dressed up like a cowboy and she's a saloon girl.

The man in the suit said, "Thank you, Mr. Bailey, we appreciate it but that won't be necessary."

They picked up their photo and offered their condolences before leaving the conference room. They were smart to do it this way, keeping me away from her remains. I felt like an actor standing backstage who didn't have to go out and do an impossible scene.

"That's it then?" I asked.

"That's it, buddy."

I folded the copy of the old-time photo and put it back in my pocket.

"I'm sorry, Jeff, but you've done what you can for her," he said. "Thanks for ID'ing her, man. Now we can find out who did this. I really want this one since you knew the victim, no matter who she was." He had the determined stare of a predator catching a scent.

I nodded.

"Were you able to find any names in your journal?" he asked.

"No. Not one."

"That's okay. Are you ready to get something to eat?"

I sat for a moment before saying, "Yeah. But I want to get a T-shirt before we leave."

———

"NOW THAT YOU know it's her, can you tell me anything about how she died?" I asked. We were driving to the buffet in Bally's, a place we liked that would be open in a half-hour.

"Blunt force trauma," Danny said. "It looks like someone beat her to death with a pipe or something. Nothing we found at the scene. At first we thought she might have fallen down."

There were no signs of a beating to her face and head.

"They didn't hit her face?"

"Well, that's how they do things now at the coroner's office," he said. "We've got guys who spend hours and hours working on photos on a computer to make the victims look like they're just sleeping. I covered one accident where a guy's head was torn off just under his eyes. I mean, the photo guy did a great job. He spent thirty-three hours reconstructing the top of his head on a computer, so the family would only see that. The victim just looked like he was sleeping."

"How long did he spend on Mindy?"

"Not as long. She was brought in the night I left a message for you."

"The night before last."

It felt like years ago.

"Do you have any leads?" I asked.

"Not much yet. We're turning up a lot of tweakers

who, of course, all act very suspicious and can't keep one sentence straight."

"Unfortunately, I know what a tweaker is."

We rode in silence. Of course, I knew what a tweaker was. I could also remember my last thought before finding out how close they were to me. *Why aren't the Christmas_tree lights on?* The moment before my world caved in.

Last December, I'd come home early from work and saw that none of the Christmas lights were plugged in. That was the depressing clue that my marriage was ending: coming home to a dark house at night over the holidays as the only person to notice that no Christmas lights were on. Then there was the moment right after I went inside that everything went completely flat line: leaning behind the tree, plugging the lights in and seeing into my stepdaughter's bedroom where her mother was lighting a meth pipe. My wife took a hit and was just handing it to her daughter as the Christmas tree lights blazed on. Their round, horrified faces looked out at me. All I could hear was that static tone that says all life was gone. Another bird with a broken wing had broken my heart.

There are just some things you can't come back from.

"We've got a description on a car that was parked at the apartment," he said. "I've got an ATL on it."

"An ATL?"

"Attempt To Locate. If an officer pulls that car over, my cell phone number will come up on the record for it. Most of her fifteen-year-old warrants were for drug use. There hasn't been anything recently, though."

"Maybe she got better at not getting arrested. How old was she?"

"Born in 1963. She flip-flopped the month and days on her arrest records so she was either born in November or December."

She was my age.

"We had a case a few months back where a pimp took one of his girls out in the desert, beat her to death, dumped gasoline on her and set her on fire. He also urinated on her in front of the other girls in his stable."

I stared at the road, at street signs, trying to erase the scene he'd just described for me.

"Melinda didn't have any arrests for prostitution in the past ten years so maybe she got away from that," he said. "I don't know if that helps or not."

I knew he was trying to sound hopeful and I appreciated it.

"Are you hungry?" he asked.

I gave a short derisive laugh. "I'm in the land of the endless buffet lines and, no, I'm not."

"Do you just want to grab a burger somewhere?"

"Sure."

"In and Out Burger sound good?"

I knew Danny liked In and Out Burgers since he could check under every soda cup to see a Bible verse stamped there, usually John 3:16. I also knew how it infuriated him to see some smart-ass punk altering their bumper sticker so it said, *IN AND OUT URGE.* I could see him ticketing every punk for desecrating the good name of In and Out Burgers. I could also see him arresting his best friend if this whole dead hooker thing turned on me.

Now I really wasn't hungry.

"They've opened a couple In & Outs in Phoenix now, too."

We crawled through traffic.

"You said they weren't into drugs at first, right?" Danny asked.

"No. Guy even threatened to kill me if I brought any around. Can you believe that?"

"When did you notice they were into drugs?"

10

Spanking For Dollars

August 1986

I HAD PICTURED the next time I saw her differently.

One of their big, dark cars pulls up to the Arrivals curb at McCarran Airport. Mindy gets out and waits at the driver's open window where Guy sits suspiciously inside, smoking a cig as his small eyes distrustfully dart at everyone coming out. Mindy's either dressed in her black casual clothes, jeans and a sleeveless top, or maybe one of her dresses for a date. Not the flashy formal stuff she wore as Angelique but something early-evening-nice. She looks relaxed, unhurried. She smiles. Those blue eyes light up. It's as if I never left. She's happy to see me. I hear Guy say, "There he is!"

I walk toward Mindy and she's walking to me. We embrace and hold each other. Her top is silk, her hair just as soft. She smells great, shampoo and fresh perfume. Guy gives us this moment. We lean back to look in each other's eyes. Slowly move forward to kiss. Those soft lips from the first night—-

Then my mother's third husband's voice booms over the airport P.A. system: "She just gave someone a head job in Bally's!"

I opened my eyes in my window seat as the plane taxied toward the gate. We just touched down. Through the heat vapors I saw the lights from the Strip outside dancing like curtains of flames in the night.

My previous trips had been during the chill of winter but now I would see Vegas in the scorching desert heat of a southwestern summer. Phoenix was normally a few degrees hotter so I knew what to expect.

McCarran had changed. The terminal was bigger, glitzier, more like a Vegas welcome than before. More slot machines too.

I called them from a pay phone and Guy answered. They were on their way. Instead of the happy welcome I dreamt on the plane, I quickly ducked into the backseat of their Lincoln Town car when it pulled up and they only glanced back to make sure it was me. A fellow gangster's greeting. At least I got the car right.

I watched the back of their heads as they chatted about the changes in the business. Everything felt different, but the three of us were together again.

"Since it's a fucking election year, the cops are cracking down on the escort services," Guy complained. "The politicians shut down the massage parlors so the business became escort services. Now that they're after the escorts, the next big thing is 'private dancers.'"

"Private dancers?" I asked.

"It's all the same thing—-that's the business of this town."

"Maybe you should try 'Solo Vaudevillians,'" I suggested.

Mindy blankly looked at Guy.

He asked, "What?"

"Solo Vaudevillians to your room! Give each girl a ventriloquist dummy and charge for a three-way."

They looked at each other, missing the joke.

"You know, just another cover name," I added, digging myself in deeper.

Great, I thought, five minutes into this trip and I'm already bombing with them.

Something else was agitating them more than my bad jokes. I caught glimpses of their eyes in the rearview mirror, brightly lit by the traffic headlights behind us. Mindy didn't say much but her blue eyes had the buzzing current of someone hopped up on something. Frying.

"We got our license," Guy said, anxious and talkative.

"Your license?" I asked.

I hoped he didn't mean a driver's license. Another difference of this trip was that I feared getting arrested with them, something I'd never thought about before.

"We're opening our own business," he said, flicking his cigarette out the window. "Our ads are supposed to hit the street tomorrow night."

"Angelique Enterprises," Mindy proudly said, making her first comment.

"We need the business," Guy grunted. "We got fucking arrested for pandering three weeks ago and it cost us three hundred dollars each to make bail. Another ninety to get the car back."

Mindy frowned at him, annoyed that he'd bring *that* up while discussing their latest venture.

I watched her from the back seat. Her black hair shimmered from the lights outside. Her eyes were a watery electric blue and her smooth skin looked pale and porcelain. She only looked at me with quick, nervous glances. I wondered what she thought of me now. How many men or women had she been with? Who was I to her? *This is the one who stays for free. He's the one who cares for me.*

When I had been up last time, I thought my role was to encourage them to get her out of the business, out of Vegas all together. As they rattled on about their latest business plan, I realized I was no longer being groomed as Mindy's Happily Ever After. With their ads coming out and their own escort service opening, they were more entrenched than ever in the Vegas underworld. Last year, they'd been aware of the degrading effects of their life-style, but now they seemed driven to succeed, proudly flaunting their cash and attitude. Hey, maybe all the running, the smoking, the hustling, the fucking wasn't that bad after all.

I wondered if I was now only their simple scribe, just another iron in their greedy fire. What had happened while I was gone?

Guy pulled the car into a gravel driveway and drove up to a large dark house on a wide-open lot. The walls of housing tracts lined the edge of the lot, but I could see the glow of the Strip not too far away.

"Wow, big house," I commented as I followed them in. I had yet to get a good look at Mindy, had only caught glimpses of her in the rear-view mirror.

The wide foyer appeared to be the center of the house. Tile floors. The smell of dog shit was horrendous.

"We've got a Doberman but she's out back," Guy huffed through the house. "So, we won't let her eat you." Since Guy looked even more obese than last time, I felt I would more likely end up on Guy's plate than in the dog's bowl. He looked huge and horribly unhealthy, worse than before.

Mindy ducked into the bathroom when we walked into the house and she returned to stand in the foyer and stare at me. Something was different about her. Without the bright lights of traffic pulsating across her hair, it seemed dull and flat. She appeared exhausted—-except for those blue eyes. She was thinner and looked sickly. The year that passed felt so brief until I saw her.

"I'm really tired, so I'm gonna say good night." She smiled.

"Tomorrow's gonna be a long night," Guy said from the kitchen.

They showed me my room and I was ready to crash myself.

Before I closed the door, I heard Mindy sniff, not as if she was catching cold but a wet, unconscious snort of air that made me think of something else.

That was the first time I'd noticed it and now I had an idea of what had happened since my last visit.

It was snowing in Vegas.

———

I DON'T KNOW how long I slept. The sun was up when Guy pounded on the door and rattled the doorknob. I woke up with a jolt and felt like I'd been running in a dream.

"Get out here, Jeff!" Guy yelled. "She's got a customer. Let's go."

I stumbled out of bed and opened the door. Sunlight glared off the tile floor outside.

"He's on his way," Guy said.

I put on shorts and a T-shirt and followed him through the house, looking down to keep from stepping on a Doberman turd. They brought customers here with that stench, I wondered.

Mindy stood in the living room at the end of the foyer. She wore a tiger-striped body stocking, spike-heeled black vinyl boots and a black leather belt with leather bracelets. And a spiked dog collar around her throat.

I stopped to stare. I'd seen her in jeans and dressed up in her glitter dress and feather boa, but this was my initial exposure to Angelique the Dominatrix. I'm sure my mouth was open. I asked myself, *I'm awake, right?*

She grinned and said, "Hi."

"Good morning," I replied, still groggy.

I shouldn't have been surprised. The year before she'd spent most of her time in the ADULT BOOKSTORE in the S&M section.

Guy's voice barked from the den, "Let's go!"

I passed a clock that said ten A.M. In the shadows of the house, I noticed several black cats darting about, chasing each other. I hadn't seen them last night but they explained why the smell was so overpowering. Doberman hanks with a spritz of cat shit. All they needed was a homeless wino pissing in the corners to get that full Modern Urban Disgusting scent.

Inside the sunken den with tall windows, Guy closed the door behind me and said, "Now, just listen." He waddled over to a desk and took a seat, putting on reading glasses and setting to work.

The first thing I noticed were newspapers spread out over every surface. Then I saw the models. Dozens of them. Military planes hung from string throughout the den, ships and other models, either partially-assembled or finished and left to dry, were on top of the newspapers. I sat down on the cool tile of the floor near the door and listened, waking myself up.

"She's had calls but they haven't been panning out," Guy said quietly. "She's blowing them on purpose...she doesn't feel like it."

I didn't know what to say to any of this.

"Her best calls are her Dominance calls," he added as he arranged the pieces of an airplane model with the focus of a surgeon.

"Dominance?" I whispered.

He looked over his glasses.

"Listen."

Within seconds, the front door bell rang and I heard Mindy's spiked heels clicking out to the foyer. The front door opened. A man's voice, but I couldn't make anything out he said. I looked to Guy. He was absorbed in snapping together a bi-plane model.

I leaned a little closer to the door. Their voices receded deeper into the house.

The crack of a whip startled me, and I jumped. I turned to Guy. He was carefully gluing together the wings of a Sopwith Camel.

After a silence, I heard Mindy's stern voice scolding

her client and then following him all the way out the front door. That didn't take long, I thought. The front door slammed and her spiked heels stomped back to the den. I jumped out of the way as the door flew open.

"He only brought thirty dollars!" she ranted. "I really felt like beating his ass and hit him once—-then I realized that was what he *wanted!*"

She looked at me, Angelique the exasperated Dominatrix, waving an oiled glistening paddle at me.

"These people!" she snapped.

———

AFTER I SHOWERED AND DRESSED, we got into their Lincoln and headed to a newspaper office to check on one of their ads. Not only was Guy putting out their own smutty handbills that would litter the Strip, he was putting ads in the smaller newspaper and auto trader personals in town. For such a media blitz, they had no other girls, despite Guy's bragging that soon he and Mindy would command their own stable. Mind would be carrying the entire workload.

"I could even get some business for you, Jeff," he said as we cruised through town.

"Don't do it," Mindy whispered over the back of the passenger seat. "It's all fruiters."

"Fruiters?" I asked.

"Fags. Guys call for guys. It's disgusting."

I chuckled to myself: Mindy Spires, the last bastion of normal paid straight sex.

"He wouldn't have to *do* anything," Guy grumbled.

I felt that they were only killing time when we drove

all the way out to a Henderson casino to eat at a buffet. We talked, but they were too preoccupied with the ads hitting the streets. If they hadn't been, they might have noticed that I wasn't quite the same wide-eyed bumpkin who rode with them the year before, all dazzled and gullible. I tried to dress better and carry myself more professionally, reserved but observant. I was working on three screenplays for my run at Hollywood.

Guy ate an incredible amount of food at the buffet. His breathing was more labored than the last visit. After he huffed back for his six or seventh plate, I asked Mindy, "How's his health doing?"

She looked to see that he was gone and said, "I have to stay on him about his meds or he won't take them."

I watched him pile up another plate as if slopping feed for a trough of livestock.

Guy was insulted when I offered to buy lunch.

Back at the house, I took some photos of Mindy on the Lincoln. She held her black cats for a couple of pics. She put the cats down and they chased her timid Doberman through the house, scrambling over monstrous turds everywhere. Most of the time, the Doberman was skittish and easily spooked, poking its head through a doorway for an uneasy peek or fleeing outside when Mindy appeared in her Dominatrix regalia. The whip probably scared the Doberman but it wasn't for pets.

Mindy beats men into orgasms for a living but she can't housetrain one dog.

Guy decided he would cook for us that night and, after sundown, we headed out to pick up some prime rib. Of course, we stopped at the newspaper boxes along the Strip and they had me run out to grab a handful of handbills to see if theirs had arrived. Not yet.

While Guy cooked dinner, Mindy and I went swimming in their huge pool. She wore a one-piece and sat on the steps in the water while I floated around. I frequently saw Guy's enormous bulk standing in the doorway to check on us.

"Are you still writing?" she asked, holding her legs together.

"Sure. I'm mostly working on the movie scripts."

I watched spotlights in the distance waving overhead from the glow of the Strip.

"What did you go to school for?" she asked.

"Film, at first. Then English Lit."

She stared down into the water. "So, you've probably read a lot of books, huh?"

"I'm working on it."

"I can't remember the last book I read," she said. "I have a hard time staying interested."

"Well, you live a pretty active lifestyle," I said vaguely and smiled at her.

"You still gonna write a book about me?"

"Yes. I'm taking notes."

I floated just beyond the drop into the deep end.

"You ever read love stories?" she asked.

"Old ones. I used to skim through my stepmother's Harlequin romances for a laugh."

"What was funny about 'em?"

"Names and characters. They're such fantasies. They couldn't possibly be real people. I would at least pick one up to read the last line."

"'And they lived happily ever after'?" she asked.

"That's what they said—-but they couldn't say it that every time. It was funny to see how many ways there were to say the same thing. Had to have a happy ending though."

She let go of her legs and sat back against the step. I could see her white face framed by her jet-black hair, and I felt a knot of tension in my stomach when I thought about swimming to her and touching her, holding her. I imagined Guy charging out of the house like a snorting bull, ripping the screen door off its hinges. *THE ADS ARE COMING OUT TONIGHT!*

"What were the old books like?" She laughed. "They probably really said, 'And they lived happily ever after.'"

"No, not usually. The books that last, the classics, don't end very happily."

"Really?"

"The ones I really like are about a guy who spends his whole life wanting one woman. They never get together because of a war or a marriage, or the lovers do get together but she dies—-or something like that. She becomes more of a symbol of what he wants that collides with the reality of who she is."

Thinking of her poems I'd read the year before, I looked at her across the pool. It felt like an ocean between us.

"Do they ever do it?" she asked, staring directly at me. "You know, get it on?"

"Sometimes they don't," I said. "I just read one where a guy, an artist, spends his whole life wanting a woman. But she's married and a little older than him. He only realizes how long he's spent wanting her when she visits and takes off her hat to reveal a head of gray hair. Their whole lives had passed them by but she was his true love. Never even kissed. Sometimes the one true love is no more than an ideal that doesn't involve sex, really."

We stared at each other, light reflecting off the water and our eyes. The moment passed.

She laughed and said, "Well, if they ever write one about just sex, I'll bet I got a whole fucking library inside of me!"

She put her head down, embarrassed but still amused.

I lowered my voice and said, "Don't think I'm not interested."

She looked up at me.

"About what?"

"Don't think that I'm not interested in making love to you someday," I said quietly. "That sex isn't important to me."

She glanced over her shoulder at the house.

"I've wanted you from the moment, no, the *second* I saw you," I told her evenly. "So, I will go along with this arrangement and I'll jump through every hoop and I will ignore everything you do to survive in this town because I want all of you. *Everything.*"

She stared back at me, her eyes wide with a smile.

"Do you tell him everything we talk about?" I asked.

"He makes me."

"Then I'll leave this up to you. I'll trust you whether you tell him about this or not."

She looked down in the water.

"Do you think about me when you're gone?" she asked.

"I have the journals to prove it. I imagine how we'll live together as a couple, start a family. I wonder how your body will look in the morning light, how you'll wear your hair in the winter. I wonder if you'll be happy."

She lifted her eyes and stared at me, expressionless. She stood up, her back to the house. She opened the towel over her shoulders and without taking her eyes from mine, she hooked her thumbs under the straps of her bathing suit and pulled it down. I glanced at her breasts, memorizing her nipples but trying to maintain eye contact with her. I didn't have to imagine what she looked like in the nude anymore—

She said softly, "Wait for me."

Over her shoulder, I saw Guy's silhouette in the door to the house. He must have sensed the air charging between the two of us. She abruptly wrapped herself in the towel and strode toward the house.

"Dinner's ready!" Guy called out.

I wanted to hold her and kiss her so badly, just like those characters in the classic novels I talked about. How would Guy react to see his scribe making a move on Angelique Enterprise's chief product?

Inside, the delicious aroma of prime rib was displacing the animal odors, thankfully. I tried to understand the meaning of a house that alternated between the dueling smells of prime rib and dog shit.

Over dinner, we discussed the meaning of life. Guy put the same Jedi master solemnity into his theory that the human race was started as an experiment by extraterrestrials as he did for his discourses on running hookers. Mindy ate and feigned interest until she threw in, "I believe in reincarnation."

"Really?" I asked.

"Do you?"

"Not really."

She cocked her head at me. "Why not?"

"Just wasn't the way I was raised. And it doesn't make sense to me. I think it's easier for people to think they'll get another chance so they don't take any real responsibility in this life. But that's my opinion."

She shrugged and chewed a bite of food. I sensed that she only comprehended that I disagreed with her, not anything about what I said.

"Do you know who Nefer-titty is?" Guy asked.

"Excuse me?"

"Nefer-titty?"

I wanted to ask, Are you saying Nefertiti, the Egyptian queen? My west coast friends pronounced it *Nefer-tee-tee* but the only way I'd heard it in the Midwest—-perhaps to avoid sounding remotely sexual—-was *Nefer-tie-tee*. Coming from Guy the pimp, there was no missing the word *titty* in her name.

"She was the Egyptian goddess of sex," Guy informed me. He pointed his steak knife at Mindy. "That's who *she* was in a previous life."

I don't know if it showed, but I thought this was the most ridiculous thing I'd heard them say. It was probably something Guy used to boost her self-esteem. She was not just a prostitute, but an erotic goddess, Nefer-titty, who happened to like watching *The Flintstones*. Back in Arizona, I looked it up. Nefertiti was a queen famed for her beauty, the mother-in-law of Tutankhamen, but she was not a goddess. I was just relieved it wasn't Isis since Guy would probably pronounce it *Ass-ass*.

Guy's pile of prime rib was incredible. No wonder he weighed nearly four hundred pounds and Mindy still couldn't cook. My cut of meat was so delicious that when I took my first bite, I was sure I felt a rush of endorphins in my bloodstream. It was that good. So good that I even boasted I could keep up with Guy's eating.

Big mistake. And, thankfully, I didn't put any dollar amount on that bet. I tried, because he cooked up an impressive amount of prime rib. But he ate enough that, despite his massive, swollen girth, it bordered on becoming a magic trick: how could one human consume that much of anything and live? A twenty-foot boa constrictor couldn't eat that much, and they can unlock their jaws!

I sat across from him, my gut stuffed, gasping like an asthmatic, a dazed fool tossed aside by a master. He chortled as he continued cutting and eating, eating and cutting.

"Good?" he asked.

I nodded, vanquished.

"Now," Guy started, "about the book."

"He writes movies," Mindy informed him.

He waved her off.

"Then it can be a movie," he said. "But it'll need to be more than one because I have way too much for just a movie. Maybe too much for your damn book."

I nodded.

"What will it be called?" Mindy asked.

Guy stared at me, waiting.

I said, "*Vegas Working Girl.*"

Mindy laughed. Guy mulled it over.

She said, "I like it!"

I was going to let them choose between that or *Nefertitty, Queen of the Strip*, but thought better of it.

"Well, once we get our business up and going," Guy said, "we'll *pay* you to come up here and write it for us. But get me an outline first."

I thought dismally, Great, my first meeting as a writer didn't happen on a Hollywood studio lot but in a Dominatrix's Vegas sex den.

"I have three screenplays ready to start sending to agents," I told them. "A horror, a comedy, and one set at my nuclear plant back home. I've heard it's always better to have more than one script to submit."

"To where? Movie studios?" Guy asked.

"Agencies. They get you into the studios."

"Fuckin' Steven Spielberg here," Guy chuckled.

I nodded. Considered what I was about to ask.

"What about that other thing?"

They stared at me.

Guy asked, "What other thing?"

"The other part...of the deal."

Guy shook his head, frustrated. "What the fuck are you talking about?"

I flashed on our previous dinner at the Aladdin. There was nothing here to keep him from pulling a gun or knife on me. Right then I was Guy's friend and I questioned the wisdom of broaching this, but I had to know.

I said evenly, "Mindy's retirement."

Mindy looked at him, calmly awaiting his reply.

This time Guy laughed.

"Are you going anywhere, Mindy?" he asked her.

"Nope. Nowhere."

"And would you like to tell Mr. Writer why?"

"Because our ads are coming out tonight."

I don't know if it was worse this time or not. The last

time I wondered if Guy would kill me but I'd had a glimmer of hope, some indication that she might be mine. The threat of bodily harm or death was gone but it hurt to feel so distant from her, to be put in my place by the girl I was here to rescue. *You just showed me your tits!* His programming worked this time although I suspected some other substance was assisting Guy's mind control techniques.

But I also remembered her whisper by the pool, *Wait for me.*

"Now let me explain something to you, Jeffy," Guy said, grinning. "She knows she's gotta earn, I know I gotta earn...and you need to know that you gotta earn. I told you that she's special. Prime rib for breakfast. So, write the fucking book and earn your place at the table."

Mindy told him, "He writes movie scripts."

"Whatever."

So much for the romance angle of *Vegas Working Girl.*

What did they think this story was supposed to be about? What happened to the man who told me that he wanted Mindy out of this business, out of Vegas, before she turned into those other "whores" he despised? Did he remember Jody Spinner, or whatever her name was? And did he really just call me "Jeffy?"

If I wanted some idea of the kind of story they were more interested in living, I found out after dinner when we watched their new favorite movie on videocassette: *Scarface.* The "remake" with Al Pacino. Mindy's eyes had lit up when she asked me if I had seen it. I probably had the same expression when they told me that Mindy was the reincarnation of Nefertiti, kind of a pained wince with a forced grin. I never liked *Scarface,* no matter how much it drew me in every time I saw it. I thought the characters were repellent and eventually pathetic so I couldn't sympathize with their coked-out downfall. A scumbag rises and falls, so what was the point? I watched it the same way I watched a car crash along the freeway: I couldn't take my eyes off it but I wouldn't exactly give either one a good review either.

The nicest thing I could say was, "Well, it's not as good as *The Godfather*."

"You know when they cut that guy in half in the shower with the chainsaw?" she asked me. "They really do that. That actually happened."

"Colombians," Guy added.

"I thought it hurt the emotional storyline to put such a shocking scene so early on," I said. Their confused glances said we were in totally different worlds.

Watching *Scarface* with them put me in mind of the has-been Norma Desmond and the hack Joe Gillis sitting down to watch her old silent films in *Sunset Boulevard*, except instead of a faded silent movie queen I was sharing delusions with a gigantic Vegas mobster wanna-be. Jeffy, the hack movie writer. My cynicism and self-loathing had started. When the phone rang, Mindy took it and came back to say she needed to go out. Guy drove her. They left me alone with the Doberman to finish the movie. I thought about fast-forwarding it but since they'd probably seen it enough times, they'd know I skipped some when they returned. I sat back, my gut bursting with prime rib and watched *Scarface* in a Dominatrix's big house in Las Vegas.

I said to the Doberman, "Hey, I forgot Robert Loggia was in this. Cool."

———

THEIR PHONE RANG but I didn't answer it. I did lower the TV volume to listen to any message. At the sound of Guy's voice on the recorder, I stood up and so did the Doberman, its rear trying to wag a tail it didn't have anymore.

"Jeff, if you hear this, you don't have to answer," Guy's said through a humming static. "Something came up so we'll be out longer. A customer's coming by around eleven or twelve so stay out of sight—"

Mindy's voice interrupted him but I couldn't make out what she said.

"Yeah," Guy continued. "If you want to go out for a while, call a cab and come back later. After one or so. Meet the cab on the corner."

Before the message cut off, I heard Mindy impatiently say, "Guy, tell him to…"

I sat down on the sofa, thinking as a muted *Scarface* played on. When I noticed the Doberman taking a shit on the tile floor at the kitchen entrance, I decided to go wander the Strip for a while.

I called for a cab and gave them the address I found on an electric bill in Guy's study. I met the cabbie at the end of the drive and said, "Take me to the Strip."

The driver, an older, fast-talking guy with stubble and darting eyes in the rearview mirror, pulled out without turning the meter on.

"How's the town treatin' ya?" he asked.

"Not too bad. Just up visiting friends."

His eyes shifted from the traffic to me, back and forth.

"You lookin' for a good time?" he asked.

"What kind of a good time?"

"Little place I know. You get a broad, a bottle, and a hot tub."

"Really?"

"Yeah, it's great. I always offer it to someone who looks like they're lookin' for a good time, ya know what I mean? I don't just say it to everyone."

"Thanks."

"Yeah, a broad, a bottle, a hot tub—-it's fuckin' great!"

Instead, I went to Caesars Palace. He dropped me off and gave me a business card with his cab number scribbled on the back.

"Just ask for me," he said after I got out. "Don't worry about payin' me for that ride—-I get money from their end, ya know what I mean?"

"Cool. Thanks."

I tipped him and wandered around Caesars.

Outside of the main entrance, at the end of the row of waiting taxis, I browsed over a scale model encased in Plexiglas of a new Coliseum planned for future construction. I wondered if they intended to bring back the gladiator games of Ancient Rome as an extreme sport. How would this fit into the cabbie's pitch? "You get a broad, a bottle, a hot tub, and you get to watch two guys kill each other—-it's fuckin' great!"

Oddly juxtaposed next to the model was a golden Buddhist shrine. It belonged on the Strip as much as a crucifix belonged on the neck of a porn star but if someone bowed down at the plaque amongst the candles and went on to win big in the casino, then I suppose it served its purpose.

I walked to the crowded corner of Flamingo Boulevard and Las Vegas Boulevard in the hot night air. More people in the summer. I looked up at the towering marquee in front of Bally's. DEAN MARTIN. He was here, the king of Vegas cool himself. I checked on the showtimes and found they were sold out. I wandered back outside, slightly disappointed but certain I'd get another chance. Frank, Dean, Sammy. They would always be here, wouldn't they? They could wheel the three of them out on their backs in separate iron lungs and people would still jostle to look in the mirrors over their faces just to watch them wink and breathe. "Hey, pallie, just keep that bourbon IV flowing and get some dame to light and hold that cig to my lips, baby."

As I walked along a line of cars parked off Flamingo next to Bally's, I spotted a pretty black girl sitting behind the wheel of a parked Monte Carlo. She waved. I stopped and looked around, wondering if she meant me. No one else had stopped on the sidewalk. I pointed to myself and she beckoned me over with a finger. I went.

"Hi," she said.

"Hi."

She had freckled caramel skin and her eyes were naturally wide. She spoke in a high voice with full puckering lips, "Hey, do you want some company?"

"What kind of company?"

"Well, do you want a blowjob?"

"Uhm...."

"Thirty dollars."

I looked into the car and could see another black girl in the passenger seat. No one in the back. I looked around the parking lot and up at the Bally's marquee on the Strip. What would the Rat Pack do? How would Frank swing? I walked around the car and the other girl stepped out to let me sit between them. They drove to the back of the lot away from the light.

I asked them where they were from. The driver said she was from Columbus, Ohio, and she smiled when I told her I'd grown up just outside in Fairfield County. She kissed me. They worked with the efficiency of paramedics —-with me as an accident victim sprawled between them. The passenger slid a condom on just a nanosecond before her mouth swallowed me. I was just too nervous, too hot in the stifling car, looking around the parking lot wondering what in the world I was doing here, doing this. My bloated stomach hurt from dinner. The passenger wasn't attractive at all and she was abrupt and pushy. I didn't believe her when she said they were both thirty years old. The pretty driver looked like early twenties. They talked to each other as if I wasn't there. The pushy co-worker said, "Phew, this is our first one and my jaws are already tired. I bet he makes his girlfriend happy."

"I don't have a girlfriend," I admitted, reminding them that the rest of me was still there. A bead of sweat rolled down the back of my neck.

What are you doing? What happened to the great Vegas love story you came for?

"We're gonna have to fuck him," the pretty one commented, but I was so nervous that I just wanted to get out of there. I felt like I'd just snapped out of a trance and could see that I wasn't this person, not the character I wanted for my story. Not really me. We were in a parking lot!

I had to get out of there. I was screwing this up—

"That's okay. Thanks. You girls were great."

"Thirty dollars," the pretty one said.

I handed over two twenties. The passenger opened her door and stepped out, saying, "Well, that'll be another ten dollars for suckin' on my titty." I'd kissed it once, but I didn't haggle, I just wanted out of there. Her nipple tasted chalky from baby powder.

I watched them drive away and wondered how this fit into anything. Again, I'd wandered into Vegas and allowed myself to be swept up in another typical transaction, but for what? *There's nothing special about you, Jeffy! Anyone can do this—*

I was so certain that Mindy was something special, something meant to be, but here I was paying for the services of another working girl. Two of them! I didn't care for the pushy passenger but the cute driver with the faint freckles and the wide-open eyes attracted me, intrigued me. The way she shrugged and said they would have to have sex with me to give me my money's worth was funny and, to me, endearing. What was her story? How did she get from Columbus to here? Was she ready to escape, to be rescued?

How pathetic did that make me for wanting to take all of them home?

Riding in a different cab back to the corner near Mindy's house, I wondered what made my story with Mindy so special if there were girls all over town whose lives were just like hers. Maybe theirs were more interesting. Maybe they wanted out more. I also wondered how deeply Mindy's hysterical racism from her traumatic past went and what she would do if she found out I'd been with black girls. This was one benefit of growing up on James Bond since I was not only tolerant of other races but I found women of all races exotic and sexy. If 007 could hop on women from all over the world, so would I. That misogynist, imperialist spy probably taught me more about tolerance and diversity than anyone else, making me the most progressive, equal-opportunity hedonist I know. Along with Elvis, of course—

I'm just a red-blooded boy
And I can't stop thinkin' about
Girls, girls, girls!

Even if any green chicks showed up—which was a distinct possibility in that town—Captain James T. Kirk taught me to go interstellar with my wee-little warp drive. I was covered for all the dames—

Mindy and Guy were still gone as I walked up the driveway to the house. As I approached the front door, I heard the clacking claws and low growls of the Doberman inside. I put my hand on the doorknob but decided not to go inside. I had enough prime rib in me that the dog might tear me apart to get at it. Instead I walked around the house and plopped down in a chair by the pool, staring at the glow from the Strip and enjoying the cooler air coming off the water.

How many sordid encounters did I need before I'd find what I was looking for? How many can be written off as "research"?

No, Mindy would be different. I did love her. I would prove it. *Wait for me.*

I was acting on a good and selfless motive. I was in enemy-occupied territory and I was trying to get someone out, a rescue as well as a romance. I was a guy who could fix it, make everything right. I had so much to offer. I could save her. I could save us both.

It was that foolish and confusing shift between love and sex that would just about get me killed.

———

THE ELEVEN O'CLOCK client seeking a good whipping or whatever form of punishment he desired didn't show up but eventually Mindy and Guy did. They were so preoccupied by their upcoming ad blitz that they didn't appear to mind. It was the calm before the storm. When I asked if we could drive down Fremont Street so I could take photographs, Guy drove us downtown but didn't spin any words of underworld wisdom or relive any memories of Mafia glory days. It was late but they were happy to get out again before the phone began ringing off the hook.

After a few hours' sleep the following morning, they had me dash out of the Lincoln and grab handbills from the newspaper boxes, and we raced through them, hunting for their ads.

I didn't eat until lunch and I wasn't that hungry then.

We stopped off at a garage so Guy could chat with his friend who ran it.

"He's in the car game and I'm in the girl game," Guy said before hoisting himself out and waddling toward him. Mindy and I waited in the car. I watched him talk with the car game guy. They were both middle-aged, horribly unfit, very friendly with each other, wheeling and dealing cars or women.

Guy waved me out. I went over to them, and Guy introduced us. (I did not write his name in my journal).

"I want to show you something," he said.

We walked around a garage as Guy told his friend that I was a writer from Phoenix, preparing a book about Mindy and him. The skeptical friend raised his eyebrows in an attempt to look impressed.

"You see that engine there?" Guy asked.

There was a motor on a black tarp in the back of an older model pickup truck.

"Yeah."

"Do you know who that belonged to?"

I wanted to say Bugsy Siegel, the mobster who started Las Vegas, but then I wondered what relevance this engine had unless it was actually involved in some historic event. Was this the engine from the car Bugsy was driving at the time when he was killed, parked outside of his lover's home in LA?

Guy said, "Elvis."

"That engine belonged to Elvis?" I asked.

I longed to remind Guy that he'd called Elvis a "punk" the year before, but it was obvious he wanted me to be impressed in front of his friend. I tried faking it. "Wow. Elvis."

Why did this particular engine have any more significance than any other engine that had been in the King's possession? I mean, he'd given plenty of other engines away—-with whole cars around them.

"There's some money sittin' there," Guy's friend said.

We spent most of the day driving to every model and hobby store in Las Vegas. Guy was looking for a model sub he wanted to build, one that he could actually operate via remote in the pool. We never found it. The only money I spent, other than during my little visit to the

Strip, was for a couple of model airplanes for Guy and a framed print of a tiger for Mindy to match her Domination leotard. Very romantic, I know.

We stopped off at their office, a nondescript space in a little business park. There were no signs or plaques outside to identify the businesses housed there. No windows, only doors and walls. It was after sunset, and all the other doors were dark. Inside Angelique Enterprises, there was only a cheap desk on a ratty carpet with a multi-line phone and a desk lamp on it. And a pile of sex ads on a chair. How many calls for escorts were made in the city of Las Vegas on a weekend? How could one girl keep up?

While Guy locked up the office, Mindy and I waited at the car across the parking lot.

"Mindy," I whispered.

She glanced back at Guy, and then turned to me.

"We don't have much time but I wanted to talk to you."

Her expression didn't change as she said, "You've found someone else."

"No. I want to know if you're ready yet."

She sniffled. Didn't she remember what she said by the pool?

"Ready to what?"

I'd noticed a difference in their behavior from the moment I'd landed in their Town car. Their sniffling, their disconnect, their distance. But I knew everything had changed when she looked at me at that moment: she had no idea of what I was talking about, leaving me hanging like a spy who'd uttered a code word to the wrong contact. Or worse, a double agent.

"Are you ready to get out of here?" I asked.

"You mean leave Guy?"

"Is he ready to go?"

She shook her head, her brow creasing as if that was the stupidest question in the world.

I said, "Then I guess I mean leave him, yes."

I could tell by the look on her face, the way her eyes looked down and her lips parted, that she hadn't thought about this until this second.

She absently said, "He's been like a father to me."

"Yeah," I said dismissively. "A father who fucks you."

There was a flash of outrage, then deep hurt, then a blank numbness.

I heard Guy shuffling across the pavement. She looked at me, completely blank. I knew she would repeat this conversation to him. I knew I was going to see that gun on the table again.

She was changing before my eyes. Wearing herself out. Aging. She couldn't have been on the streets very long when I first met her, and that would've been the moment to get her away from Vegas, from Guy, from the frightening physical toll of surviving minute by minute on the streets.

Maybe I should've run off with the black girls. The driver was so pretty and the whole interracial element would be new and interesting. I couldn't play the naïve, love-struck rube anymore, as if that had been an appealing character in the first place. Any love, like their version of success, was getting buried under a pile of fantasy bullshit.

I hugged her goodbye at the house. I could feel ribs this time and she sniffled in my ear.

"You take care of yourself," she whispered.

"You too."

Guy drove me to the airport, talking most of the way. He pulled up to Departures and I got out, closed the door and looked back in at him through the open window.

"I'm tryin' to pay ya a compliment," he said, exhausted.

I missed what he'd said. I thanked him anyway for whatever his compliment was.

As he drove off, I realized how late I was for my flight. I sprinted through the airport and nearly missed my plane. The gate attendants were taking down the numbers from the flight info board and the plane was preparing to push away.

I developed the photos when I got back. Mindy looked small and wilted as she sat on the hood of the Lincoln. Even the dim night shots when I'd jumped out at red lights on Fremont Street made the neon spectacle overexposed and underwhelming. I wouldn't be able to count on photographs to recall the awe of gliding into those lights for the first time. I just had to keep the memory from drifting further and further away.

But, as anyone who's been to Vegas in the past ten years can tell you, you can't drive down that street anymore.

11

Two Packs Of Sugar

APRIL 2005

I SAT in Danny's SUV as he dodged through the heavy traffic on the way to In & Out Burgers. My stomach growled but I wasn't hungry. Instead I felt wide awake but sluggish from exhaustion, the usual stayed-too-long-in-Vegas fatigue.

Danny got off the Strip and took Koval Lane heading south. I guessed he was heading for the In and Out across the Strip on Tropicana. We stopped at a traffic light on Flamingo. I could hear a police siren in the distance. I looked at the light and the intersection and said, "Two packs of sugar."

Danny said, "Yeah."

We were sitting at the intersection where Tupac Shakur had been shot on a Saturday night, September 7, 1996. Danny was one of the first responding officers on the scene. Over a dozen shots were fired into the car after a Mike Tyson fight and nobody in the crowd saw anything. "Suge" Knight, the president of Death Row Records, sitting in the driver's seat right next to Tupac, didn't see a thing even after a bullet grazed his huge shaved head (all the other bullets hit Tupac). The car filled with their bodyguards behind them didn't see a thing. Nobody saw anything. Danny told me that the Vegas PD was so angry at the wall of silence from everyone who saw everything that they referred to the victim as Mr. Two Packs of Sugar when interviewing the bodyguards, deliberately trying to provoke them.

"It's Tupac, man!" the bodyguards raged.

"Yes, that's what I said, Mr. Two Packs of Sugar," the cops calmly repeated.

None of them took the bait and attacked the police so Suge Knight and the bodyguards went back to L.A. It's still an open murder case, the Internet is abuzz with endless conspiracies, and Tupac still puts out CDs, fueling Elvis-type rumors that he's still alive.

"Oh, no," Danny assured me. "He's gone."

"Yeah, I know," I said. "I saw an autopsy photo of him that was leaked online. The Y incision and everything."

At the In and Out Burger, we got our order and sat down to eat at a small table next to a window. A line of vehicles inched to the drive-thru outside while eat-in order numbers were called out over the throng at the counter.

I knew Danny would want to say a blessing over our burgers so I waited. He glanced at me and we bowed our heads.

"Heavenly Father, we ask your blessing on this meal and thank you for this time of fellowship together," he said rapidly. "We ask for you to give rest to Melinda and remember the lost girls on our streets everywhere. In Jesus' name we pray, Amen."

I opened my eyes with my head still bowed. I could see Danny salting his fries. It broke my heart to think that nobody prayed for Mindy in her final years. She had fallen out of my own thoughts so long ago.

"The lost girls," I mumbled.

"What's that?" Danny asked, sipping his milkshake.

"She was so lost," I said. "Now she's on Shadow Lane. Some guy she knew twenty years ago had to come identify her."

"At least she had that. We still have a lot with no one stepping forward to ID them."

"I've seen the coroner's website."

"It's sad. I see it all the time."

I took a drink of my soda and felt the cold run down the empty walls inside my stomach.

"He has to be dead," I added.

"Guy Reinhart?"

"It'd be too crazy for him to survive—-but this whole thing is insane."

"Stranger things have happened. And usually to you."

I nodded. "Yes, they do."

"He probably died under a different name," he said. "Maybe somewhere else."

Danny bit into his burger. I picked at my fries.

"I never thought he'd leave Vegas. He was always bragging about his Mob connections but I figured he was just full of bull. Real mobsters would never waste their time on someone like him." I was sure he just died of natural causes somewhere, brought on by unnatural appetites.

"The Mob's not really here anymore," Danny stated.

"This was back in the Eighties, just before the town went Disney and the FBI cleaned them out. Guy drove around in a big Lincoln, wearing his big fedora. The funny thing is I'll bet my dad back in Ohio had more face time with real mobsters than Guy—-and he was a truck driver!"

"Your dad?"

"Teamster."

"Oh, okay," he said, understanding.

Danny ate more of his burger. I could tell he wasn't interested in discussing criminals in any other way but busting them. Mobsters shouldn't be admired, they should be incarcerated.

"My dad would see rioting at a college or in the Middle East on TV and he'd say, 'They ought to let the Mafia run those countries. You wouldn't have any rioting then! You don't see anyone tearing up the streets in Vegas.'"

"Doesn't matter who's in charge, they're going to protect the money," Danny threw in. "The Mafia's been run out of here for a while. Now it's the gangbangers out of L.A. trying to move in. Mexico too."

I asked him, "Did you see *Casino*?"

"No."

"The guy Joe Pesci played. Tony Spilotro."

"Tony the Ant. I know who he was."

"He was beaten to death back east and buried with his brother in a cornfield in the summer of '86. I was up here running around with Mindy and Guy that summer, watching *Scarface*, while the FBI was chasing the mob out of Vegas."

Danny said, "It's a different place now."

"Yeah. Not as good as *The Godfather* though."

He allowed a grin.

I blurted, "I'm going to divorce my wife."

His grin vanished. This felt like a moment from one of the classic novels I'd told Mindy about: the understated bombshell dropped during tea, a confession stated stiffly in polite society—-except it was casually uttered in a Vegas In-n-Out Burger instead of an elegant London parlor a hundred years ago.

"There's no other way?" Danny asked.

"I caught Allison smoking meth with her daughter on Christmas Eve. In our house. In my house."

Danny stared. I could tell his mind was madly calculating that into his Christian equation, trying to add everything up to anything but divorce. He didn't have to remind me about my vow to God when I married Allison. He had stood right next to me as my best man when I made it.

"There are just some things you don't come back from," I finally said.

"I'm sorry," he said.

"I knew Allison used to have, uhm, a problem. I never knew it had been as bad as it was before we got together. She told me that if she had a stable home and happy marriage, she wouldn't want to do that anymore. We hoped for the best."

"So, what happened?"

"Her daughter moved in with us. Dawn didn't get along with her dad and I knew she'd come to us. Daughters want to be with their mothers."

"I'm glad I have two boys," he said.

"I hear that. Everything was going fine until the teen rebellion thing hit. Allison just completely buckled. I would tell Dawn to be home by ten o'clock and she would remind me that I wasn't her dad. If Allison ever thought about backing me up, Dawn would tell her that Mommy always loved the men in her life more than her own kid, which destroyed Allison. She caved every single time."

"And you caught them?"

"I got off work early on Christmas Eve so I thought I'd surprise them. Try to make a good holiday out of it. Things had been falling apart for months. Lies, open defiance. I walked in the house and the tree wasn't lit. Allison had the decorations up Thanksgiving weekend and there are no lights on for Christmas Eve! So, I walked over to the tree and leaned behind it to plug in the lights. From there I could see into Dawn's room. They didn't even see me, never heard me come in the house. When I saw my wife pass that glass pipe to her daughter, my marriage ended. Time of death: one-thirty-five A.M., Friday, December 24, 2004."

After a moment, Danny asked, "There's no working it out? Has anything changed?"

"Oh, they're both in treatment. Four months now. I guess they're clean. Staying with friends. I haven't filed yet because I want them to use my medical benefits from work to get themselves together."

"But that's it?"

"She says she's sorry about the drugs and the drama," I told him, "but I know there's one thing she's not sorry about. She's not sorry about choosing her daughter over me. It's the mistake we'll never get past because Allison doesn't see it as a mistake."

Danny frowned. "Even if the kid is totally wrong?"

"Dawn's boyfriend was also her dealer. They kept him away from me and I never met him. And Dawn's still seeing him. Oh, they're in love! I just had an argument with Allison a couple of weeks ago because that worthless piece of shit—-sorry—-is still around. But what do I know about love? When did I ever find it? And when the dealer knocks Dawn up, I'll just have to deal with that. Then he'll be more blood than me. *Their dealer* will mean more than me."

Gradually the sounds of the restaurant around us could be heard again. I wondered if I would ever get beyond this deafening hurt and rage.

"You see," I said, "I could justify divorcing Allison because of her miserable parenting skills or the drugs or what have you, but the truth is they let me know I was nothing in my own house, nothing to my own family. They're all blood and I'm not. From their point of view, I'm the one who's messed up. I'm the one who doesn't belong."

Danny sighed. I knew he was trying to think of something to say.

I quietly added, "I didn't belong as a kid. I've known that feeling my whole life. I wasn't about to live that way as an adult. Not in my own house."

Another rescue gone wrong, I realized. I could've written my marriage story and put a happy ending on it...but the villain, the monster of addiction, wasn't permanently vanquished, just left behind for a time. I could write it to the point where I married Alison and we had a happy home for a while, but the monster came back and the damage was done. It would be years later before I realized that it wasn't her addiction that killed us, it was the hidden wound of loneliness in me. The little circle of addicts—mother, daughter, dealer boyfriend—cut me out of my own life so I destroyed everything.

As usual, my own fingerprints were all over the weapons that killed me. But first I had to deal with this dead hooker thing—

We finished our meals and watched the cars in the drive-thru line.

"Hey, the boys have a Little League game tonight," Danny said. "You can come along if you want."

Before I could answer, Danny's cell phone rang and he snatched it off his belt.

"This is Olsen."

He listened, then bolted up and marched outside. I heard him formally answer someone named Officer Sanchez before the door closed behind him. He paced outside, talking quickly, his brow creasing and his stare intensifying at the ground in front of him. He hung up and looked in at me. Something's happened.

He came back to the table without sitting down.

"We've got someone," he said.

"The car from the apartment complex?"

He nodded.

"The guy had several IDs on him. One of them is Guy Reinhart."

I opened my mouth to say *that's impossible* but Danny looked too excited, too pumped to notice the dread in my eyes.

It's all going to come out now. This is what you get for feeling relief that Mindy was gone. This is what you get for marrying somebody else and hiding it.

You had your own secrets to hide.

———

DANNY PULLED ONTO THE FREEWAY, speeding down-town to get us to the jail as I was trying to deal with a flurry of questions: Was this the guy who killed Mindy? Was he Guy? What else would he tell the cops about us?

"He's already booked into jail," Danny said.

He called his partner on his cell phone and said he was heading downtown. It sounded like the partner was already on his or her way too.

"How did they find him?" I asked, trying to hold down my panic.

"He was picked up but the arresting officer must have missed the ATL on the bottom of his computer screen. The booking officer at the jail noticed it and they called me."

"So, they just picked him up?"

"Yeah, today."

I looked ahead at the trail of brake lights on the free-way. Downtown Vegas appeared as a cluster of buildings to the right, coming up way too fast.

"Can I see him?" I asked.

"Yeah."

"Will he see me?"

"No, we don't do the six-pack anymore."

"Six-pack?"

"Police lineup. Lawyers don't like 'em."

I would've asked why but I was already reeling at the idea of Guy still living and seeing me. I kept telling myself, he can't be alive. He was a gasping, chain-smoking, morbidly-obese cocaine addict eighteen years ago. He was supposed to be dying.

"Does he have to know I'm here?" I asked.

Danny looked at me. It was the same curious look he gave to the RADIOACTIVE WASTE sticker on my journal.

"No. You're not that involved with the crime."

I stared straight ahead. My present life away from Vegas was in shambles while the ghosts of my Vegas past were calling out to everyone.

"Do you remember when a bunch of us came up here from the plant?" I asked.

"Yeah, why?"

He found an open lane and floored the accelerator. The engine bellowed and we cut off onto an exit ramp. We were downtown, blocks from the jail.

"I'll tell you later."

We stopped at a red light.

"Why do you ask about that trip?"

I could see myself reflected in his sunglasses. Small, jumpy, shrinking.

I offered weakly, "It's not like I didn't try to get Mindy out of here."

12

She's Not You

September 1986

I WATCHED a familiar scene at a gaming table behind a rail, a hushed area encircled by columns and tall potted plants. Guarded by solemn men in stiff but sleek black suits, this table was separated from the main casino floor but remained accessible to the gawkers and small-timers —-if they didn't mind watching reverently from the rail.

This was where Baccarat was played, the game I'd seen countless times in spy films when it seemed the fate of the free world depended on each deal of the cards. I had no idea how it was played and never bothered to find out what the French words used during the game meant, I just knew it was something phenomenally cool. As I stood as close as I could to a real table, near an actual game, I leaned against a column and watched the expressionless people huddled over their chips. I also glanced at a free pamphlet from the hotel lobby explaining the rules. The first crack of irony in the Baccarat cool of my childhood illusions was to find out that the game came from the Italian word *bacarra*—-zero, nothing.

The dry dealer crisply drew cards from the shoe, still the coolest gambling motion since Sean Connery's fingertips first appeared in *Dr. No*. There were only three players this afternoon: a blank-faced Japanese couple, totally unreadable in their middle age and steely concentration, and a caricature of an older Texas oilman. His big ten-gallon hat, wide bolo tie, and tall stacks of high dollar chips reeked of Western excess but also made him look physically sunken and shriveled.

Their chips moved back and forth across the table, either pushed out in neat stacks by the players or unceremoniously scooped away by the dealer. Wow, I thought, so that's what a twenty-five-hundred-dollar chip looks like.

I studied each player who lost, trying to detect any reaction as their lost bet—-ten chips totaling twenty-five thousand dollars—-effortlessly slid away from them. Nothing from the loser. Hardly a blink. Maybe an almost imperceptible tightening of the jaw that quickly passed. And that one hand would've paid for my entire college education, if I had stayed in school.

Someone tapped me on the shoulder and I turned to face Gil Rozell, my roommate in West Phoenix, and probably the funniest guy I'd ever met. I was back in Vegas but I didn't come alone this time.

Drink in hand, Rozell asked, "What the fuck?"

"I just found out James Bond is a total fraud," I told him.

"Where is he?" he demanded and looked around as if I

could point the superspy out.

"You just missed him."

Rozell muttered a curse and took another belt from his drink. He'd started drinking heavily at the airport back in Phoenix, explaining that the best way to do Vegas was to be "completely fucked up the entire time." (He also insisted that the best way to watch the Jerry Lewis Muscular Dystrophy Telethon was to spend the entire twenty hours frying on acid). The only way to experience pure kitsch or show biz sleaze was to be completely impaired and unable to fully trust your senses. It made sense to me but not enough to break my 23-year sobriety streak.

The stewardess on our short but bumpy flight had unsuccessfully tried to pry his drink away from him before we landed but I saw him buzzed and still sloshing his cup as he passed the open cockpit.

"What the hell kind of landing was that?" he bellowed at the flight crew. "You boys need more simulator time!"

As we stood watching the Baccarat game our first day in Vegas, I wondered when Rozell last ate solid food.

"Baccarat, Bond's game of choice," I said quietly, holding up the pamphlet. "It's pure luck. All those games 007 pulled out of his ass against those super villains? He had no idea what the next cards would be."

"Maybe he was just a good bluffer," Rozell suggested with a little burp.

"It requires no skill at all. It's just blind luck."

"Just like life, huh?"

"Unless you win every time."

"Let's get some chips and find out."

I glanced at him and noted, "You see those white

chips? Those are the five hundred-dollar chips and they're the *lowest* valued ones on that table."

Rozell turned back to the casino and asked, "Is there a five-dollar table somewhere? Because I can be the most bad-ass bluffing card shark in the fuckin' world...for about twenty bucks."

I shook my head.

"No skill at all, huh?" he asked.

"Not really."

He gulped down the last of his drink and said, "I always suspected those movies were bullshit."

Even wasted on a steady flow of alcohol, Rozell kept his mocking comic edge, feigning the proper amount of disappointment upon learning that the James Bond films didn't accurately portray the real world. That was one of the funniest things about Rozell: how unfunny he looked. Average height, average build, he kept his short wavy Marine cut, wore stylish glasses to fake a thoughtful, even dignified expression, and he appeared far too mundane to say or do most of the outrageous comments he uttered on a daily basis. I saw him as a stand-up comedian who never took the stage but was always performing.

I folded the Baccarat pamphlet and said, "Another childhood illusion destroyed."

"Well, just the gambling scenes," he said, lifting the empty glass to his mouth. "I'm sure the rest of that shit is real. You know, like pussy galore."

"You think Pussy Galore sounds like a real name?" I asked, incredulous.

"I wasn't referring to a name."

He noticed his drink was empty and peered hard into the glass.

"Where's that stewardess?" he asked.

"Do you think you should eat something today?"

He turned to me, teetering but serious.

"Hey, this is Vegas, baby. You either destroy its illusions or they destroy you! That's what makes this town such a beautiful fucking nightmare!"

Rozell was my closest friend at the nuclear plant but he knew nothing about Mindy and Guy. He knew nothing about my beautiful nightmare.

He spotted a leggy cocktail waitress striding through the nearby slot machines.

"Yo, serving wench!" he loudly called out to her.

The serious men in black suits around the Baccarat table turned to stare at him like he was a circus clown who'd just came honking and laughing into a funeral home. I got him away from there as fast as I could.

———

THERE WERE about a dozen of us, nuclear security officers from the Los Arcos plant and a couple of wives. Danny Olsen was along but since he'd recently married, he hung with the couples on a very short leash, not that he would submerge himself into the heathen Vegas depths anyway.

We all flew together from Phoenix and checked into several rooms at the Marina Hotel and Casino across the street from the Tropicana. The 5000 rooms of the MGM Grand are now stacked on the corner of Tropicana Avenue and Las Vegas Boulevard but in 1986, we stayed at the 714-room Marina.

It was my first trip to Vegas without Mindy and Guy but they occupied my every thought.

I felt like a spy, looking over my shoulder from the second we landed at McCarran, scanning everywhere as if we could bump into each other at any moment. It's funny how small the world becomes when you don't want to be seen. I felt like I could run into them anywhere, everywhere.

Or...I could try to see her like any other customer. The idea stopped me in my tracks before we even arrived at the casino. I could call her to my room and no one would know, especially Guy. He usually stayed in the car, out of sight, and he never saw most of her johns. He'd never know as long as she never told him. My main problem was that I had to trust her.

Just as I was naïve enough to believe that love could conquer all, I also felt that any good would be rewarded, namely my good and honorable desire to rescue Mindy. (I had to admit to myself that getting tag-team head last time from two hometown sistas threw my moral gyroscope off and my shining knight armor was getting a tad tarnished on this quest since I was still knocking off a piece in AZ every once in a while). But no matter how I justified this new plan, this mission was now a betrayal. The pimp who was so touched by my love for Mindy was about to be deep-dicked by the punk who would pass himself off as a john to steal her away.

I wanted to be Mindy's soulmate, Guy wanted to see her off the streets, and Mindy wanted to meet someone who knew where she came from and still loved her. A love she'd never known before. Her own family couldn't even do that. At least that's how it looked when it started.

How was Guy looking out for her now? By producing street ads to bury her deeper in the Vegas sex trade? By allowing her to toot up on cocaine, the very offense he'd warned me against, punishable by death? "I'll kill you if you bring drugs around her"? What bullshit.

I just needed to see her alone. We could replay the scene of our first meeting, except now I could take her away. I knew enough about her life to risk it all now. I could say everything I really wanted to tell her, make all my insane promises and heartfelt offers of a normal life, a Happily Ever After. That's what was missing, that connection of the two of us alone, that crazy electricity from the first night.

No, Guy betrayed us. His "business is business" line meant nothing to me anymore since he was also on the shit too.

Vegas could have him but I wasn't going to let it devour her, not without a fight.

First, I needed one of the rental cars.

———

THE STRIP WAS CHANGING. During my previous visit, I saw Guy's tired, flabby face under his fedora behind the wheel of their Town car as we drove past the Sahara. He was staring at the new gigantic kiddie water slide they'd just erected. A fucking kid's ride. The domain of the Rat Pack had been invaded by the kingdom of a mouse named Mickey, and I don't mean Mickey Cohen. Vegas was just starting its corporate makeover to be "family friendly" and watching Guy's look of incomprehension at that slide was burned into my memory. Fuck a bunch of ankle biters.

Now I was driving a rented Town car down the Strip

with three buddies from work. I couldn't shake them.

Cooper (we all went by last names at the plant), a chunky club hopper who could dance, latched on from the moment I asked for one of the rentals while the couples were at a show. He had made the arrangements for this trip so he annoyed everyone with his mother hen micro-managing.

In the elevator on our way down to the casino, Cooper asked, "You knew Skoof worked security up here in Vegas, didn't you?"

"No. I just knew he lived here before."

Milkos Scoufalis, the Skoof, was a supervisor who came along on this trip and was somewhere down in the casino.

"Yeah. Just don't mention Jerry Lewis in front of him."

I looked at him and asked, "Why not?"

"It still pisses him off."

I was about to ask how the mere mention of a comic legend beloved by children and France could piss off my otherwise mellow supervisor when Cooper said, "While we're out driving around, I wanna find Plato's Retreat."

"What's that?"

"An orgy."

The elevator doors opened with a loud *ding* to the casino.

We found Rozell teetering outside a lounge, moving awkwardly to the band's jazzy rendition of Bob Seger's, "Old Time Rock-n-Roll," the only tune from my era to make it into the Vegas lounge songbook. Every act included that song to keep up with the times, Vegas-style, of course.

"I think I'll quit Los Arcos and come up here to be a

lounge singer," Rozell said with complete conviction, devoid of his usual mocking tone. But that was one thing about Rozell—-he ridiculed everything so you could never take anything he said seriously. Nothing. Sure, he was your funniest friend but he was also the most insincere person you would ever meet.

"Do you have a stage name yet?" I asked.

Cooper rolled his eyes. There was a slithering orgy of asses, legs and tits out there and we were discussing lounge acts.

"Dondino's already taken by that fuck downtown," Rozell sneered, mentioning someone we'd seen earlier. "That's such a perfect Vegas lounge name."

I knew he was overplaying his anger at Dondino since Rozell loved every second of his act earlier.

I'd spent most of the day following Rozell from one lounge to another in his drunken, misguided quest to find the cheesiest, most obsequious lounge singer in town. Our fathers may have had the original Rat Pack but we grew up with Bill Murray's Nick the Lounge Singer from *Saturday Night Live*. We applauded every act we found, each one a major dollop of Vegas kitsch with names like Rocky Cool & the Rumblers or Vic LeMasters, and nobody lived and breathed kitsch more than Gil Rozell.

"Where do you think you're going?" Rozell asked.

"An orgy," Cooper said.

"Just driving around," I added.

"Outstanding!" Rozell bellowed. "You got your camera? I gotta get my picture in front of the wall where Evel wrecked."

Cooper's face appeared to implode with distasteful impatience as he carefully worded, "What?"

"New Year's Eve, 1967," Rozell rattled off, "Evel Kneivel jumped 144 feet over the Caesar's Palace fountains and slammed like a hamburger puppet into a wall. One of the greatest moments of the century but you wouldn't know that, would you, you ice-fishing, upper-peninsula Michigan fuck!"

"You're such a moron, Rozell," Cooper shot back. "Why should I let you use a car for that?"

"Why don't you drive down to the buffet and tape another twenty pounds of chow to your fat ass, 'cause that's exactly where your next meal is going!"

I spotted Milkos Scoufalis across the casino and left Cooper and Rozell to debate Evel Kneivel or orgies for the evening's itinerary.

I couldn't miss Skoof's large head of dark wiry hair and broad shoulders hunched over a video poker game. His drink looked tiny in his big, bulky hand.

"Hey, JB, what's up?" he asked as I sat down at the machine next to him.

Milkos Scoufalis was one of my Los Arcos supervisors, although he looked more like a bouncer at a biker bar. He was a big Greek from Cincinnati, and everything about him looked heavy and thick, his nose, ears, fingers. He had a dark stare but rarely employed it to intimidate people. In fact, he was a gentle guy who liked a good laugh, the only loud thing about him. It was easy to mistake his quiet manner for pure menace. The guys either called him Mikos, without the 'L,' or Skoof.

"Having any luck?" I asked.

He turned to me and asked, "You see that girl over there?"

Two rows of machines ahead of us, a pretty lady,

dressed nice, made up and alone, sat playing video poker. She held a disinterested but self-conscious pose.

"Yeah," I answered.

"Do you think she's a hooker?"

We watched her. She never looked up.

I observed, "I'm not really sure how you can tell."

My inner voice said, *She's a hooker.*

Skoof saw Rozell and Cooper and asked, "You guys going somewhere?"

Rozell and Cooper were still bickering as we all walked to the parking garage. I tried to drop them off downtown but Rozell didn't want to hang with Skoof and Cooper, and the other two were afraid I wouldn't come back for them. After wandering the Fremont Street casinos for a while, I gave up on shaking them and brought them along on my stakeout.

Skoof sat up front as I drove. Rozell and Cooper sat in the back and drank.

"Where are we going again?" Cooper asked.

"There's a girl I know up here," I said. "I just want to check her out without letting her know I'm here."

"You think she's a whore, don't you?" Rozell shouted from the backseat, feigning a defiant outrage.

I looked in the rearview mirror and asked, "What?"

"You heard me," he said, turning to Cooper. "Vegas. Female. It's all there!"

"Don't be ridiculous," I snapped at him.

Skoof asked, "Then why do you have to stake her house out?"

"Married," Cooper threw out.

I wondered how far to go with my cover story. Despite imbibing copious amounts of alcohol, my partners were still capable of thoroughly scrutinizing my situation in Vegas. Women were obviously a very sobering topic.

"If you guys aren't into this, I could drop you off somewhere and come back for you," I again offered. "I promise I won't leave you stranded somewhere."

"I want to find Plato's Retreat," Cooper repeated.

Skoof asked me, "What is it you're trying to find out?"

I decided on telling them, "I just want to know if there's anyone else." I immediately regretted saying that since I realized we could potentially see a steady stream of customers going in and out of that house. I could already hear Rozell's mad cackling at the stupidest cuckold in the southwest if the procession of johns appeared.

But I was, wasn't I? I couldn't have felt any more ridiculous, driving a carload of drunken friends to watch the house of a Vegas prostitute while secretly formulating a plan to get her out. I had a cool *film noir* scene in my head that I might have pulled off if I had been alone. I'm behind the wheel, by myself in black and white, smoking a cigarette and staring at the house with the smoldering burn of sexual obsession in my eyes. Kind of like Robert Mitchum in *Out of the Past* (by the way, his name in that movie was Jeff Bailey—*my name! Ha!*).

As usual, I wasn't in the scene I wanted. I didn't even smoke.

"Don't throw up in this car, Rozell," Cooper yelled. "I mean it!"

"I don't throw up, you fat fucking lightweight," he casually replied.

"You guys need to be quiet," I said to them. "This is a residential neighborhood."

I coasted to a stop along a wall on Mindy's street.

197

Trees and the rooftops of tightly packed tract homes stood behind the walls around us. We were too close to a streetlight but the spot offered the best vantage point to their long driveway and the dark house behind the shrubbery.

"Wow, that's a pretty good-size house, JB," Skoof noted from the passenger seat. "What's this girl do for a living?"

"I'm not sure," I lied. "I think she's a showgirl."

"What's she look like?" he asked.

I described her.

Skoof raised his eyebrows with a nodding frown and said, "Nice."

"I bet she's a titty dancer," Cooper guessed. "Girl that young, livin' in a house like that? Titty dancer."

"Or she's a whore!" Rozell blurted out.

I looked into the rearview mirror at a defiant Rozell. Cooper and Skoof didn't laugh at first, probably holding off to see if I would be insulted.

"She's a whore living in some drug king pin's *casa*," Rozell continued. "Guns, drugs, sex slaves. If we see a bunch of machete-wielding beaners in there and an army of DEA Agents going in, let's join the fun!"

Skoof laughed, "Shut the fuck up, Rozell!"

As we sat in the silence, occasionally hearing the sounds of suburban domesticity and the hiss of traffic from the nearest boulevard, I lied, "No, it's nothing that interesting."

We watched the house. Were they in there? A dim light behind the unkempt shrubs and window shades suggested an abandoned night light.

Cooper said, "Hey, maybe we can get out and walk around it."

"They have Dobermans," I told him.

"You've been in that house?" Skoof asked.

I nodded.

"They? It's more than her?" Skoof asked.

"Are you sure they're not drug dealers?" Rozell said. "Because my next guess would be vampires."

An irritated Cooper asked, "How long are we gonna sit here?"

"This is Vegas," I pointed out. "We've got all night. Isn't that right, Skoof? You used to live up here."

Skoof nodded.

"You used to work security up here?" I asked him, glancing at Cooper in the rearview mirror. Cooper narrowed his eyes at me. This was going south so I decided to push the nuclear button: I would ask Skoof about Jerry Lewis.

"I hear you've got a thing about Jerry Lewis," I said. "Something that happened here?"

Skoof's face hardened into a tight, solid expression that made his head look even larger. I sat back, feigning surprise.

"Did they tell you to say Jerry Lewis in front of me?" he said in a low growl, jerking a thumb toward the backseat.

"No. What's the deal?"

I could see he was trying to swallow his anger, pull it back. He actually had to calm himself down.

"I used to work security at the Aladdin in the Seventies."

"Okay," I said.

"I worked the Muscular Dystrophy Telethon. They'd rotate us around, just like at the plant. You'd spend some time on the floor near the stage, then cover doors, parking lots. I was posted on the floor between the door where the talent came in to the stage, ya know, just hanging out. The best place to stand to watch what was going on with the telethon was under this monitor. So, I'm standing there and this guy with a headset comes over to tell me that I have to move. I look around and ask why. He says, 'That's where Jerry walks.'"

Skoof nods and continues, "So I step back and he leaves. I'm wondering if the guy is messing with me when another guy with a headset shows up and stands right where I was standing, right under that monitor. Now I don't tell him anything. I thought I'd just see what would happen. In walks Jerry. He had a Winnebago out in the convention center with David Hartmann, you know, *Good Morning, America,* and Ed McMahon—-they each had their own—-and they'd go back there when they weren't on. The moment Jerry Lewis sees this guy in his path to the stage, he completely melts down. I mean he's screaming that this *motherfuckin' cocksucker* is standing in his way—-"

I laughed uncomfortably. Skoof's voice began to rise as he continued, "I'm serious, he just lights into this guy and this guy takes off, getting out of there as fast he can, and Jerry goes on. So, I'm not looking to beat that first guy's ass for messing with me."

"Wow. That still pisses you off to this day?"

I remembered reading how Jerry was out of his mind on painkillers for most of the Seventies, starting with stories in the *National Enquirer* about how he was rude to elderly people. Now one of my friends was a first-hand witness. Kooky, baby.

"Oh, no, it got worse."

"Jerry yelled at you?"

Skoof shook his head, the anger returning.

"You can do a lot of things to me, and I won't care. I can see a lot of things, and I still won't care," he said, "but you do something to kids, then I can just lose it and I just about killed that fucker."

"You almost killed Jerry Lewis?"

I flashed on how the media would portray Skoof as an uncontrollable animal who killed a beloved humanitarian-entertainer adored the world over. France, unable to come to terms with its grief, would dust off its guillotine and offer to behead the Skoof monster. It would be ugly, but great television in the name of justice. It's what Jerry would've wanted.

"Well, I got rotated to the door leading out to the convention center. Don't let anybody but Jerry Lewis, David Hartmann, and Ed McMahon through to the Winnebagos. Do you remember Chad Everett?"

"Sure. He was the doctor on *Medical Center*."

"Yeah. Nice guy. Good man. I don't know if that's why they didn't let him have a Winnebago with them or not, but his was across the hall in another big room, and there was plenty of room in theirs. Anyway, here comes Chad Everett with these four little kids. They'd collected some money and wanted to personally give it to Jerry. Chad heard about it and was bringin' them back. They were all dressed up like KISS, ya know, the rock group. Faces all painted. And they said they walked all the way from Nellis Air Force base to give this money to Jerry. So, Chad Everett is asking me to let these kids go back—-and I'm a soft heart for kids—-so I'm stepping out of their way, when they see Jerry with a drink outside of his Winnebago. The kids run toward him, saying, 'There's Jerry! There's Jerry!' He totally loses it again. *'Who let these motherfuckin' brats back here?'*"

Skoof quoted Jerry at full volume and I winced as I looked around outside.

"Dude, our windows are down," I told him.

"Just screaming his head off at all of us as he's trying to get through the door. Chad's shielding the kids, they're all crying. Jerry doesn't shut up...*THESE GODDAM FUCKING BRATS*...and I'm trembling. I mean, you be cruel to a little kid or an animal...and I'll just go fucking berserk. All I can see is red, the color I see when I'm gonna lose it. That, and Jerry Lewis' neck. I was going to reach over and snap his fuckin' neck."

"Hi-yo!" Rozell laughed.

"But I didn't. He just ranted on his way back to the stage. Chad calmed the kids down, got 'em to stop crying, and he got a limo to take them all home. Chad Everett's a cool guy."

Skoof sat back in his seat, letting the rage run its course. I was just grateful he didn't turn green and tear out of the rental car as if it was made of aluminum foil.

"And Jerry Lewis never knew just how close he came to dying that night," Skoof added. "Raise all the damn money you want for kids but if you fuck with one...then I don't care who you are anymore."

Rozell began drunkenly singing, *"You'll never walk ah-ha-ha-lone!"*

Anyone on the other side of the wall would've heard Skoof's near-execution of Jerry Lewis. Hell, Mindy, Guy and their Doberman could've heard him.

"Are you guys sure you want to do this?" I asked. "I'll take you anywhere and I promise to pick you up."

"Let's go find Plato's Retreat," Cooper said.

"What's that?" Skoof asked.

"It's a private club," Cooper answered.

"You told me it was an orgy," I said.

"Yeah, a private club for orgies," Cooper explained.

"I'm not going anywhere with Cooper without a chaperone," Rozell announced. "He's too horny and I'm too drunk to properly guard my bunghole."

I could see a glowering Cooper lift a middle finger at Rozell.

Rozell bellowed, "You can't afford me, fatboy!"

I opened my mouth to yell "Shutup" at them just as the police cruiser turned onto the street in front of us. I ended up only saying, "Uh-oh."

The cruiser shot directly at us and stopped with its blinding red and blue flashing lights coming to life on its roof. A bright white light pierced through the windshield on us.

"Oh, shit!" Cooper said.

Skoof said over his shoulder, "Rozell, lose the drink. It's illegal to have an open container in a car here."

"But I can carry a bucket of vodka on the Strip?" he asked scornfully.

"That's the law here," Skoof muttered.

"I fucking *love* this town!" Rozell exclaimed in the flashing lights of the police cars.

"We're just here looking for a friend of mine," I quickly instructed them as two uniformed officers rose out of the cruiser and approached us. They both held bright flashlights on us. A casino couldn't have poured more foot candles into our car. Any brighter and I would've lost my eyebrows.

After a few questions and a quick check of my driver's license, the officers ordered me out of the rental car to perform a test for alcohol. Me, the guy who never drank in his life, went through the humiliating motions as a carload of my drunken co-workers watched. Four clean-shaven guys with short hair probably looked like rowdy military guys on a reckless bender. Kids gathered on the sidewalk as neighbors peered over their wall from their backyards. I tried to keep from facing Mindy's house but glanced over several times.

I thought I saw the blinds part in one of the windows in the distance. Someone was watching from there. Guy? Mindy? As I went through their ridiculous pantomime to prove my sobriety, I wondered if Guy kept binoculars at his windows, along with perhaps an automatic weapon.

Through binoculars or a rifle scope, Guy would see that it was me in front of his house with the cops and would probably in some cocaine-fueled fit of rage think I was leading a raid on him. As the officers lectured us about drinking and driving off the Strip, I wondered if my head would explode at any moment from the first round fired from the house. That would suck.

"You see, officers, I'm here for a girl…"

BOOM!

Why couldn't the cops have given me a psychological test and haul me in? I would not have fared as well as I did with the sobriety test.

After the Las Vegas Metro Police determined that I was unimpaired enough to operate a vehicle on their streets, they let us go and I drove the car back toward the

Strip, relieved that I didn't die in a stupid and mistaken shootout. Guy must have been elsewhere.

Rozell snickered in the backseat while Skoof and Cooper dummied up. I left Mindy's street with no idea whether they saw me or not.

"Is this a girl you really care about?" Skoof asked.

I realized that when it came to Mindy, even my friends became strangers to me, outsiders who could never understand.

Embarrassed and afraid to say anything more, I asked, "So where is this Plato's Retreat?"

Cooper directed us down Industrial Road, a darker back alley of a street that ran parallel to the Strip, and we pulled into a cheap shopping center where a small sign read, *PLATO'S RETREAT, Private Club*. Next door was a large strip club with older model cars and trucks parked with motorcycles out front.

"This is it," Cooper grinned.

We opened a glass door and entered a tight, brightly-lit vestibule. A window that reminded me of a medical office slid open and a middle-aged, heavyset woman without makeup appeared. Just as I questioned the decision of having the gravelly-voiced Gerty working the escort phone lines, I had to wonder why the management behind an orgy would post such a matronly old woman at their reception desk. Nurse Ratchett was a showgirl next to this beast. The setting was seedy and sordid enough but making grandma work the door screamed SCAM in monstrous red letters.

"Hello," she said.

Cooper asked, "How much is it to get in?"

"Fifty dollars for guys, ladies for free."

"Are there any women in there now?" Cooper asked.

Her reply sounded like a hollow, over-rehearsed line: "Yes, there are lots of beautiful women inside."

"Bullshit," Rozell said.

We didn't go in. I offered to wait in the car if they wanted to go but Rozell said he needed a fresh free drink on the Strip and Cooper looked reluctant to step inside with Skoof, another chunky guy whose arousal expression looked scary and desperate.

Even if all the hot strippers next door were overcome with a sudden and inexplicable desire to run next door and ravish every revolting sad sack in Plato's Retreat, I didn't want to throw away fifty dollars on such distractions. During the last trip, I lost forty dollars on the Bally's sistas and I needed my cash for Plan B of Mindy's rescue.

———

"YOU REMEMBER that girl in the casino?" Skoof asked me the next afternoon. "The one I asked if she looked like a hooker? After we got back, she was still sitting there at the poker machines."

We sat in a buffet and overate. I'd only had a few fitful hours of sleep.

"Wow, that was hours later," I said.

"I asked Cooper what he thought and he went over and asked her."

"What did she tell him?"

"He got head for three hundred bucks from her."

"Three hundred?" I asked, a little too loud. I knew it was about one hundred just to talk to a girl and that there were girls who did everything for that amount, or less. But I also remembered that the girl was very pretty, so the thought of her blowing a shaved ape like Cooper quickly made me wonder why she hadn't charged more. My Vegas weekend with co-workers felt like a ridiculous mix of high school carousing and decadent Roman hedonism since the sexual near-misses for some of us were actually comical. I was up to my eyeballs with sex but the only action I found so far was a sobriety check from the police.

"I didn't say anything to him because I didn't want to follow him," Skoof said. "Ya know, sloppy seconds. And I'm sure he'd tell everyone at work. Since I made supervisor, I wouldn't give him the satisfaction because you know he'd make a big deal of going first."

He was right. Cooper would brag about Skoof paying to wallow in his leftovers.

The rest of the day went quickly since I had a plan to meet up with Mindy after dark. Rozell continued to drift into alcoholic comas and amused himself by trying to place bets on professional wrestling at all the sportsbooks on the Strip. He did a brilliant job of faking shock and outrage each time the old men behind the cages informed him that he would not be able to cash in on his hot tip regarding the Hulk Hogan-King Kong Bundy match set for next week. He also got his photo taken at the wall where Evel Knievel wrecked. I gave up on reminding him to eat any solid food and he finally passed out in the hotel room well after midnight.

I sat on the other bed and thought about how I was going to call Mindy. As usual, I'd been up too long in a town with too many temptations to think clearly about anything. I only knew that I had a chance to hold Mindy, kiss her, and have a private moment with her without wondering if Guy would shoot me.

I walked down to the metal newspaper boxes outside on the Strip and casually plucked a couple of handbills. I stuffed them in my shirt for the walk through the casino and up to the room. The other rooms were quiet as I keyed back into mine.

Rozell snored. I opened the ads. Guy and Mindy's ads had hit the streets with pics of her interspersed with the purloined porn star pics normally featured. Guy obviously hadn't hired a professional photographer, so Mindy looked plain and poorly-lit alongside the glossy, filtered fantasy babes. In one photo, she was wearing her tiger-striped body stocking and black boots while waving a whip. She looked fried and haggard with dark rings under her eyes. Instead of appearing wild and sexy, she came off as threatening and crazy.

I sat next to the phone and stared at the number in the ad.

What if Guy answered? What if he recognized my voice?

What if Rozell woke up and heard me talking in some goofy accent? What if he woke up at any point after she showed up?

The same persistent recklessness that compelled me to make that call on that first trip pushed me to call again. I had no idea what was going to happen next.

I picked up the phone and dialed. On the fourth ring, a woman's voice answered, Gravel Gerty's. "Private Dancers, how can I help you?"

"Yeah, hi. I'm looking for a girl with black hair."

"A brunette?"

"Not just brunette. Jet black hair. Her name is Angelique."

"Dark hair?"

"Yes, she has dark hair," I said.

"Where are you?"

I told her the Marina and room number. She said she would be there in thirty to forty-five minutes.

"Angelique, right?"

"If she's available, yes." Click.

I hung up. I stared at my hand on the phone. Here I was again, calling for an escort to come to my hotel room —-but what a difference a year made: I knew her this time, I felt the thrill of pulling off a covert spy operation instead of just trying to get laid and I had no idea how she would react when she got to the room.

I turned on the bathroom light and shut off the other lights in the room. Rozell kept right on snoring. At least I knew he hadn't drank himself to death. I stood near the door, listening, watching the clock radio's red numbers on the nightstand count off the minutes. I imagined seeing her through the fish-eyed peephole in the door, opening the door, pulling her inside and, without a word, kissing her. The feelings all came back as I imagined holding her. Our love story was back on track.

I leaned against the door and stared with one eye out the peephole. An old guy walked by outside and I heard him enter a room further down the hall.

Anything felt possible.

"Run away with me now," echoed through my thoughts. Her blue eyes responding. I pictured us fleeing in one of the Town cars and checking in somewhere else. I would come back and explain to everyone that something was going on. They could deny knowing me while Mindy and I escaped to Arizona. Somehow. But they wouldn't know how serious this was, and they would probably give up my name pretty easily to Guy. "We work with him at the nuclear plant in Arizona," and he would know it was me and where I worked. He knew I worked nuclear security. He would know how to find me.

In the forty minutes before the rap on the door, I went from the exhilaration of pulling off my little covert operation, to the fear that I was foolishly risking not only my life, but Mindy's. I could tell Guy that I was just doing research. My excuse for everything stupid in my life. Yeah. I was researching what it would be like to call for an escort and the amazing Angelique appeared in my room—-

But I was sure that Guy would see it as a deception by me and cheating with her. Our very weird form of cheating.

I jumped at the knock on the door and looked out the peephole. And saw blonde hair. Was she wearing a wig?

I opened the door and came face to face with another girl, a different escort. She wore purple spandex pants, chewed gum, and had curly blonde hair with black roots. Her cheeks were high and her face looked puffy. I could smell a pungent perfume and cigarette smoke from her.

"Did you call for me?" she asked.

"You're not...Angelique," I said.

"Who?"

"I asked specifically for someone," I said, standing in the doorway.

"I am someone."

"Someone else."

"Doesn't mean we still can't party, does it?" she asked, stepping closer.

I thought of Mindy's crossed eyes in the Polaroid and the quote she wrote under it, *That's right, sir, $105 for everything.* This escort was probably one of *those* girls.

I reached into my jeans pocket for some money.

"I'm sorry," I sputtered. "It's not you, it's—-I was looking for someone I already know—-I'm sorry."

She stared at the twenty, so I handed her another twenty. I actually felt for her. She was coming up to sell herself for a hundred dollars and was getting rejected. It probably didn't mean much to her and it didn't matter to me who it was, but I will always feel for a woman who suffers rejection. The hurt in their eyes was just agonizing for me to see in anyone. She just looked annoyed.

"I'm sorry for your trouble," I said.

She took the money. Just as the married co-workers walked by. The wives put their heads down and walked on, appalled and embarrassed, and the husbands did a lousy job of stifling their giggles. Danny stared at me, at first surprised and awkwardly amused, then embarrassed for me.

"Okay, no biggie," the escort said and headed back toward the elevator.

"I'll put the tray out when I'm finished," I said, loud enough for the others to hear. "Thanks for bringing this up."

"Whatever," she answered. "Asshole."

I closed the door, put my head against it, and said, "Fuck!"

Rozell called out from his drunken coma, "Hi-Yo!"

```
┌─────────────────────────────────────┐
│                 13                  │
│                                     │
│          Code Five Inmate           │
└─────────────────────────────────────┘
```

APRIL 2005

DANNY FLASHED his badge at the parking garage officer and parked his SUV in the first open spot.

"Do you remember coming back late and seeing that girl outside my room?" I asked him.

"Yeah. Was that Melinda?"

"No. I was trying to call Mindy to my room to see if she was ready to run away with me, but they sent the wrong girl."

"Everyone got a good laugh out of that, catching you with a hooker outside your room. It kind of bummed me out at the time though."

"Because it ruined your opinion of me?"

"No. Because I knew it meant you were lonely."

I wanted to laugh but didn't.

"Did Cooper and Rozell know about any of this? Your Vegas thing?"

"I didn't mention it to them until way later," I said. "I started to tell Rozell but when he asked me if her name was Sharon Peters, I figured he wasn't the right audience for that story."

We rode down an elevator and then walked outside of the building, hurrying around to the Booking entrance.

When I did a ride-along with Danny back in '93, he'd brought in another officer's suspect so I could see the jail facility. The two sets of sliding automatic glass doors, the white sterile walls, the bright blue trim around the windows, and the uniformed officers gave the Booking entrance a sterile façade of formal processing. The various suspects dragged or carried into Booking provided the noise and chaos, bringing their rage or terror or even some laughter with them. While waiting for Danny during my first trip to Booking, I watched a battling drunken couple brought in wearing separate handcuffs. The husband, dressed only in jean shorts and flip-flops, looked bewildered and barely conscious on one end of the bench with a big angry knot on his forehead. The wife, her hair tangled and eyes boiling with fury, wrenched at her cuffs on the other end. The next suspect to arrive was a baseball umpire still wearing his black and white stripes, caught driving under the influence after a game.

Plopped down between the restrained couple, he looked stunned and dejected in his cuffs.

I was chatting with the Booking Officer when he saw the umpire and casually asked, "Hey, ump, can you give us a hand here with these two?"

The umpire noticed he was between the feuding couple and blurted out, "Don't get me involved!"

Everyone laughed except the fuming wife.

Danny and I walked through the sliding glass doors and entered the jail.

"I'm going to go in to see him," he told me. "Hang out here. I'll be right back."

He flashed his badge to the Booking Officer and moved on to the back counter to speak with the Processing Officers there.

I didn't want to sit on that now empty bench. That was where suspects under arrest were placed. I could've ended up on that bench so easily when I was with Mindy and Guy. Accessory to pandering, trespassing, weapons charges. When did they start carrying drugs? Probably a lot sooner than I thought.

In a nearby corner, I spotted the low black chair on rollers where the unruly new arrivals were strapped in and bound by several black seatbelts until they calmed down.

I hated the anxious helplessness and dread I now felt. I was so oblivious to the risks when I was hanging with Guy and Mindy. Now I was more exposed and vulnerable, jumpy and afraid to be swept up in a fast-moving investigation by Las Vegas Homicide than when I was running as a young moron with real criminals. There was no way Guy could be alive, I kept telling myself.

The doors slid open behind me. A petite but sturdy woman, professionally dressed with dark red hair in an all-business perm, marched into Booking carrying files, her eyes hidden behind sunglasses. She didn't look overtly masculine but the way she carried herself suggested there was a gun and a pair of non-recreational handcuffs somewhere in her pantsuit. I stepped out of her way as she headed straight for the counter.

Danny emerged from one of the doors behind the counter, holding a sheet of paper. He knew the lady and I watched them talk. She put the files on the counter and gestured to them. Danny told her something and they both looked at me. I stared back. Danny waved me over.

"Jeff, this is Stephanie Killman, my partner."

I smiled as I shook her hand. She removed her sunglasses and said, "Hi, Jeff, how are you?"

Her warm smile and soft, friendly voice surprised me after her bold entrance. I wondered what she looked like dressed for a night on the town, when she wasn't a detective.

"I have a printout of this guy's mug shot," Danny said, holding the sheet toward me. "Is this Guy Reinhart?"

I took it and stared at it. The man in the color printout hunched forward and glared into the camera through dark, thick eyebrows. He looked burned out, hollow. Gray hair, uneven stubble, empty, bloodshot eyes. A tweaker, not a cokehead. And it wasn't Guy.

"That's not him," I said.

"Are you sure?" Danny asked. "It's been a long time."

"This guy looks older than he probably is, but he's not old enough to be Guy."

"He knew the victim, you said?" Stephanie asked, gesturing at me.

"He's a writer," Danny told her.

I winced with embarrassment as I handed the paper back to Danny. Writers know unsavory people, as lame and misguided as that sounded now. Danny and

Stephanie went into an animated conversation as they tried to catch each other up on the case.

I was ready to sit down. Even on the bench of shame in downtown Booking. Relief spread through me like a shot of Novocain flowing through my bloodstream, easing all the suspense and numbing all the tension into nothingness. It wasn't Guy. Their lives and squalid deaths, at least Mindy's at this point, might let go of me and I might remain only a material witness to this whole mess.

"He's obviously frying out, ranting and raving," I heard Danny tell his partner. "He says he'd never heard of the victim, said someone loaned him the car. It's his car. He was carrying some antique gun on him when he was picked up."

Antique gun.

Stephanie asked, "What kind of antique gun?"

"One of those handguns from World War II. German, with the long barrel. Kind of a cool-looking gun, I thought."

"A Luger," I interjected.

Danny nodded. "Yeah, one of those. It didn't look like it'd been fired in years. The firing pin is broken and it's totally neglected. Useless as a weapon."

Stephanie was watching me.

"Does that mean anything to you, Jeff?" she asked.

"That was Guy's gun."

"You've seen this gun before?" Danny asked.

"Guy Reinhart carried a German Luger. I saw it several times. That was probably the one thing Mindy would've kept of his, something he really valued."

The Homicide Detectives looked at each other.

"I'll get him in an interview room," Danny said.

Stephanie scooped up the files.

"Hey, Danny," I said as they headed behind the counter.

He stopped and turned back to me.

"I'm gonna take a walk, if that's okay."

"Take your time."

Excited by this new scent in the hunt, they left me standing in Booking and disappeared behind a door.

———

I STEPPED OUTSIDE as a Metro police cruiser pulled up and stopped. A lanky young officer lurched out and rushed over to activate the sliding doors. He called inside, "Code five inmate!"

I peered into the back of the cruiser. A dark shape rolled up from the backseat, wild hair, no shirt. His round, crazed eyes glared out at me and I could see his mouth contorting with rage as he wrenched at his handcuffs. Officer Lanky returned with Officer Burly as they both pulled on latex gloves. Another officer stood by with a camcorder to record getting Charles Manson out of the cruiser and into Booking. Judging from the bellowing obscenities and flying spittle rolling out of the cruiser when the officers opened the door, the black restraining chair inside the jail would not stay empty for long.

"What do you need a camera for?" the deranged inmate bellowed. "Hey, motherfucker, what's the camera for?"

I heard the camcorder officer calmly state, "It's for your protection as well as ours, sir."

ATL, six-pack, Code Five Inmate. I was picking up all kinds of cop lingo this trip.

Still dazed myself, I wandered down toward Fremont Street.

Tourists shuffled past the casinos and souvenir shops under the canopy of twelve million lights for the Fremont Street experience, a nightly light show extravaganza. During the day, the canopy looked like a monstrous awning shading the five-block promenade section of downtown Vegas. The only lights to jump out during daylight hours were on the marquee featuring strippers dancing and beckoning customers inside the Glitter Gulch, mostly gyrating bodies in bikinis or close-ups of licking and kissing lips.

I walked under the marquee, so relieved that I felt dazed. Guy had to be dead, as I'd always thought, but the panic I felt at the jail that he might be alive rattled me. Anything was still possible in this town. As Danny and his partner (Detective KILLman!) grilled their tweaker suspect, I loitered on Fremont Street like a tourist, relieved that their murder investigation was veering away from me. I'd only known Mindy, their homicide victim, years ago and no one knew what happened to Guy so I calmed myself as another face in the crowd.

I walked into the Golden Gate (not the Glitter Gulch) on the corner across from the Union Plaza. They served one of the best ninety-nine cent shrimp cocktails in the tiny cafeteria behind the casino. Not like the plastic cups half-filled with shredded lettuce down on the Strip. I ate one while listening to a pianist play an excellent rendition of "Beyond the Sea."

I decided to head back to the jail. I had no idea how

long Danny needed to question their suspect and I wasn't sure how long I'd been wandering.

At an intersection, I turned away from Fremont, taking side streets back. Along the wall, I glanced at a line of dirty transients reclined or slumped on the sidewalk, reeking of sweat and urine and dressed in soiled rags only yards from the shuffling tourists. I wasn't surprised to see the homeless in Vegas. With all the buffets, they probably also had the most plentiful and diverse dumpsters for all their diving needs.

The Phoenix homeless were normally an older and sluggish heap, worn and leathery in the harsh desert sun. Their brains ravaged by substances, their livers resembling a chunk of polluted coral, their identities robbed of them, they haunt the parks and alleys or sleep on city bus benches like stinking zombies. Worse, really, since our society would do something if they were real zombies. After a lifetime of very bad choices and/or very wicked addictions, their tragic lives allowed them just enough vital organs to keep breathing, to keep existing without living. I always think the same thing when I see them: They were someone's babies once.

But these were just kids off Fremont Street. If they hadn't looked so filthy in their ratty old t-shirts and stained jeans and so foul in their airspace, they could've been a bunch of high school kids hanging out at the local arcade. Their dirty fingers held cigarettes and gestured wildly as they rapidly conversed. Tweakers and burn outs, I cynically thought. Some chattering in the sun, others sleeping, a few glaring angrily at passersby. They appeared to have money for tattoos, piercings and cigs although they were surrounded by Styrofoam containers with someone else's discarded meals. They were too young to look so completely lost and ruined.

I thought, My God, they *are* someone's babies.

I heard a loud voice, bellowing over the noise and traffic. A disturbingly filthy homeless man limped out of an alley on an old leg brace. Following me down the sidewalk, he ranted, "Same shit, different day...same circus, different clowns!"

I stopped at the next corner and looked back at him. His wild eyes blindly glanced around the buildings, his mouth shouting from a scraggly beard. He swung his leg brace past me, still raving. I knew this feeling. I understood what it was like to be in the vicinity of madness.

"Everything's all fucked up...I can't wave a wand and make it all normal again!"

That's funny, I thought, because that's what was going through my mind.

14

The Blizzard of 1987

FEBRUARY 1987

ABOUT A MONTH after my first non-Mindy trip to Vegas (I still wonder what would've happened if Gravel Gerty had sent the right girl), I drove to L.A. for the first time to meet my new Hollywood agents.

One of my first screenplays had been about aging Weather Underground and Black Panther fugitives banding together in one last blaze of glory to infiltrate a nuclear power plant (I took the job at the Los Arcos Nuclear Power Plant for "research," of course). I registered the script with the Writers' Guild and sent dozens of query letters to agencies. Within a month, three responded to ask for the script. Another month later, one of them called to tell me the script was "gold" and sent me a contract so I drove to L.A. to meet my new agents. Their offices were on Wilshire Boulevard and I made sure I was early enough to find a place to park. I'd never seen so much glass and chrome in my life as I entered their building.

On the elevator ride up, I recognized an up-and-coming actor I'd seen in a couple of movies but couldn't think of his name. He hadn't had the big parts yet but I knew who he was. He grinned. I could tell he enjoyed that I recognized him, even if I didn't say anything. I'd seen him as a ghost in a Peter O'Toole comedy called *High Spirits* and he'd just done *Darkman*. This was years before *Schindler's List* but I'll always remember that happy but humble moment before he was really Somebody. Two grinning guys, one of them Liam Neeson, in an elevator on the edge of Hollywood's dreams.

I quietly entered the agency office and introduced myself. Almost instantly I was sitting in a conference room with the head of the agency, an older well-groomed man who appeared fascinated by this Midwestern creature who drove out of the Arizona desert, the thing from the flyover states. I was glad I wore my biker boots from work. Two of his androgynous agents flanked him, a man and woman who both wore glasses and short hair. Their clothes were so casual and comfortable that they appeared blandly asexual, which didn't make me feel any less tense and anxious.

As pleasantries subsided, I thought of Charlton Heston before the monkey council in the original *Planet of the Apes*. Not because these laid back, friendly L.A. professionals reminded me of simians but because I felt like I was the one from a different planet.

"Well, we love the script," the head agent announced.

Good. I would like this new planet.

We talked about nuclear plants—-the setting of the

script—-and they said they could set up a reading with Sean Penn. The agency had packaged his last movie so they had an "in." He might be interested in one of the lead roles.

I think I said, "Wow."

"What else have you got?" the male agent asked.

I was working on a teen comedy I'd started in high school. There was also a vampire script.

Everyone seemed so nice in Hollywood. Polite, direct, complimentary. They were soft spoken and enthusiastic at first but I felt like I was losing them. In my first meeting with my agents, I soon felt like the nuke plant script had been a fluke when they didn't sound as excited by my other two ideas.

Flustered, I blurted, "I know a hooker in Las Vegas."

All three of them stared. I had them back.

"I'm supposed to write her story," I said. "I've spent a few weekends with them to see how they live."

The female agent asked, "'They?'"

"She lives with her business manager." Even in the safety of L.A., I felt uncomfortable enough to hesitate before adding, "Her pimp."

"So, they're cooperating?" the head agent asked.

"Oh, yeah, I stay with them. The AIDS thing has scared her into Dominance so she doesn't do the hooker thing as much."

They were excited again, happy with anticipation. I was worth something again.

I didn't see anyone else famous on the elevator ride down. Alone, I felt like another rube not ready for Hollywood. *What else do you have?* The other two didn't have the authenticity of the nuke script. I was too young to have much experience to draw from and most of my screen-play ideas were just derivative echoes from late night TV I'd grown up on. Getting here wasn't easy but now it looked like the hard part was just beginning.

I left L.A. chagrined that the only real story in my life was playing out in Las Vegas and that the next best shot I had at a killer deal depended on a coke-snorting Domina-trix slipping further and further away from me. I thought about telling Mindy and Guy that I'd mentioned their story to my new Hollywood agents, but decided to only tell them about the agents. And maybe the Sean Penn thing.

After the holidays, I called Las Vegas. They were very excited for me and they were going to let me know how excited the next time I flew into town.

———

OH, yeah. *That.* That first kiss goodbye, those young lips so tender and even a little innocent then, the kiss that made me feel less stupid for jumping into this insanity. It was in that one clear moment that I felt for her, an emotion of such purity and forgiveness that I would do anything to be with her. Wipe away her horrible past, forgive all her sins, discard my own safety to get her away from Vegas, away from Guy.

Did I lose it somewhere? I will admit that my silly ego chose to focus on my incredible amount of self-sacrifice and forgiveness instead of dwelling on her sucking and fucking for cash every night, but what on earth was I trying to prove? To Guy and Mindy, I was a sucker. To anyone else with a brain, some desperate idiot.

Even as our love story descended into just another cocaine crash, I stubbornly hung on to Mindy as my hopes and dreams dwindled and the mission became more humanitarian than romantic: Mindy the addict needed a different kind of rescue now. The odds got higher while my role grew thinner. I went from a sentimental kid wanting to save a young girl's heart to a flustered adult trying to figure out how to intervene and then restore what was left of her.

When they picked me up at the airport, I got the welcome I'd wanted the last time: Mindy got out of the car and threw her arms around me, her hair smelling of perfume and cigarette smoke. Her bright red lips jabbed a quick kiss at the corner of my mouth.

"Welcome back, stranger!" she said, smiling.

My mouth hung open. I'd scheduled my flight within hours of my last twelve-hour shift for the week so I'd been awake for nearly twenty-four hours. Not a smart move but it gave me more time with them. It was late enough in the evening that I figured we'd all end up asleep anyway, unless the phone rang.

"Come on," she said. "Guy has a surprise for you." She quickly stepped back and jumped into the passenger seat.

"Get in, Hollywood," Guy's voice said from the dark interior of the Lincoln.

I got in the backseat with my bag and Guy accelerated, my body pushing back into the seat. I got the welcome I always wanted but I was too exhausted to appreciate it.

Mindy looked over the seat at me.

"You still gonna write our book, aren't ya?" she asked.

She sniffed and sniffled and swiped at her inflamed nostrils constantly. Even in the dark, in the flashing streetlights and headlights, I could see tiny blue veins webbing out from her eyes. Guy was sniffing, too.

"Yeah, of course I am," I told her.

"What'll happen if they make your movie?" she asked.

"Then maybe I can write full time. I won't have to guard nuclear power plants anymore."

"What's the guy's name?" Guy asked. "The big actor?"

"Sean Penn."

"He was that stoner guy in that one movie," Mindy said. "The one who calls that old teacher a dick. You know. It's funny as hell."

I imagined Mindy all dolled up on my arm at a Hollywood premiere and we run into Sean Penn. And he punches her for gushing over his role as Spicoli in *Fast Times at Ridgemont High*.

I looked at the back of Guy's fedora.

"So, what's the surprise?"

He drove us downtown. I could see the glow of Fremont Street down the block when we parked along the sidewalk. Across the street I saw a busy office with people walking in and out with the all the windows lit up.

"Let's go," Guy gasped and hefted himself out of the car.

We walked across the street and Mindy held my hand as Guy led the way. I look confused and gestured at Guy's back. She waved him off and squeezed my hand. She was wearing her spiked black boots, black jeans, and a nice blouse. Not much different than what she wore that first night but her sniffling made me think she wasn't the same girl. Her hand felt cold and bony in mine.

At the top of the steps, I saw the letters in the windows, *Clark County Marriage Bureau*. The office was open until midnight. Happy couples were entering and exiting.

I slowed to a stop, already numb from a lack of sleep. I felt like I was having a delayed reaction to everything. Mindy stepped in front of me, happily smiling, expectant. The young girl was gone. Guy stopped and turned back to us.

"What's happening?" I asked.

"You're gettin' your wish," Guy said, as if he wished otherwise.

"My wish?"

"Ya feel like gettin' married tonight?" Guy asked.

"Tonight?"

Guy chuckled. "Listen to him!"

I'm sure we all stood there longer than I knew.

"I'm sorry, I haven't had much sleep. I just—-I haven't even proposed," I stammered.

Guy took a step toward us.

"Then go ahead and do it," he said.

She was right next to me. I took her in my arms but my fatigued mind was trying to figure out Guy's angle on this. Was he giving her to me? Was there some aspect of wedding her that I was missing? She would be mine now. This couldn't be right.

I dropped to my knees and held her thighs, looking up at her. One of my hands held her ass cheek but Guy couldn't see it. I could feel bones. Her wired blue eyes looked down at me.

"Mindy, will you marry me?"

Please don't look at Guy before answering—-

Her hands felt cold on my face. Lack of circulation, or just a chilly winter night?

"Yes."

I hugged her tightly and pushed my face into her belly, what little there was. Her fingers combed through my hair as I held on.

"I love you, Mindy," I said into her blouse. I don't think she heard me. When I looked up, she was staring at Guy with an evasive grin. I stood up and embraced her. She kissed me again with the same jab I got at the airport.

Guy held the door open for us. We got the marriage license and found the first chapel with a marquee that said OPEN near downtown. Twenty-four-hour weddings. In and out faster than if we ordered a meal. The tired old couple on the backshift informed us that we'd just missed their Valentine's special rate. Wired and on the verge of collapsing, grinning like an idiot in an all-night chapel on the Vegas Strip, this was how I finally married Melinda Spires. My first wife, the one no one ever knew about.

We didn't do it the way I would've wanted to write about it, but it was performed and duly recorded. A matter of record.

I wondered if they would've been in such a hurry if they understood that signing with a Hollywood agency didn't make me a million-dollar screenwriter; it just meant that there was now someone there to take ten percent if or when a buck was made.

Instead of anything remotely romantic or triumphant, I stumbled along like a drunk making a huge impulsive mistake. How could Guy maintain his hold on her if she was my wife? There had to be something I was missing, something the old hustler was holding back.

She didn't get in the back with me when we left the chapel. She rode up front with Guy. I didn't say anything.

I just sat slumped on my bag and listened to them sniffle on the way to their house.

My first real look at her was under the bright fluorescent lights in the chapel, right after I said, "I do." I realized that each time I saw her there was less and less of the girl I'd met before. She was physically changing from a pretty teen to a coked-out street skank and I'd just married her. Her arms and legs were thinner but her bloated body lost her curves from just a couple years before. And then there was the constant sniffling. I didn't do the math but she was sliding into an absurd self-parody of herself on an Elvis timeline. The sad, drugged-out version of the king had appeared only a few years after his trim and triumphant Hawaiian satellite show of 1973. The end came quickly.

So now we were married and we would soon consummate our union. I would make love to her; I would do what I always imagined. Then we would be like everyone else, every other couple just doing what they're supposed to do (technically). All the sudden, our story didn't sound so interesting anymore. I had to admit to myself that, in some goofy way, I felt so *worthy* pursuing her and not trying to have sex with her. Once we had sex, she wouldn't feel so special and different anymore. *Vegas Working Girl* would be a dead project because I got what I really wanted. We could seal that file and move on with our lives.

"There's where Famous Dead Fruiter Number Two lived," she remarked as we drove through the dark side street to their latest house.

"What's that?" I asked.

Guy slowed down.

"Famous Dead Fruiter Two," she repeated. "Liberace."

I looked outside and saw a black iron fence surrounding a large one-story house on a corner. Only a few feet of yard could fit between the house and the fence, so the property looked crowded by the wide house. In the center of each section of fence was a gold cursive "L."

The master showman had died two weeks before as that highly-publicized epidemic's silent tentacles reached into America's darkest fears. Gay men and drug addicts were dropping like flies while housewives and heteros were afraid of mosquitoes and salad bars ("All a waiter has to do is sneeze near the lettuce!"). The media fought over what had claimed Liberace and he went to his grave blaming a strange watermelon diet gone awry. Everyone knew it was AIDS. If he had been struck by a meteorite, there still would have been talk of AIDS. A strapping, handsome leading man like Rock Hudson stunned everyone; a flamboyant, effeminate pianist flying across the stage in feathers and sequined knickers did not.

"Liberace lived there?" I asked.

"Yep," she said. "Famous Dead Fruiter Number Two."

We stopped outside a driveway and Guy hit a control. In front of us a gate slowly rolled open and the car pulled into the driveway. Wow, they could afford a house with an automated gate. I got out and pulled out my bag, looking over their latest digs under the streetlights.

"Nice," I said. By the time I thought of carrying Mindy over the threshold, they were already inside.

The living room was wide and sunken with a fireplace. The entire house was tiled. Guy bragged that it once belonged to an Italian mobster who brought the tile over from the old country. Another Mafia link, whether true or not. In the backyard was another pool, smaller than the one they had before, but with a grotto and waterfall. A hallway led to several bedrooms and bathrooms.

Undisturbed newspapers were uselessly spread out near the sliding glass doors and the whole house smelled of dog shit. Now they had three Dobermans that mostly stayed outside. The entire backyard and concrete around the pool had black sausage-looking turds scattered everywhere.

"Here's my throne." Mindy smiled and motioned to a huge chair in the living room. It looked like it had been made from railroad ties.

"That's definitely a throne."

After putting my bag in a guestroom and getting the tour, we sat down at the long table in the dining room. Guy sat across from me. Mindy hovered at one end of the table. I wondered if now was a good time to ask if my new bride would be sleeping with me but I saw something that knocked even that out of my brain.

Spread out on the table was a cocaine processing operation. Scales, mirrors, razor blades, piles of product on sheets of paper, vials, white plastic containers.

"We were thinking about cutting you in on a little business proposition, seein' as how you're practically family now," Guy said, grinning, his eyes narrowing. This was the look he got when he thought he was doing someone an incredible favor.

I looked over their little table-top operation.

"What is it?" I asked.

"We need some funds to get started right," Guy said. "If you invested fifteen hundred dollars right now, we'd invest it, and you'd get seven hundred and fifty back within a month. What we're doing is taking half and putting it back into the operation. Then you'll get another seven hundred and fifty the next month—-which you'll have your original investment back. But you'll keep getting the seven hundred and fifty a month while we're up and running."

Whatever energy I had vanished. I didn't know how long I'd been up and I had again stepped into their world with no sleep. Maybe if I'd been spun up on coke with my senses all sharper and popping, I could've avoided marrying Mindy instead of blindly jumping in. But hadn't I been doing crazy shit like that all along without dope? Staring at their cocaine factory, I was now sick to think that Guy allowed Mindy to marry me to bring me into their dealing. I missed the Guy who had threatened to kill me if I brought drugs around them. Now I felt like I was slumped on the set of *Scarface Two*. Two years after his threat, they were cutting me in on their drug operation.

Guy explained how they would cut the coke with the white powder in the containers, selling twice as much to the desperate cokeheads who couldn't tell the difference. I wondered if Mindy or Guy could.

"I'm really tired, Guy," I slurred. "I need some sleep. But it sounds good."

I was lying. It sounded dangerous and terrifying, and I was sitting right next to enough coke to send me away for the rest of my life. I said it sounded good because I didn't want them to shoot me in my sleep if they realized in their coke-fueled paranoia that I would never be part of such a thing. I knew that drugs made people distrustful and suspicious, and I also knew that they didn't know me. They never knew me if they thought I would become a part of this, married to Mindy or not. Was this why Guy allowed our hasty nuptial? To draw me further in?

I stood and walked to the hallway. When I realized neither of them had moved, I turned back and looked at Mindy. She stood behind Guy at the end of the table. That would've been a good shot for their movie, Guy and Mindy behind the scales and cocaine mounds on the table.

"You need to rest up before the honeymoon," Guy said evenly. "You look like shit."

I went to bed alone on my wedding night but I didn't really care. I passed out thinking, this is not the way I would've written this scene.

No one would've written it this way.

Unless the author really hated me.

———

EVERYONE HAS moments when they find themselves in a place so bizarre and removed from their normal life that they have to spend a few moments retracing their steps to see how they got there. Standing at midnight in a Vegas chapel with an escort and her business manager might be one or sitting across from same business manager with a mountain of cocaine on the table would certainly qualify as well, but another moment would distinguish itself over that weekend.

I was aware of the phone ringing, the loud chirping from the kitchen counter and the harsh clanging from the master bedroom on the other side of my wall. The nearest ringing made me think of a machine gun firing into a copper drum. I woke up alone. I heard the phone and looked to a window to see if the sun was up. It was gray through the curtains and I slid back into sleep. When I heard the clacking of Mindy's heels on the tile, I wondered whether to try and stay awake or not—-

Until Guy pounded on the door.

"Yeah?" I called out.

"Don't come out for about twenty minutes," came Guy's raspy grunt through the door.

"I'm not even out of bed yet."

"Good."

I tried to figure out how long I'd slept. Had I slept enough to attempt a coherent thought about the past twenty-four hours? I stared at the ceiling, listening, then I looked over the room. Bland wallpaper, a dull gold carpet over the tile. The sheets were clean. My stuffed bag and sneakers in front of the empty closet were the only personal items in the room. My solitary honeymoon suite.

Why did he let me marry Mindy? What was Guy's angle? Did he believe I'd already made it in Hollywood because a name actor was reading my script?

Mindy's sharp heels clicked across the floor outside the door. Her belt and bracelets clanked and jangled. The Dobermans' claws scratched in the distance as Guy herded them into the garage. Something was going on.

I felt so different and none of my feelings had anything to do with the fact that we were now man and wife. She looked so different now.

Still dozing, I heard her say, "Hi," at the end of the hall in the living room where her throne stood. But I could also hear her voice through the wall behind me. Over a speaker. As she chatted with a man in the living room, I realized Guy was listening in from the master bedroom.

I couldn't make out what they were saying. It was business.

Then I heard the whip.

At first it was only a distant *thwap, thwap*.

"How's that?" she asked. I heard that.

The man said something in a concentrated nasal whisper.

Thwap, thwap. Thwap.

He said something to her.

Crack!

I stretched out and stayed perfectly still in the queen-sized bed and wondered what I was doing with my life. Guy had the marriage certificate. I had signed it as did Mindy but Guy folded it in half and slipped it into his sports coat's inside pocket. Then they brought me back to this alleged mobster's house and showed me their drug operation. Congratulations! What considerate father-in-law wouldn't try to bring his baby's new hubby into the family business? Obviously, I possessed a dangerous zeal to prove that I was the world's worthiest and nicest guy. Unfortunately, I was proving it to extremely hardcore criminals. *Great job, Jeffy!*

I felt like the stupidest dupe on the planet until I added up their hospitality and generosity. They never asked for anything after my first visit, except to get their cocaine biz off the ground. Guy was always insulted anytime I offered to pick up a meal. Was I the only normal guy in their lives? Did they know anyone else? *What was I missing?*

I heard the man say in grateful submission, "Yes, Mistress."

Customers called and showed up at all hours. I

managed to shower and dress before the next Dominance seeker called. When I went out to the living room, I noticed that the coke factory had been removed from the long dining table and was replaced with black candelabras, giving the room a cheap horror film look. Mindy was snorting a few lines from a mirror on the kitchen counter. I noticed she now wore leopard-spotted body stockings instead of tiger stripes.

"Hi," she said.

"Good morning," I said.

She didn't kiss me. That was her in the chapel last night, right?

"I don't even hook anymore," she said, her silver chains rattling as she stood up, sniffing. "I don't have to! There's enough guys that get into all kinds of kinky shit, and I don't have to so much as kiss them! No body contact. It's great."

"Sounds a lot safer," I admitted. "With AIDS and everything."

"It's fun too," she explained. "I get to turn the tables on these assholes for a change. I tie 'em up with what I got in there—-"

She gestured at the tan suitcase on the fireplace near her throne.

"—-and abuse them all I want. And they *love it*!"

Standing at the sliding glass doors, I said, "And that's it?"

"I leave one of their arms free to jerk themselves off so, yeah, that's about it."

The phone rang. Another customer on his way. Mindy told him to ring the bell at the gate with a can of Sprite in hand, so she would know it was him.

Guy waved me back into the master bedroom, still shuffling around in a t-shirt and baggy briefs. I walked in, he closed the door. He dropped his weight onto the bed.

"Have a seat," he said.

I didn't feel comfortable sitting on their bed, so I sat on a thick rug with my back to the wall. The German Luger was on the nightstand. Next to it, the speaker crackled as Mindy answered the door.

"You don't have to sit on the floor," Guy snapped.

"No, I'm fine."

The next customer spoke rapidly and was very specific. "Okay, basically what I want you to do is beat me and tell me how bad I've been. I've got these rubber underpants I wear, so that's all I'll be wearing. It doesn't matter to me what you call me -as long as it's bad. When I'm about ready to come, I want you to spank my balls."

I wanted to laugh. Guy read an old issue of *Newsweek* magazine, his reading glasses perched on the end of his nose. He rarely reacted to anything, and the most he would do was shake his head at me.

Another customer, trussed up and licking and slurping her boots as she sat on her throne, gasped, "Can I touch your tit, Mistress?"

"No, you cannot touch Mistress' tit!" she roared at him. *"How dare you ask Mistress that!"*

Guy glanced at the speaker. Or at the gun next to it.

As that customer cleaned himself up, he said, "You're good."

The microphone for the listening device was tacked under her throne, so the lip-smacking or panting of her customers on the floor crackled loudly in the bedroom. I never saw these guys who were paying around two hundred dollars for her to whip and abuse them, but I wondered who they were and where they came from. Most were gone in a half-hour.

One guy showed up and asked for a champagne enema. Two hundred dollars. He sat on the toilet in the little bathroom near the front door while Mindy held up the bottle of pink champagne with the enema tube. They casually chatted during this procedure and then fell silent toward the end. I assumed Mindy stopped talking to allow him to quietly ejaculate. After he left, Mindy stomped back into the master bedroom and tossed the cash on the bed in front of Guy.

"I can't believe he took the whole bottle!" she said. "You should have seen how red his ears turned!"

No matter how wrong everything was, I doubted if anything broke any existing laws when you think about it.

That empty bottle of champagne remained in the bathroom garbage can for the rest of my visit. Some bubbly to celebrate this weekend? No. Some guy wanted to fill his asshole with champagne. Love is grand, no?

The steady procession of masochists and perverts kept us occupied as Mindy and Guy ignored our quickie Vegas wedding and I ignored their start-up *Scarface* home business.

Later that day, sitting in the back master bedroom with an obese pimp, listening to a Dominatrix—-my newlywed bride--beat her kinky customers, I mulled over my Vegas experiences, remembering my tiny hometown in the Midwestern cornfields that conjured up every cliché of American normalcy, and reassessing how I'd left one for the other to write screenplays in Hollywood. I ended up here, in Vegas, a week or so after Liberace expired of AIDS down the street, listening to these warped sex sessions, wondering--

How did I get here?

———

YOU KIDS JUST MISSED our Valentine's Day special, I thought dismally to myself. That's what the old couple at the Strip chapel had said. Another amusing little detail that now screamed like another ignored warning that I was really hosing up my life, big-time.

Sitting in someone else's bedroom, listening to the wet sounds over a static-filled speaker of kinky sex several rooms away, I kept sifting for the scam of marrying Mindy while realizing how little sex anybody was getting. I was sure every other couple who came to Vegas to get hitched on or around Valentine's Day were, in the words of my degenerate nuke co-workers, "balls deep in love." But not in my life, not in this house.

I sat on the floor, still a virgin as far as Vegas knew, paying for sex a couple of times but never getting a happy ending, throwing out cash but unable to consummate any transaction so far. Guy was plopped down on the bed like a corrupt burgomaster, smoking, listening to the speaker and counting his tribute. Who knew when he last saw his dick, let alone used it. And out on the main floor was Angelique the sniffling Dominatrix, thrilled with her snarling persona and loving the control and distance it gave her. She got off on how far away she was from the hands, the lips, the genitals and the semen.

Calls came in and scenarios were played out, money was handed over and fluids were mopped up, and nobody touched anybody. Sex was everywhere in a city dedicated and enslaved to the flesh but the closest anyone around me to finding the rapture and euphoria of making love was the sick son-of-a-bitch jerking off on the living room floor.

———

WHEN WE WENT out to get something to eat—-prime rib, what else? —-I saw at close range just how addicted they had become to cocaine. Guy, always a physical wreck, now looked so doughy and sweaty that I expected him to keel over at any moment. He had a cigarette in one hand and a fork of prime rib in the other.

If he'd reminded me of Jackie Gleason in *The Hustler* before, he now reminded me of the gasping Orson Welles during his last appearances on "The Merv Griffin Show."

Mindy was ruined. The once beautiful contrast of her jet-black hair and pale white skin now only accented the scary mask of a frazzled cocaine fiend. I'd never seen anyone with tiny blue veins around their eyes. They stood out more than her brimming, bloodshot blue eyes. She constantly sniffed and rubbed her nose, even sneaking a snort from a small brown vial she carried wherever we went. I had to fight to keep the words *coke whore* out of my thoughts. In two short years her youth had been cut up on a mirror and snorted into oblivion.

Even Guy noticed her constant snorting—-or noticed that I noticed. That morning, they staged a ridiculous charade for me in the dining room. Guy sat reading a newspaper at the table when I came out and took a seat across from him. A Kilimanjaro snowcap of cocaine stood on a sheet of aluminum foil on the counter behind him which was not unusual. Mindy came out from the master bedroom, looking groggy and dressed in a robe.

Guy said to her, "Good morning!"

I think it was one o'clock in the afternoon.

"Hey," he grunted at her and motioned to the mound of coke on the counter.

She curled her lip and waved him off, walking through.

Guy turned to me and said, "See? She's not addicted. She can say no whenever she wants."

I knew my face wasn't buying into it, so I just nodded. Either before or after her performance, I figured Mindy found another pile elsewhere or hit her little brown vial. She knew where the pure shit was.

We acted as if the wedding never happened. My participation in their cocaine distribution plan never came up again either so it was a very weird stalemate.

The Dominance customers kept calling and arriving frequently enough to keep us distracted from any awkward silences or confrontations. When I went to get some sleep, I didn't try to communicate anything to Mindy that she should come with me. I don't think either one of them slept anymore as long as there were white piles of inventory everywhere. Mindy was too wrecked for me to even feel any sexual desire for her. Great, I told myself, *now* you want to hesitate, now you want to back away?

Still, the steady parade of perverts arrived at the gate as each one displayed the soda can of Mindy's choice so she could answer the door as the cruel mistress.

My curiosity got the best of me the second day and I

slipped behind Mindy's throne to peek out of the heavy drapes at the customer ringing the bell at the gate. He was about average height, black hair, white skin, thick five o'clock shadow. Small eyes, but he was squinting in the daylight. He was the first customer I saw and he looked like any other guy walking the streets. In the restaurant that evening, I looked at the people around us and wondered what twisted little secrets they were all hiding?

After our prime rib dinner, I asked if we could take in a show. They both stared at me.

"I'd like to check out a Vegas show," I shrugged. "I'll even buy the tickets."

Guy snorted contemptuously. The big spender swept aside my insulting offer to treat and wanted to find one of the bigger shows on his dime. As bizarrely entertaining as listening to Mindy's spank-and-moan sessions were, I instead wanted to stay out of a house with cocaine piles on the tables and counters.

The first marquee I wanted to check was Bally's to see if DEAN MARTIN was still spelled out in huge letters. Dino was gone. In smaller letters to fit were the names JERRY LEWIS & SAMMY DAVIS JR. Dino's ex-partner with one of the Rat Pack. They would have to do.

Although the showroom was full, we got right in and were seated near the back. If only Dino had been this easy, I thought sourly, I wouldn't have blown forty dollars out in the parking lot with the two black girls from back home.

We were surrounded by white and blue hair in every direction and we were probably the only people under the age of sixty in the entire showroom. Guy and Mindy both sniffed and snorted and I impatiently waited for the lights to go down. Now I was the one thinking of *Scarface*, remembering the restaurant scene where a coked-out Pacino loudly announces to offended diners about Michelle Pfieffer, "My woman don't wanna *fawk* me no more!"

Thankfully, the show started. Sammy Davis Jr., one of the original tuxedo icons, a real live Rat Packer, appeared limping and frail, and I couldn't get over how tiny he looked. But he could still sing, belting out tunes and giving as much as he could, the last gasp of that ring-a-ding time warp that defined old school Las Vegas. Gil Rozell would've been in kitsch heaven: we were seeing a revered relic from the ultimate era of Vegas cool.

I got the feeling that Sammy still needed this. He breathed performing like he needed oxygen, and he would cease to exist if the crowds went away and the spotlight went out. Looking smooth in his shiny tux as his knuckles glittered with jewels and rings, he softly addressed the auditorium like a best friend sitting next to him. He had dedicated his life to pleasing millions of people who never knew him.

"A lot of things have been written about me over the years," he said, and I figured he was referring to a recent porn star's tell-all book that detailed her sexual antics with both Sammy and his wife (and the porn star's hubby thrown in as well), "but it's you people who really matter, the folks who come to see me and hear me sing."

The elderly crowd applauded enthusiastically. I was glad that Rozell wasn't here because I found myself deeply touched by the love and appreciation between a performer and his audience. Rozell would've mocked me for the rest of my life for wiping a tear from the corner of my eye.

The show opened with both Jerry and Sammy doing a number before Sammy was left to do his set. When it was Jerry's turn, the crowd was just as adoring but I was at first confused and then embarrassed. Jerry told Pollack jokes, scratched his balls, and mugged incessantly during breaks in his monologue. At one point, Jerry rode a bicycle across the stage and, after disappearing for too long behind the curtain, the tinny recording of a crash blared over the sound system. He also left the stage before the sound of a flushing toilet and his relieved groan played over the speakers to gales of laughter.

"He's still got it!" someone called out near us.

I turned to see who said that. When Jerry appeared as himself in a cameo in his movie *The Bellboy*, he surrounded himself with sycophants who laughed at everything he said, even expressions of grief. When Jerry as Jerry talks of losing a family member, his entourage erupts in laughter and a voice calls out, "He's still got it!"

I didn't see who said it in the showroom but I'm sure I was the only person on the planet who made the connection to *The Bellboy*.

Wiping and pinching her nose, Mindy stared at the stage, expressionless, detached but posing as someone having a good time. Guy sat glowering, unimpressed by Sammy and thoroughly annoyed by Jerry. I grinned weakly and tried to enjoy the show, but Jerry's foul mouth kept me wincing. When a woman presented Sammy with a bouquet of roses, Jerry turned to the crowd and complained, "I didn't get no goddam flowers!" His constant curses, along with too many lame references to

Sammy as "one of those people," had me wishing Skoof had been along to get his chance to snap Jerry's neck.

At least he did some good things for handicapped kids, I told myself. And made *The Nutty Professor*.

When I spotted Mindy snorting from her little brown vial, I felt a twinge of panic in that sea of laughing senior citizens. Was the eye in the sky in here? I knew there were cameras over every table in the casino but what about in the showroom?

Who could see me sitting there with the coked-out whore and her ridiculous pimp, fidgeting uncomfortably in my obscene caricature of a honeymoon? Could anyone see me? Somewhere in the building, there were people at consoles monitoring the action, hidden at video monitors and watching for scams; security keeping an eye on things, pit bosses staring, waiters attentively standing by, hustlers seeking and scanning, tourists swooning and gawking. I could see all of them, the legions of wildly-diverse characters who populated my Vegas story, but I also felt someone was watching me, someone far more creative and knowledgeable and better at crafting these stories than I could ever be. Someone who would surprise even me in my own story.

Someone I now feared because I was on the wrong side of my storyteller. In Hollywood, they called it "losing rooting interest."

I felt like the doomed character who was about to have his ass handed to him.

———

I DIDN'T SEE her last customer on my last day, but I heard

his creepy voice. Guy stopped reading and leaned toward the speaker, so it wasn't just me. He told Mindy he was "hardcore," and wanted to be harshly beaten. We could laugh at the others, but just by the sound of his voice something hit us wrong about this guy.

"Don't be afraid to hurt me," he said.

He grunted hard as she whipped him. From the sound of the *cracks*, I could tell she was using the longer bull-whip. I could hear the actual sounds across the house better than what came over the speaker. And he kept telling her, "Harder."

I grimaced and looked at Guy.

"Don't you have anything harder?" the customer demanded.

"Hang on a minute," she said.

She burst into the room, tossing the bullwhip aside and paced back and forth.

"I don't know what to do with this guy," she said, flustered.

"Calm down," Guy told her.

"I am drawing blood out there! His back is bleeding and he still isn't getting off yet."

"Melinda. Calm down."

"I don't have anything else hard enough for him!"

Guy looked at me. I sat back against the wall.

"Give her your belt," he ordered.

"What?"

"Your belt. That's leather, right?"

"My dad gave me this belt," I said.

"I'll get ya a new one—-give her the belt!"

I removed my belt and handed it to her. She took it, but her eyes told me she didn't want to go back. That was the look I'd been waiting for: get me out of here. But I never saw that look from the young girl I met two years before. She stomped back down the hallway.

I paced. As with the bullwhip, I could hear the cracks of my belt through the door as clearly as they played over the speaker. I could also hear her desperate whimpers and the customer's excited breathing from the speaker.

I turned to Guy.

"I'm gonna go get her," I told him.

He lifted his head and turned his bored eyes to me.

"What did you say?"

"Don't you think that's enough?"

"He's gettin' what he paid for," he grumbled.

I took two steps toward the door.

"Hey!" Guy hissed sharply.

I whipped around to face him. "That's my wife out there!"

"You married her...but I *own* her ass," he growled. "And now I own you!"

I didn't know what to say. Of course, marriage meant nothing to him. This was Vegas. You could get married in a fast food drive-thru and get fries with that here. Elvis could perform the ceremony and your best man could be a clown, so what did something sacred mean here? *Nothing was sacred here—*

"This is business," he said through gritting teeth. "You want a say? Then sit your fuckin' ass down and write our book. *That's* your business!"

"Sean Penn is reading one of my scripts," I said and opened the door, stomping down the hallway.

"Hey!" Guy called out behind me.

My breaths were short as I wondered if Guy would

shoot me in the back. I made it to the end of the hall and stopped to see the scene in the living room. Mindy stood over a nude man bound on the floor, her hand shaking as she held the belt. Her eyes were wide and crazy and she looked like she was coming out of a trance. The naked man looked over his hairy ass at me and then up at Mistress Angelique.

"Is this part of the scenario?" he asked in a calm voice.

"No!" she barked.

I wanted to ask her if she was ready to leave. We could just run outside as we were and get out of here. This was Vegas. Nobody would think twice about her S&M outfit —-until we landed in Phoenix.

"If I could get fucked in the ass right now," the naked perv said, "that would be great."

Powerful hands grabbed me from behind and angrily dragged me backwards to the bedroom. Guy hurled me across the bed and I crumpled on the floor. The old man still had some strength in him. We both caught our breath as the pervert's voice came over the speaker: "Is he part of the scenario?"

"No," Mindy answered firmly. "He's not part of our scenario!"

I heard her lash him with the belt and repeat several times, *"He is not part of the scenario!"*

I looked up at Guy, the big ole coked-out teddy bear. Now it was his complete lack of humanity along with his size that reminded me of a bear. The cocaine had taken away anything I'd known about him. We stared at each other.

The sounds of the beating stopped. A thin satisfied

groan came over the speaker. The customer got what he paid for.

"You're the best," he moaned.

As he cleaned himself up and paid her, he chatted amiably with her. I could hear that she just wanted him gone.

"Do you live alone?" he asked her at the front door.

"No," she said simply.

Seconds after he left, Mindy burst through the bedroom door and stood before Guy, steadying her breathing. She tossed the bills on the bed in front of him.

"That actually worked," Mindy said. "I think he came faster because Jeff was there!"

I sat up, straightened my shirt. Winded, Guy dropped onto the bed. Mindy went to him and put her arms around him and they held each other. She sniffled as he comforted her. I appreciated that she'd tried to cover for me but she was holding him, not her husband.

"Here's your belt," she said when she opened her eyes and saw me. "He didn't get anything on it, and I didn't hit him where he was bleeding."

I mumbled, "Thanks."

Like so many other American families, we pretended like nothing happened. Just like the wedding and their coke deal. Guy tried to make jokes, chuckling that maybe I should've whipped the last perv with my own belt since he might have ejaculated sooner.

They took me to the airport that night. I felt I was seeing them for the last time. Guy remained quiet and suspicious. Mindy rattled on to keep the awkward silence away. She got out of the car and kissed me hard on the mouth, saying she couldn't wait until I came up next time.

"It'll be different next time. We'll have a real honeymoon or whatever you call it," she said with a smile, teasing and insincere. Guy stayed in the car and I saw the glow of his cigarette burning over the steering wheel. She added, "I don't care what he says."

She got in the car and it glided away.

In the airport, I bought a t-shirt that said VEGAS 86 but couldn't find one that said, "I married a hooker in Las Vegas and all I got was this lousy T-shirt!"

I definitely didn't want to be around cokeheads, let alone vast piles of the stuff itself. I thought of Brando warning the other Mafia families in *The Godfather*, a line as prophetic in real life as it had been in the movie: "This drug business will be the end of us." But Guy and Mindy wanted to live another movie, a totally different scenario: *Scarface*. There was no talk of getting Mindy out of Vegas anymore or retiring her ass to a life with me in Arizona. Okay, so I married her but that didn't matter because they had *made it*; living in a mobster's house, spanking for dollars with piles of blow and clothes, finding their happy ending. Just like their hero, Tony Montana. And the truth was that since this was real life, they didn't have to stick to that script and play out its bloody climax. They could make this work. But even if I wrote their story with their happy ending, I would never believe it.

I imagined my agents handing this script back to me, saying, "What kind of a piece of shit is this?" I wondered what their critique notes would be if I tried to pass my life off to them as a story. What would they want to do to me in the next rewrite, how badly would the next writers on the project make me pay for being so stupid?

I would just have to dream something else up, no

matter what happened next. Be creative. Try not to be heavy-handed about making Mindy and Guy answer for their crimes and their sins.

As I flew back to Phoenix, I kept telling myself that I didn't owe Mindy or Guy anything. Guy pocketed the marriage certificate but I didn't plan on going back to them. I could write whatever I wanted because I was never part of the scenario.

15

The Appalling Murder of a Henderson Car Salesman

APRIL 2005

I GOT BACK to the jail to find Danny impatiently pacing at the side entrance.

"You really need to get a cell phone," he said. "This guy cracked as soon as we told him we knew the gun was Melinda's."

He raised his hand and I absently slapped it for a high-five.

"We also hit him up about having an ID for Guy Reinhart, who originally had the gun."

"Did he know what happened to Guy?"

"He said no. Melinda gave him the Reinhart ID. She had it."

Danny hurried back to the parking garage like an anxious quarterback trying to get the game-winning play to the stadium where the team was waiting. I kept up with him.

"Stephanie left a while ago to start doing checks on the gun itself," he said. "Because of the type of gun, it shouldn't be hard to find out if it was ever used in any other crimes."

Danny's tires squealed twice on sharp turns in the parking garage.

"I'm not going that fast," he complained. "Happens every time I drive my POV here."

I barely heard the quick squeaks of rubber. I was remembering how the Luger sounded when it fired and counting Guy's shots from memory.

"Did he say why he killed her?" I asked.

"Because he's a whack job."

I snapped out of my own thoughts and looked at him.

"It doesn't sound like they'd been together too long," Danny said. "They were getting short on cash and long on jones'ing. He wanted to pawn the gun and she refused. They fought. She hit him with the gun. Then he took it away from her and beat her to death with it. He's saying self-defense."

"Self-defense? Right."

"Do you mind if we go by my office? I figure you'd want to see what Steph finds."

"Absolutely."

We immediately found ourselves locked in rush hour traffic, which probably started shortly after lunch when the morning rush ended. We crawled back to Homicide.

"Man, I want to thank you for this," Danny said.

"For what?"

"For coming up here on such short notice, helping with the case. Who knows how long it would've taken to sweat everything out of this guy if you hadn't been here to ID Melinda and the gun."

"You know I'll do anything to help out," I mumbled, looking outside.

It took everything to keep from imitating Fred MacMurray in *Double Indemnity, "It was all right in front of you, Keyes..."*

"I know you cared for her. I'm sorry it had to turn out this way."

"Well. It's not how I would've written it but life rarely cooperates with my outlines."

We sat through several traffic lights at each inter-section.

Steadying my breathing, I said, "You might want to check on that gun in Arizona too."

Out of the corner of my eye, I saw him whip his head to look at me.

A blaring voice roared inside my head, *What the fuck are you doing?*

"Why?"

"I think he killed some people down there."

"How do you know that?"

I felt as if I was teetering at the edge of a deep, molten abyss. It's all going to come out now and I didn't care anymore.

"She told me."

"Melinda told you that Guy shot people with that gun in Arizona?"

The words *I shot somebody* stung like a paper cut on the end of my tongue but I couldn't say them. I was sick of the burden of all my secrets. Worse, I was bored with them. Just not enough to let them all out at once.

"The last time I saw them was in Phoenix. July 1987. They were passing through on their way to Mexico. I'm sure it was to pick up a shipment of coke. She told me one of their deals went bad."

He looked like he wanted to ask more but he snatched up his cell and called Detective Killman.

"Steph, hey. We're heading to the office," he said into his phone. "If you can, check for the Luger in any homicides in Arizona. Summer of '87. We'll be there in a bit." He looked at me. "Phoenix?"

"Tucson," I said.

"Tucson area," he said into his cell. "Thanks."

He snapped his phone shut.

Frustrated, Danny sped onto side streets, which felt like progress until we found ourselves back on crowded boulevards.

"It was over after that last trip to Vegas," I said. "When they showed me their cocaine distribution center on their dining room table. When Liberace died. I never expected to see them again but they showed up in Phoenix. That really was the last time."

"You saw them then?"

"Yeah. On their way to Mexico or wherever they were headed."

"On the way down?"

"Yes."

Don't tell him too much.

After parking in the lot, I quickened my step to keep up as we plunged into the building and up an elevator. We came out to a floor of cubicles but the walls of each one were only waist high. You could see across the entire floor. No one else was there but in one cubicle stood a hat rack and perched atop it was a big rubber buzzard.

"She's not here," Danny said.

"You just talked to her, didn't you?"

He walked to his desk and scooped up a thick file. I saw the name plates on the two desks in this cubicle. DETECTIVE D. OLSEN and DETECTIVE S. KILLMAN. A post-it note was stuck on the thick file. The handwriting was feminine. *Here's one—-Steph.* She'd drawn a smiley face as well.

Danny scanned the file, then put it down.

"Have a seat," he said, gesturing to the chair next to his desk. "Let me see where she went."

He left me alone. I sat down, looked at the rubber buzzard standing over another cubicle and then stopped on the file on his desk. *Here's one.* I wondered. Another homicide with Guy's Luger? I was intrigued by a woman who would draw a smiley face on a post-it for a murder file.

I glanced at the doorway. Looked at the file. I could hear muffled conversations and distant phones ringing in the building around me. *Here's one.* I reached out, lifted the cover. My thumb also caught the top sheets and I ended up seeing a Xerox of a newspaper story deep in the file. *Appalling Murder of Henderson Car Salesman.* I dropped it when someone walked by the doorway.

Murder of a car salesman? Guy's friend, the mechanic who showed me the Elvis engine? Did Guy get so coked out that he killed his friend over money or even the Elvis engine? Was that buzzard watching me? Why was there a big rubber buzzard mutely perched over Homicide?

Did they have a gift shop too?

I was reaching to open the file again when Danny and Stephanie walked in. I jerked my hand back, looking guilty and embarrassed. They both saw me.

"The printer isn't working here so Steph's been printing files down the hall," Danny tersely explained.

"Oh."

"We got one hit here in Nevada on the gun, so far," Danny said, "and we just found another case in Arizona, outside of Tucson."

"Oh."

Danny picked up the first file and leafed through it.

"We'll have to wait for ballistics to confirm that it's the same gun but that type of weapon was used in these cases —-which is rare."

"When did they happen?"

Danny looked into the file.

"The Nevada one was February of 1989."

A year and a half after I'd last seen them.

"And the Arizona shooting?"

Stephanie Killman's steady gaze was locked on me.

She said, "Bodies were discovered in July 1987."

"The last time you said you saw them, right?" Danny asked.

They were both staring at me now.

I said, "That was when they passed through Phoenix."

"And Mindy said Guy killed people in Arizona?" Danny asked.

I nodded.

"How many?" he asked.

"She wasn't specific. She just...made it sound like a drug deal gone bad."

I felt like both detectives could see right through me.

"They were so coked out that I didn't know what to believe. Guy always tried to sound like a gangster." I shook my head. "Most of the time they played me like an idiot, I think. I was, then."

A long pause hung in the air.

"Can I ask who they killed?" I asked.

Danny laughed and nodded at the file next to me. He said, "Didn't you see?"

I grinned and shook my head again. Danny's laugh diffused some of the static pressure I felt. He opened the file and looked through it.

"A really brutal homicide. They didn't just shoot him, they totally butchered this poor guy."

"Who?"

"A car dealer over in Henderson. They beat him with hammers and sliced him up. He looks like he'd been tortured before he was shot with the Luger. It's the same gun. Probably the last time it was fired. Forensics says they waited a while before shooting him."

I was wondering where Guy and Mindy could have been mentally to commit such barbarism, where their addictions had taken them when Danny held up a printout of a driver's license belonging to Charles Blythe, the butchered Henderson car salesman. I took it in my hand, my mouth opening.

"Did you know him?" Stephanie asked.

I turned the printout around and held it up to them.

"That's Guy Reinhart."

———

THE NEXT HOUR WAS A BLUR. I wasn't sure an hour or a day passed.

Danny and Detective Killman read and compared files, trying to put all the info together into a practical if not logical timeline. I stared at the manila file with "Jane Doe" crossed out and "Melinda Spires" handwritten over it.

The gruesome murder of Charles Blythe, a car dealer, had baffled police since his body was discovered in 1989. Some traces of cocaine were found in his autopsy and some residue turned up in his residence but nothing that sent up any red flags. A car dealer with a little blow, especially in this town, shouldn't have ignited such vicious brutality in anyone. Detectives wondered if Blythe smuggled drugs in car shipments but that led nowhere.

Now that the detectives knew who he really was—-Guy Reinhart the pimp and small-time coke dealer with Mexican connections—-they were ready to close another lurid murder case.

Danny said, "This simple ID is turning into a gold mine for us."

"Ya got any other open files?" I wearily asked. "I got a pretty hot streak going here."

He smiled. Stephanie's grin was tight and mirthless.

The Mexicans had finally caught up to Guy. At first, I asked myself why he hadn't left Vegas, why he'd only gone as far as Henderson, but I knew he could never leave town, not *this* town. What other place was there for someone like him, a Mafia wannabe who believed his own bullshit, an obese pimp and coke dealer buzzing around the neon like a gaudy moth circling the brightest bug zapper of them all. Any place else was just a dark empty night.

You got your *Scarface* ending, Guy, I thought. And I'll bet it hurt like a bitch. You probably didn't even get a shot off.

I heard Stephanie ask Danny, "So how did Mindy end up with the murder weapon?"

Danny rustled through the Blythe file.

"Body wasn't discovered for several days," he said. "She could've easily come home to find him. Taken it then. Who knows. Maybe she was there and they left her alive."

I had been quiet for a while. "Or she finished him off. He might have been just hanging on when she found him. He would've begged her to."

"You know that's what happened?" Stephanie asked.

"No. But I can see it."

I stared at Mindy's file but could feel a look pass between Danny and his partner.

"I do have one question though," I said.

Danny asked, "What is it?"

I pointed back over my shoulder and asked, "Why is there a big rubber buzzard over that cubicle over there?"

"Oh, that's our way of knowing who's up for the next homicide," Danny explained. "There's a rotation for us as cases come in. The buzzard goes to the next pair of detectives so we can see where we are in the rotation." He turned to Stephanie. "It doesn't have a name yet, does it?"

Stephanie shook her head.

"You know what I would call him?" I asked.

Both Homicide detectives stared at me.

"Boris."

They glanced at each other.

"Hey, that's a pretty good name," Danny admitted. "I like that."

Stephanie nodded. "Best one I've heard, so far," she said.

Danny told me later that most of the others in Homicide liked the name as well so the rubber buzzard became known as Boris the Buzzard of Las Vegas Homicide. My contribution to Las Vegas. Didn't expect it to be that.

"Well, I should probably get you back," Danny said.

I shook hands with Stephanie and she thanked me. She was a little friendlier, more like the person who drew smiley faces on post-it notes, when she knew I was leaving. Danny said he'd be right out. I wandered back to the parking lot and waited at Danny's SUV. When he hurried outside, I said, "I can't believe the sun's still up."

"You can pack a lot into a day when these things start coming together."

We jumped right back into heavy traffic.

"Phoenix is getting like this," I noted.

"It's worse here."

"Your partner looked uncomfortable."

"She didn't like it that you didn't ask how many were killed in Tucson."

"I never knew. They never told me."

"So, you weren't there?"

"No," I lied.

"Did you write about that visit in your journal?"

"I didn't write about Mindy and Guy in Phoenix."

"Why not?"

"I knew what they were into by then so I stopped writing about them. I just wanted out. Wasn't the story I wanted."

Danny's cell phone rang and he answered it. His wife. He told her to go ahead and feed the boys. He could still make the game. He looked at me and said I would be there too. I nodded. He hung up.

"The report on the Tucson victims indicated there were two shooters."

"Two?" I asked.

"Do you believe that Melinda was capable of shooting anyone?"

I thought about it. I remembered an old biker saying but kept it to myself.

"Yeah. She could've shot somebody." We were snarled near an intersection on Industrial Road. I added, "You don't know who you're getting when they're doing drugs. Don't know what they can turn into. Someone strung out is capable of anything, right?"

"That's a lot to carry around all these years," he said.

"Maybe that's why she got on drugs. Maybe that's why she had to be high all the time."

"I meant you," he said.

"I never knew what happened to them. Now that I know, I'm not surprised. About some people, you just keep waiting to hear bad news."

"Happens every day."

"What should I have done?" I asked. "Turn them in? Or get completely pulled into their world?"

"No. I understand."

I wanted out of Danny's vehicle.

"Hey, I'll just jump out here and walk the rest of the way," I offered.

"No, we're almost there!"

"From here you can whip around and get back on the freeway."

"Are you sure?"

I released my seat belt and opened the door, stepping out onto the curb.

"I know you want to get back. What time do you want me to come over before the game?"

"Seven."

"I'll be there."

Before I closed the door, I said, "If you need anything more, let me know."

I closed the door and he turned into a parking lot, squealing the vehicle around and heading back toward the freeway.

I watched him drive away and felt safe enough to allow relief to spread through my body. I tied up a lot of loose threads and the investigation was moving on, away from me. Some secrets were going to stay safe. Boredom looked easier to deal with on the outside of a prison cell than in one. As I walked down Industrial Road, not too far from where Cooper wanted to find Plato's Retreat in the Eighties, I imagined the bloody corpse of Guy Reinhart a.k.a. Charles Blythe looking up from the coroner's slab to blurt out, "Did that rat fuck tell you what we did in the desert?"

But he was dead, gone, and he would never say anything to anyone ever again.

I quietly said aloud, "So long, Guy."

Alone and melancholy, I again thought about burning my journal when I left Vegas. What did any of it add up to? A sad ending of drugs and descent, too typical to be worth anyone's interest. A former Vegas working girl beat to death by a raving tweaker boyfriend. Her father-figure pimp savagely tortured and shot to death with his own gun. Even I knew you didn't steal and kill from Mexican drug runners and only move across town afterward. Maybe everything wouldn't come out. Now that I had some breathing room, I thought of Mindy. I just couldn't shake the feeling that I'd let her down, that I could've done something more. Something to help save her.

My feelings were as gridlocked as the traffic idling and spewing smog next to me. You can't save a dame or anyone else from themselves. Something caught my eye and I stopped dead on the sidewalk. A thirty-foot Elvis Presley was across the street.

———

SO, I spent an hour or so in the Elvis-O-Rama Museum behind Treasure Island, immersing myself in kitsch for a while. Looking at the albums my dad owned on the walls, listening to the music, I was relieved that my day of reckoning didn't look like it was going to be today. I could still enjoy some music. I bought postcards and a TCB keychain.

Back at the Stardust, I propped up the postcards and placed the keychain on my RADIOACTIVE journal and Old West photo with Mindy, everything atop the morgue T-shirt. My temporary Jeff Bailey Vegas Museum, a display somewhere between the Elvis-O-Rama but probably closer to all those little white crosses of the dead in the desert.

I could still hear the mournful echo of a sad Elvis song in my thoughts.

Well, I'll never, I'll never love another
Oh, my heart, all my dreams

Yea, they're with you
In that long black limousine

I knew that part of Elvis' lasting appeal was that he made our innermost agonies sound freakin' awesome.

I also realized that Mindy wasn't even going to get to ride in a black limousine anywhere, definitely not back home. I doubted if anyone would even claim her. But I've never heard a voice hit such a note of hurt or sound so mournful and alone as Elvis did in "Long, Black Limousine."

I still listen to his songs because I know what a broken heart sounds like.

And if nobody claimed her, I would.

———

THAT EVENING, as the sun dropped behind the mountains, I sat back on aluminum bleachers and watched a Little League baseball game as Danny's sons played. I offered my denim jacket to a mother in front of me who didn't think the breeze would cool off as much as it did. Danny sat next to me. Elated and relieved, he looked like he was coming down from the rush of nailing a case. He had a confession in the murder of Melinda Spires and he at least had more info on the cold case of Charles Blythe.

"Tucson Homicide will want to talk to you about the '87 homicides," he said. "They'll probably come to Phoenix so you won't have to go down there. They might even interview you over the phone."

"That's cool," I said.

I'd had enough years to get my story straight.

"I can't thank you enough—-"

I raised my hand. "Hey, I'm glad I was able to help."

If Danny had a football, he would've run down onto the baseball diamond and spiked it in front of the Little Leaguers.

"I'm just embarrassed that I ... I involved myself with people like that," I said.

"Well, you had your reasons."

"Yeah."

"They weren't *good* reasons but you had 'em," he laughed.

Since we were discussing cases, Danny's wife sat down on the bottom bench with other mothers to cheer her boys on.

"I'll keep you in the loop," Danny said. "We shouldn't need you for the trial or any follow-ups but I'll let you know."

We watched a few plays of the little boys and girls swinging and scrambling out on the field. After wandering the Strip since my arrival and visiting the Coroner's Office and Homicide, this casual game in its suburban tableaux of normalcy felt oddly surreal. I never felt comfortable here. What passed for the usual reality, the small towns and suburbs, gave me comfort but never made me feel as if I belonged. I shivered at a chill in the night air and tried not to regret loaning out my jacket.

"Pride goes before a fall," I said aloud.

Danny asked, "What's that?"

"I always thought I was so together," I confessed. "That I had so much to offer a woman."

"Well, you do."

"I'm not sure what they see," I said. "They might want a

knight in shining armor but then it pisses them off if anyone sees them as a damsel in distress."

"So, stop picking psychos in distress."

The cool spring breeze blew over the bleachers. The mother wearing my jacket hunched forward and drew it tightly around her.

"Well, I definitely take on the hardest cases, that's for sure. I keep trying to prove what a nice guy I am. But for what? What good have I done? What do they want from me?"

"When you figure that out," Danny said, "then write it all down because you will have answered one of life's greatest mysteries. Then you'll have your big best seller."

I glanced at Danny. He stared down at the first row of mothers watching the game.

"Yeah," I agreed, watching them as well, "I'll really have something if I figure that out."

We fell quiet again for a while. It was obvious that some of the kids were getting bored and their attention drifted. Parents shouted from both sides to keep them focused. I never knew this life. I was just the moody little shit who got left behind at the TV set.

"Maybe I'm trying to fix myself along with all their problems," I said.

"What do you mean? What's wrong with you?"

"Mindy, then Allison. All the women in my life were beautiful but badly damaged. My folks had an ugly divorce when I was a kid and I was so determined to be different. I would get it right." I turned to look at him. "If I could rescue the girl in the worst-case scenario...then I could rescue myself. How lame and predictable is that?"

"Yeah, you need to think up a happier ending for yourself."

"I thought I had one with Allison. I thought she could beat her addiction," I said. "I told her that when she smoked that stuff, she wasn't just killing herself anymore, she was killing me too."

"That didn't work?"

"No. We died."

Out of the corner of my blurring eye, I saw Danny glance at me.

"I wasn't enough," I added, "and I have to let her go."

I closed my eyes.

"We're here for you, buddy," Danny said.

I caught myself and pulled all the grief back inside. I didn't want to lose it watching a Little League baseball game. I opened my eyes.

Danny said, "Keep positive, it'll turn around."

"Three people can keep a secret if two of them are dead," I mumbled.

"What?"

"Just an old biker saying I remembered."

"What made you think of that?"

I shrugged.

"Nothing. Everything."

"Steph wanted me to ask you one more question to close out our initial report."

"What is it?"

"You said Melinda told you about Guy killing someone on the way *to* Tucson, right?"

"No, it was those bodies found outside Tucson."

"But you said you saw them when they were on their way to Tucson."

"Then I must have talked to her afterward," I said.

I glanced at Danny and I must have looked guilty as sin. He saw it. The sky was completely dark now.

"You didn't write any of that down?"

I stared beyond the baseball diamond, beyond the lights of Vegas, looking deep into a desert night in the past.

"There was nothing more to write after that."

Danny shrugged and offered, "Maybe there will be now."

16

Some Serious Shit Happened

JULY 1987

THE TITLE PAGE CAME EASY.

I sat at my IBM Selectric typewriter and rolled in the first sheet of paper at the dining table in Cooper's house. I'd rented a back bedroom the previous spring and would haul the Selectric out to the dining room when working on anything. I was ready to begin.

I locked the caps and the underscore key to type:

VEGAS WORKING GIRL

Beneath that I typed:

A Novel by Jeffrey Bailey

A novel, a work of fiction. As if I'd made it all up. I imagined an interviewer asking me, after the novel's publication, if it was difficult to write as such a stupid and unreliable narrator. No, it wasn't, I would humbly assure him, because I was a genius.

Proud of my title page, I yanked it out of the carriage and rolled in the next page. Page one, double-spaced. If I was working on a screenplay, the Selectric would be set on single-space but I hadn't touched a script in weeks. Not since my agents called to tell me that Sean Penn had passed on my nuclear script.

"We still believe in the project," they told me. "We're submitting it around town." They also had notes for the vampire script I showed them: drop all that religious shit at the end. Obviously, Hollywood wasn't going to be so easy either.

I stared at the blank page, thinking, Where could I even begin?

The night I met her. I replayed the memory of her walking away from the Stardust room as snow fluttered through the darkness. I typed, *I love you.*

I realized we had been doomed from that moment; doomed before she ever met a nice guy, doomed from the second I fell in love with her. That was when I should've tried to get her out, get her away before I ever met Guy Reinhart. It was foolish of me to think I could operate in her world, let alone pull off such a daring mission.

The next vivid memory was Mindy by her pool, just as the cocaine was first showing the effects of its draining claws in her red eyes and pale flesh. She had lowered her swimsuit, facing away from the house. She probably only swam at night since there were no tan lines. I tried not to stare at her exposed tits but I wanted them seared into my mind, my eyes burning to possess them at least as a memory. I still see her watery eyes and pink, puffy areolas and I typed: *Wait for me.*

I sat back in the chair and stared outside, wondering how to make this work. Maybe I wasn't the guy to write this. I looked back at the page. *I love you. Wait for me.* That was the first and last thing I'd written about Mindy after the winter of 1987. They almost completely disappeared from my notes and journals after my Vegas visit of February, after I married her. I never wanted anyone to know I had seen them again.

But they showed up in Phoenix that summer.

Anyone going through my journals would find two lines for the second week of July. On Tuesday, I sardonically noted, "Wife called (didn't call back)." On Saturday, "Mrs. B called." Mrs. Bailey. She'd been reduced to code names only I knew. The rest of my entries were movie titles I watched, people I met for lunch or dinner, and the restaurants where we met. Then a couple of blank weeks.

I'd hear a song from that summer and those lost days would come roaring back at me like the sound of a gun in the desert night and I'd see bullets slam through bodies right in front of me. Such sudden flashbacks only meant that those particular memories, those specific dates intentionally left blank in my carefully recorded life, were never that far away from me. I never had to write anything down to remember about that night.

Three people can keep a secret if two of them are dead. The same ratio holds true for five people.

As long as it all came down to one—-to me—-I thought I'd be safe.

———

I KEPT LOOKING at the door, thinking that all I had to do was walk out of it.

Mindy and Guy showed up in Phoenix on a hot afternoon, cruising down Grand Avenue to meet me in a parking lot next to a Circle K convenience store. They had called me from the pay phone there.

I was renting a room from Cooper, the same guy who wanted to get into Plato's Retreat so badly the September before but had ended up with Skoof's hooker. Cooper was absolutely fascinated to hear about my relationship with Mindy and Guy and was thrilled at the idea of meeting them. But his live-in girlfriend, who had just moved in, was horrified at the idea of my Vegas friends staying in the same house for even one night. I heard her shout from the kitchen, "I don't want some *whore* staying here!"

I had to chuckle: Cooper's new girlfriend surrendered every orifice to him the first night she'd met him in a bar, moved in two weeks later, and now she was telling Cooper who was and wasn't welcome in his house. I moved out a short time later, but the week Mindy and Guy showed up in town, I was still at Cooper's. He came into the living room to tell me sheepishly that my Vegas friends would not be welcome. He also asked if he could ride along with me when I went to see them. I informed him, "I'm sure your girlfriend wouldn't approve." (She didn't last much longer after I'd moved out and he begged me to move back, but I refused).

I actually asked my mother if we could visit her place, but she didn't think her new husband, Daryl, would like it. They had just been married the previous New Year's and I assumed he'd let me know he was the new head of that house. Daryl hadn't warmed to my association with these

Vegas folks since saying to me, "You'll meet her for dinner somewhere and kiss her...and she just got done giving some old fat guy upstairs a head job," but he'd said little else about them since. I didn't tell Mom they were in town and also decided against telling her that Mindy had been her daughter-in-law since February.

So, I met Mindy and Guy at a convenience store and I was embarrassed that I didn't have a place for them to stay. I got a kiss on the cheek from Mrs. Bailey. I followed them to a nearby seedy motel along Grand Avenue. They checked in. Mindy had one of her Dobermans with her and it actually managed to bring most of the stink of their houses with it. She had it dressed up with a silver choker chain and a red bandana around its neck.

I sat on a chair at the table and Guy dropped his enormous body on the bed, sweating and gasping and smoking a cigarette. Mindy also smoked as she inspected the room with its faded curtains and threadbare carpet. She considered the bathroom and turned on the light. Her Doberman sat on the other side of the bed and watched her.

"Guy, you're not gonna be able to get in this bathtub," she said from the bathroom.

He was reading a newspaper and lifted his head. Glancing from the bathroom to me.

"I don't care," he eventually said. "I don't feel like looking for someplace else."

I asked him if I could see the section of the newspaper he finished. The front page. I was following the PTL scandal in all its ugly, glitzy melodrama; the greed of the televangelists' fleecing of the flock, the exposure of the sex scandals, the TV meltdowns and a zealous self-righteous media gone wild. The depressing truth was that tele-vangelists were getting more action than me.

"I want to get her on a biplane," Guy announced.

I looked up from the news article.

"What's that?"

"I want to get her on a biplane. A plane ride."

"A biplane?"

"They have them here, don't they?"

I'd seen biplanes plenty of times outside of Phoenix, diving and plunging as they dusted the fields beyond the spreading tract homes, but I didn't think any of them offered rides. We weren't in Vegas, where everything was offered as some form of entertainment.

"I've seen crop dusters here," I told him.

"I'll pay whatever it takes."

I turned to see her standing in the bathroom door, her hands on each side of the doorway, leaning out and staring at me. She was thin and pale, still constantly sniffing and wiping at her nose. There were now dark circles to go with the blue veins around her eyes. I noticed she chewed or cut her fingernails down too much and the nail polish was worn and neglected. She grinned.

"That Dutchman's Gold is somewhere around here, isn't it?" Guy asked.

I heard him snort and looked over to see him licking the last of a hit of coke off his hand. I wondered how much they brought with them.

"The Superstition Mountains," I said. "East of here, on the other side of the Valley."

"What's that?" Mindy asked, stepping over to the bed and sitting down across from us.

"It's a legend down here," Guy explained, studying his

hand for any leftover granules. "An old miner found this big, ole strip of gold in them mountains but wouldn't tell anybody where it was. He said a shadow pointed to it every day, but nobody's found it yet."

Intrigued, Mindy looked to me.

"That's pretty close," I said.

Guy looked directly at me, narrowing his eyes with that proud and defiant stare of superiority.

"See, I know things, even here," he said.

"So, all that gold's still there?" Mindy asked between sniffs.

"If it ever existed," I said.

"Oh, it's there," Guy said.

I was waiting for some story about Guy's association with crazy old prospectors, the way he bragged about his Mafia connections in Vegas, but he didn't go into how he knew there was gold in the Superstitions.

"So where are you guys on your way to?" I asked.

"We've got some business associates to meet from Mexico," Guy said.

"Our suppliers," Mindy blurted.

Guy's eyes burned at her like an industrial laser cutting through metal.

"It's just Jeff!" she said, raising her voice.

"Melinda...," he growled.

"You ought to come with us," she said, turning to me.

Guy looked at me.

"Have you ever been to Mexico?"

I bit my lip. Mexico? With these two?

"We're not going into Mexico this trip," Guy said, his voice still low with smoldering anger. "They're meeting us on the US side. Our side."

"Well, it's down that way," Mindy said. "How far away is it? I wanna say I left the country someday."

"It's a couple hundred miles to the border, I think," I said, trying to keep the conversation moving instead of lapsing into uncomfortable pauses where Guy glared at Mindy. "I've been down to Tombstone. That's southeast of Tucson."

Mindy ignored Guy's steady stare. He looked like he was trying to cut her in half with his eyes.

"Where the gunfight at the OK Corral happened," I added.

"Was that Butch Cassidy?" she asked.

"Wyatt Earp. And Doc Holliday."

Guy turned his gaze at me. "Are you free the next day or two?"

I only had two seconds to consider lying to them about my schedule, but chose not to. Even coked out, Guy would probably see right through me.

"Well...yes."

"Would you like to ride down with us?" he asked.

Mindy was petting her Doberman.

"You're not going into Mexico?" I asked.

"How much do you make at that job of yours?" Guy asked.

"Enough to live on."

"Are you ready to make it big, son?" he drawled.

"What do you mean?"

I looked at Mindy. I could tell by the way she continued petting her dog that she knew what was coming.

Guy asked, "What do you call it when someone secures a writer to write something? A retainer?"

"No, an advance. Or a development deal."

Guy grinned, his eyes twinkling with the excitement of good news.

"How would you like a big, fat advance on your future?"

I shrugged.

"How does fifty grand sound? Is that big enough for those Hollywood assholes to match?"

"You mean come up to Vegas and write for you?" I asked.

"You'd be working for us exclusively," he said.

"We could put him up in his own apartment," Mindy interjected. "So, he can concentrate."

Guy's brow furrowed as he glanced at her, his greedy mind obviously calculating that cost. He admitted, "We could do that."

My greedy mind was foolishly running with this new plan. Could this jumpstart my career? Sure, the nuke plant paid me to read and write all night while earning a living but I wouldn't have to wear a uniform and commute and punch a time clock. I'd be a paid writer, living in Las Vegas. My Hollywood agents and future biographer would love it!

"Ride with us," Guy said. "We'll talk." He grunted an unsavory laugh. "We'll do lunch."

My mouth opened to say something but I just nodded.

Guy's pale, sweaty face nodded. I looked at Mindy. She was still petting her dog but she was grinning, pleased.

———

AS I RODE in the stale cigarette stench of their dusty Town

car, heading south of Phoenix and across the desert toward Mexico, I kept thinking about that door out of their seedy motel room. About how I should have walked out and never seen them again. But I didn't. Guy knew which bait to use this time, as he always did. It didn't take long for me to realize that biting on that brightest of all shiny lures would be the biggest mistake of my life.

I only had myself to blame. Guy and Mindy were who they were and it was entirely my fault for foolishly risking life and limb by entering their world. How stupid could I have been to pursue a brainless romantic quest with a whore and her pimp as they both disappeared under the avalanche of blow blanketing Las Vegas? Research? The arresting officer would buy that, the judge, my new cell-mate—-all the way up to God Himself. Yeah, Jeffy, go with that.

I'd worn my naïve hope for saving Mindy like some type of talisman, as if my love, as misguided as it was stubborn, was enough to protect me from the increasing risks of each contact with them. I felt like the crazy soldier who stands and walks through a hellish firefight, amazing everyone on the battlefield when not a bullet grazes him. But the longer I stayed around Mindy and Guy, the longer I found myself out in the open and the more I could feel the invincibility fading as the crosshairs closed in, especially if now I was around them for cash to fund my own selfish dream instead of the lunatic Happily Ever After.

Even though I realized that they both were now not just fried-out coke fiends of the lowest order but complete scumbag dealers, I still got in their car and rode south with them for wherever they were going. They believed me when I told them I was a writer; they opened up and welcomed me when I wasn't sure if my own blood relatives noticed I was gone. If Mindy and Guy thought I was a moody little shit as well, at least they didn't let me know. I was an author to them and they believed I would make them immortal in a story everyone would want to read. They were my characters and they became my family, even as their dangerous lives were leading me straight into hell. They, not Hollywood, were going to give my first fat check, my first big break.

On paper, I thought, everybody wins.

———

I RAN BACK to Cooper's, threw together an overnight bag, and drove back to the seedy motel on Grand Avenue. Guy paid for the room for the next three days, so we left my car there and we took off in their Lincoln for Tucson. Mindy drove and I sat in the passenger seat. Guy and the Doberman were in the back seat.

As we drove down Grand to catch I-10 south, a car pulled out in front of us and Mindy slammed on the brakes. Guy braced himself in the back, and the dog, the only one who didn't see it coming, slammed into the seat behind Mindy.

Guy exploded, shouting at the top of his lungs, *"YOU GODDAM HOOSIER!"* Guy had to be from Missouri, like Mindy, or somewhere in the Midwest. Somewhere across a river or state line from the goddam Hoosiers.

During our first quiet moment, I said, "I just found out that Sean Penn has passed on my nuclear script. My agents called me last week to tell me."

A part of me wanted to hear Mindy say, *"That's okay, we're not really married."*

"Hey, Mr. Writer," Guy huffed from the backseat after we got on I-10 and headed out of Phoenix. "I got a story for you. It might get me killed to tell it, but I don't give a fuck anymore."

Mindy cut in to ask, "What about our movie script?"

"Have you got an ending for me yet?" I asked.

She asked back, "Aren't you gonna make one up?"

I thought bitterly: I wouldn't be here if Sean Penn liked my script.

"Did you know who Nikita Khrushchev was?" Guy continued.

I watched Mindy glance at him in the rearview mirror.

I answered, "The Soviet premier? Just that he was a Russian leader and he beat a podium with a shoe and said he'd bury us, right?"

"That's the one! Well...I was part of a mission to assassinate that Commie prick in the Fifties. Top secret. No one knew about it. I told you I was a pilot back then, right?"

"I knew you were into planes," I said, thinking of the dozens of airplane models he snapped together the year before.

"You wouldn't know it to look at me now," he chuckled, "but I use to fly fighter jets before you were born. And I flew on a top-secret mission into Russia to kill Khrushchev. I would probably be killed for talking about it."

I didn't know what to think. As he rambled about the assassination plot, I wondered where he got this Intel. Everything else he'd ever told me sounded vague and exaggerated, the tough-guy boasts of a mobster wanna-be, but he was filled with details and drama about the Khrushchev plan. Was it possible that the most ridiculous yarn he spun was the only one that was true?

Guy asked me, "What kind of medical benefits do you have at your nuclear plant?"

"Not much."

"I mean as far as spouses go," he added.

This was the first mention of my marital status with Mindy.

"I'm just a contractor so there are no medical benefits," I told him.

"We made seventy-two thousand dollars last year from her Dominance customers," Guy said. To her, he asked, "I'll bet between that and our other business, we'll make well over two hundred thousand this year."

I wondered why he would ask about benefits for a job I was going to quit to come write for them.

"Should we show 'em what we got in the trunk?" Guy asked Mindy.

Her wired eyes darted from me to the mirror at him.

"It's just Jeff!" he mocked her, repeating what she said earlier.

A wave of anxiety rolled over me. We could not have looked anymore suspicious, and now I knew there was something in the trunk on its way to "almost" Mexico.

We didn't have Las Vegas to distract everyone from how guilty and ridiculous we looked in the real world.

We were completely out in the open.

———

MOST OF WHAT I remember about those hours just south of Tucson was heat, darkness and bugs.

Several times I was leaning against the car while Guy talked on pay phones and Mindy took the Doberman into the dark to relieve it. I stopped thinking about that door back in the seedy motel room. Now I looked out at the lights deep in the desert darkness and thought about running toward them. It had to be money in the trunk. This had to be pickup for them. This had to be The End for us. Fifty grand or not, this wasn't me.

Never been drunk, never even tried weed, and here I am—

"Pop the trunk," Guy barked at Mindy, then turned to me and said, "Jeff, you sit in the back with me this time."

"Where are we going?" I asked.

"We're going to meet some business associates out of Mexico," he said with a hint of nervous impatience. "We're not going into Mexico so we'll be all right. Fuckin' beaners."

That didn't make me feel better.

Mindy brought a black gym bag up and Guy struggled into the backseat like a bloated mammal burrowing into its lair. He took the bag and ordered us into the car.

"He said we're just about there. Take the second exit and go west, which is...."

"Right."

Guy looked at me, winded and sweating.

"West. Right."

I felt something small and metal press against my leg. I saw Guy's arm reaching toward me in the dark.

"What's this?" I asked.

"Take it."

I reached down as he withdrew his hand, leaving a snub-nosed revolver in my hand. I held it up to see it.

"What the fuck is this, Guy?" I snapped.

"You're gonna want more than your dick in your hand tonight."

Exasperated, I popped the cylinder open and saw the glint of all chambers filled. I wanted to shout, *"That line's from The Godfather! This isn't a fucking movie, Guy!"*

Great. My life finally became a movie—-just not the movie I wanted to play in.

I cursed myself for the next several miles. I was paying for all the reckless chances I'd taken with them. Not only did we have to get to this rendezvous with the suspicious gym bag but after meeting these associates I had to get back to Phoenix without getting busted by anything from Arizona state troopers to the US Border Patrol to the Drug Enforcement Agency. And I was armed too.

"Right," Guy said as we pulled off the highway. "Go right."

"I am," she said impatiently.

I watched the Doberman in the seat in front of me. It could sense the tension building in all of us. Quivering, it kept looking at Mindy as she drove.

"Goddammit, Melinda, slow down!" Guy shouted.

"Shut the fuck up, Guy!" she shouted back.

"Mindy, we have to see the dirt road to pull off."

"There was a dirt road back there," I said.

"Did it go to the left?" Guy asked.

"It went both ways."

"Turn around and go back," he ordered her.

She made a four-point turn with that big Town car and headed back. She slowed and turned south, the tires rumbling over the dirt and rock. Rocks pinged and banged on the undercarriage. Probably what bullets sounded like hitting against the car? The dog whimpered.

"It's okay, baby," Mindy told it.

I kept thinking the words: *Fuck me running*.

Guy grunted, sat up, peered out the windshield. A rubber orange cone appeared along the dirt road and he said, "Slow down. Stop."

The dust the Town car kicked up rolled over us and Guy cursed her for driving too fast as we coughed.

"Keep that dog in here," Guy said.

"Why?" she asked.

"Do you want to get it shot, Mindy?" he snapped at her. "They don't know we've got a dog, you dumb bitch!"

This was not the playful name-calling banter of Vegas. I could tell they were both as jumpy and frightened as I was. Mindy would've torn into him for calling her a dumb bitch but she took it.

"Let's go," Guy said.

"All of us?" I asked.

"All of us," he said, his voice low with menace. "Except the dog."

"I thought I wasn't supposed to get involved," I said quietly.

Guy growled at me, "You wanted material? You're getting it. Did you think you were going to be in our lives for free?"

I flushed with anger. My fear and anxiety made me feel stupid and helpless even though I was armed but anger was an emotion I could do something with.

We got out of the car and I looked at the open desert around us. I could only see a few feet of rocks and dirt before the ground disappeared into the night. I slipped the .38 revolver in my belt under my shirt behind me. We were miles from the glow of the highway and I could see the craggy black mountains under the stars in the distance. I took a step away from the headlights and the instant onslaught of bugs. Anything out there would see us too clearly.

"Jeff," Guy said quietly.

I stopped.

My eyes began adjusting to the night. At first, I could sense something near, something big and unmoving. By the time I saw the metal bumpers glinting in the creosote bushes, I realized it was a pickup truck. With two men standing next to it.

"Jeff."

I turned. Guy stayed at the car and held the gym bag out to me.

"Take this over to them."

"Me?"

"Don't fuck around here," he harshly whispered. This was the first time I'd ever seen fear in his eyes.

I was standing in what could very quickly become a cross fire. I did not want my final thoughts to be *Fuck me running*.

I looked at Mindy, who stayed behind the car in the powdery road. Did she have a gun too?

I walked to Guy, took the bag, and started walking toward the truck. Guy followed a few steps behind. My tennis shoes crunched on the rocks and dirt. There had to be thousands of dollars in that bag.

They were Mexicans. Both lean with gaunt faces and glaring eyes. I couldn't tell if anyone was in the truck.

They were dressed like most of the migrant workers I'd seen around Phoenix. Western shirt and faded jeans, battered cowboy boots. One of them held an identical black gym bag at his side. For people who seemed to know each other—-and this appeared to be a pretty routine transaction—-I felt an incredible amount of tension from everyone.

I wondered if they were feeling the same anxiety, if we were all just playing some tough guy role. Just be cool, like *Scarface*. I really hated that movie, especially now that I was looking into the shit hole it glorified—-

Fuck me running—-

The first shot hit the Mexican holding the gym bag in front of me. It was so loud over my right shoulder that I thought I'd been shot in the back of the head. He clutched his gut and crumpled backward. I wondered if my body jumping and my muscles seizing were what it felt like to be shot.

The next shot was at the other Mexican, who turned to run. Two more quick shots and he fell to the ground. I could smell kicked-up dust and the smoke from Guy's gun behind me.

I didn't move. I stood holding the gym bag and staring at the Mexican holding his stomach. He was saying something, curses I think, but I couldn't even tell if it was English or Spanish.

I kept waiting for Guy to shoot me. I don't know why, but I didn't want to see it coming. Guy would get to keep his fifty grand.

The gut-shot Mexican on the ground in front of me reached behind him and pulled a silver gun from his belt. He groaned and rolled to aim it at me. I was looking into the dark barrel when I reached back and pulled the revolver from my belt. *Line of sight* flashed through my brain. I brought the gun up, lined up the rear and front sight on his face and tried not to jerk the trigger. The nuke plant training was there—-line of sight, squeeze trigger—-*BANG!* The white flash from my gun seared a throbbing splotch of brilliance in my vision. I tried in vain to look around it.

The bullet hit him just under his left eye and he flopped back onto the ground. His arm still held the big silver revolver aimed at me for a second before it lowered without firing a shot.

"Guy!" Mindy screamed from the car behind us.

"Jeff!" Guy shouted at me.

I slowly turned and looked at him. I wondered why I wasn't dead.

"Get the bag and let's go!" he hissed at me.

"Guy!" Mindy screamed again.

"*Shut the fuck up!*" he yelled back at her and then turned to me, still holding his German Luger. "Get the bags and let's go, goddammit!"

I looked at the dead Mexicans. Stiffly I walked over to the one holding the gym bag. I dropped my gym bag and bent down to get his. I looked at his face. He was gone, but his hand was still warm as I pried it off the bag. Blood was pooling next to his head and his left eye had swelled shut just above the bullet hole, puffing up like a boxer's.

"Oh, God," I breathed heavily.

I picked up both bags with one hand and stumbled back toward the car. I kept my gun pointed at the ground. Guy was trying to calm Mindy down.

"She's gone, Guy!" she stammered. "She jumped out of

the car and took off! Guy!"

"Mindy, we've got to get out of here *now*!" he told her, still gripping the Luger.

"No! I won't leave without her!" she screamed, hysterical.

When Mindy turned and called out to her Doberman, I thought Guy was going to raise his gun and cap her right in the back of the head. But he didn't, so I didn't shoot him.

That's it! I thought. That's the end of their crappy movie! The stupidest, most naïve idiot who believed in love, the rube with blood all over him, is the only one to walk away. And the dog jumps in the car as he leaves everyone's bodies behind.

"*Shut up, Melinda!*" he shouted, his voice echoing into the darkness. "You're going to get us busted!"

He grabbed her and shoved her into the backseat.

"Jeff, you drive," he said.

I walked around the car and threw the bags onto the passenger seat. Mindy was openly sobbing in a heap and repeating the dog's name as Guy wrestled in next to her.

Still holding the revolver, I turned the car around and threw dirt and gravel as we sped away, back toward the highway. The panic of getting caught lifted a little as we pulled onto I-10 north, back toward Tucson.

I looked into the rearview mirror and saw Guy stroking Mindy's hair and shoulder. Huddled in his lap, she repeated, "Fuck your shit, Guy."

"I'll get you another one," he told her. "Hell, I'll get you twenty more, if that's what you want."

I said nothing as we headed north.

"There's another chapter for you, Jeff," he said after a while.

Another chapter? Suddenly, I was now horrified at the thought that this story would get out. I realized then what a sociopath was. He wanted me to put this night on paper?

"Write about this?" I managed to say.

"You did fuckin' good," he insisted.

I drove the speed limit and could see the glow of Tucson ahead. I knew the drugs completely had him now. If he was smart, he would've left me back there with a couple Luger slugs in me.

"Here, gimme that gun," he said.

I hesitated but then handed it back to him.

"So, there's money in one bag and cocaine in the other?" I asked.

Guy said, "We probably won't be doing this down here anymore. This was to get us started on our own."

"Does the dog have tags on it?" I finally asked.

"What?" he asked.

"The Doberman. Does the Doberman have tags on it identifying either one of you as the owner?"

I regretted it as soon as I asked. Guy might order us back to the murder scene to find those dog tags.

"No," he said. But he sounded like he was still thinking about it.

We rode on without saying anything, the hot desert air whistling through the half-open windows. I could see Guy's burning cigarette in the rearview mirror. I couldn't get the image out of my head of the Mexican's eye swelling after I knew he was dead, nor forget the warmth still in his hands as I yanked the bag away. The bright flash of my shot was now a faded star in my vision.

As we pulled into Tucson, I could see Mindy sitting up in the backseat across from Guy, her face still wet with tears. As the streetlights passed overhead, I saw her in flashes and glances. Her whole face glistened from tears and sweat and mucous.

"Why did you do that, Guy?" I demanded. "Why did you do it?"

I could see his eyes darting as flashing headlights passed over his face.

"I needed some capitol," he finally said. "And you weren't coming through with any of that movie money."

He was blaming me? My characters had hijacked my life and were trying to kill me.

"They find dead Mexicans in the desert down here all the time," Guy said aloud.

"They usually don't find them with that many bullet holes in them," I said with the petulance of a smart-ass teen.

I heard Mindy snort her entire vial of coke. Well, it wasn't like they didn't have more.

———

THERE'S something that happens when someone dies. No description in a book, no recreation or (even real footage) on TV, not any scene in any movie ever fully conveys the experience of someone dying. Especially if you have something to do with it. There's more than what you see or hear happening in physical space, something different than your own perceptions or reflexes convey to you.

For one nanosecond, for something that can't even be measured by time, you are aware of the other. Not just life but life leaving. And death. Something more. As big as this glimpse into eternity goes, it's still nothing compared to the unnatural weight of guilt that falls upon you if you are responsible for it.

You are blind in a universe of darkness but you know the eyes of God are on you.

You can't screw up any bigger than that.

———

WE CHECKED into a luxury resort in Tucson. Guy stayed with the gym bags in the Town car and let Mindy and me go into registration, handing over about six hundred dollar bills he'd peeled out of one of the gym bags. This, of course, meant that we would register under my name. Since we didn't have reservations, we couldn't get rooms close together, so I took a smaller room down near the main lobby, while Mindy and Guy got a bungalow near one of the pools.

We went to their bungalow first, which was a far cry from the seedy motel back in Phoenix—-but they were suddenly in a higher income bracket now. Mindy, her face still wet and puffy, checked the place out, announcing from the bathroom, "You're not gonna like this tub, Guy."

"Fuck it," he said. "I'm gonna hit the pool."

I was going to remind him of the sign I saw that the pool closed at eleven but remembered all the times I'd heard Mindy tell flustered waitresses, "He sits where he wants." I was sure that went for swimming pools as well.

He needed some type of hygiene. Rancid from hours

of desert heat and perspiration, he should at least drop into the pool fully-clothed to wash them out as well.

I stared at the two gym bags on the bed.

"We'll meet you at the pool," Guy said. I looked up at him. His suspicious stare told me that he knew I was looking at the money and the coke.

"I'll be in my room."

I left them and walked through the quiet maze of doors and dark windows and hissing water sprinklers soaking the tiny but perfect strips of grass along the sidewalk.

I felt too rumpled and dirty to be stalking through such an opulent setting. I felt like a trespasser or worse to be loose in such a posh resort with the grit of desert dust in my mouth and the ringing of gunfire in my ears. In my room, I turned on the light, tossed my overnight bag on the floor, and collapsed on the bed. Someone will see that truck tomorrow. Or maybe even buzzards over the bodies. The motel manager in Phoenix knew they had a Doberman when they checked into that seedy motel.

You just shot somebody in the face—-

A part of me hoped Guy would leave me here.

There was a knock on the door.

I knew it was Mindy when she impatiently knocked again before I could get to it.

She lunged into the room and grabbed on to me, burying her face in my chest.

"I didn't think he was going to go through with it," she half-sobbed.

I put my arms around her and held her. She felt so thin. Like she was someone else. She calmed down a little, holding me. Her hair smelled like desert dust and cigarette smoke. I took hold of her arms and backed her up so I could see her face.

"Why are you here?" I asked. "With me?"

"I want to get away from him."

"Now?"

"I want to go with you!"

"Why now, Mindy?"

"I want it to be over. I want my own life without him all over me all the time."

She stepped closer.

"I want to be your wife. I *am* your wife!"

Who was this girl?

She said, "He's really got something wrong with him this time. I know he wants to spend most of the money on his hospital shit anyway."

"You mean treatment?"

"Doctors. Whatever's wrong with him. I don't know why he doesn't just die!"

"I don't know if now's the time to do this," I said.

"Sure, we'll just take the car and go."

"And just leave him here?"

"Fuck him! He's a murderer!"

She pulled her anger back and tried to look vulnerable with a hint of hope.

"Isn't this what you've always wanted?" she asked. "Now's our chance."

"How?"

"He wants you to come down to the pool while he's swimming. There's something he wants to tell you. Then don't come back here, just go out and wait at the car. I'll be out as soon as I can."

I said slowly and clearly, "Mindy, he has a gun with my

fingerprints on it."

"I'll get it, I'll get it."

I stared into her frantic eyes, the pretty blue almost lost in the bright red eyeballs and dark circles around them. Her hollow cheeks, brittle hair. She was the wreckage of a lesson she would never learn.

She lunged toward me and kissed me, but not tenderly or honestly. Her lips and tongue against mine were sloppy and loveless. I wondered if she had any diseases.

I felt absolutely nothing for this girl. There was nothing left to salvage. They had finally pulled me into their shit and I was completely covered in it. My heart drowned in it. I didn't win anything. I just stuck around until there was nothing worth having.

"Give me a minute and come out to the pool," she whispered. "Then, after we go to our rooms for tonight, go out to the car and wait."

She left me standing in the open door. Her spiked heels clacked on the smooth walkway toward the pool. Rage boiled up inside of me. Guy was going to help me conquer Hollywood the same way he helped Mindy beat Vegas? He had turned Mindy into a snorting dried-up coke whore and left me with a huge pile of bullshit stories to try and mold into a piece-of-shit movie I wouldn't even watch. And now I had participated in two of his murders. *I shot somebody.* For money. So what if our victims were drug-running illegals, they were human beings as much as whatever was left of us. How were we any better?

I closed the door and went into the bathroom to splash the dust off my face before heading down to the pool.

I could see Guy's enormous flabby body floating in the water as I stepped through the gate and sat down on a lawn chair. I noticed Mindy sitting on the other side of the pool, both gym bags between her feet. No one said anything. I only glanced at Mindy since I knew Guy would be catching all looks between us. I knew he would kill me if he had any idea of what she was planning—-but I also knew he didn't have his gun in the water with him.

He looked like he was paddling in his boxer shorts. He moved like wheezing manatee, his breath grating while I waited for it to stop. But it never did. If anything, Guy Reinhart was an exhausting reminder of just how durable the human body could be.

"Once we get back to Vegas," Guy eventually said, "We'll be a lot better off."

I felt that this was the moment for our big confrontation, the point in our story where I exposed him as a corrupt and even evil fraud. Right before I would finally take her from him, leaving him wrecked and alone, ignoring his threats to kill us or to turn us all over to the police. It wasn't because I loved her anymore. The drugs, the killing, the bullshit sent whatever was left of my heart running off into the desert with her Doberman. If Mindy was going to have any kind of life, with or without me, she had to leave now.

I was still willing to rescue her but I also wanted an annulment. If she straightened herself out—-who knew what would happen then—-but this had to stop, it had to end.

"And I'll tell ya something, Jeff. I'm not gonna forget this. I've got something special for you."

I glanced at Mindy. She was staring right at me.

"Oh, yeah? What's that?"

He rolled over onto his back, keeping his face out of the water.

"You like that punk Elvis Presley, right?"

I reluctantly allowed a quick laugh.

"Yeah. I like Elvis."

"I'm going to give you his engine."

He raised himself up to look at me. He had that grand expression of a king bestowing his kingdom on a commoner, as if he just said, *I'm giving you the keys to Graceland.*

"The Elvis engine?" I asked.

His eyes narrowed.

"That's right. Think of it as a wedding present. Other than Mindy, of course, and the 50k retainer. So, don't say I never done nuthin' for ya."

I'm still not sure why, but all my outrage and anger dissipated in that moment. Joe Gillis knew this moment too, at the end of *Sunset Boulevard*, when he realized that Norma Desmond was totally insane and his movie dreams were completely over. But Gillis ended up face down in her Hollywood swimming pool with her bullets in his back. I was going to walk away from this one. I got to see that Guy's temptation was a total fraud, and survive, but *Vegas Working Girl* was dead.

"Thank you, Guy. That's too cool."

He waved me off.

That's what I missed. From the moment they hustled me down to the chapel, I wracked my brain trying to figure out why he allowed me to marry Mindy. What was Guy's angle, his scheme? I realized that maybe Guy didn't have an ulterior motive. The part I missed was that Guy, alone with his rap sheet and his whore, damned by appetites and addictions, thought of me as his friend, maybe even a son-in-law. I was probably his last living friend on earth.

I was relieved he was in the pool. If he hadn't been, I was horrified to think he might have hugged me.

————

THERE'S a beautiful old Spanish mission just south of Tucson called San Xavier, which is pronounced completely different from the way it's spelled. The first time I ever saw it was near dusk on a road trip through southern Arizona. I could see it miles in the distance and the setting sun turned its white walls pink in the settling haze. I thought about that church out there, just south of where I waited for Mindy to sneak out with the cash for our escape. I needed more than escape. I needed to dive deep into a baptismal pool to wash away the guilt and shame of running with these people, of thinking that their lives should be chronicled and glorified. As their hack, I was now as guilty as they were. I was worse: I had known better. Life may have kicked them down this far, but I chose it.

Was Mindy ready to be embedded in a sober, normal life? When I carried the gym bag, it felt stuffed with money. Who knows how much was in it. Enough for a house back east, plenty to get Mindy into rehab. My Midwestern friends would be thrilled to have me back. My family would be suspicious of my new girl, the one who had to go straight into rehab. Should I give up writing and just get a regular job?

It wasn't as if I had much in Arizona. An old man's job

shaking door knobs at a desert nuclear plant and a room I rent from a buddy. My name wasn't on a mortgage. I gave cash to roommates for the utility and telephone bills. Mindy and Guy had rap sheets, I didn't. As far as plugging my name into data banks and records, searching for my paper trail, I had already vanished. The only hit on my name might be on a marriage license in Nevada if anyone thought to look there, but it wouldn't lead anywhere.

Would I eventually feel guilty for betraying Guy, leaving that gasping fat man alone with a bag filled with cocaine and no wheels? Just when the Elvis engine was mine, all mine!

But what minor infraction, like her freaking out that she lost a dog while trying to flee a murder scene, would cause Mindy to betray me like she did Guy?

What about Vegas? A city I adored; warts, kitsch, and all. Would this rescue mission banish me from the neon paradise?

Even this far from Vegas, I could see that our odds were impossible. I thought about praying but I was afraid of what God would tell someone who'd just shot a guy in the face over a drug deal. What would I do that she would one day turn on me and say to someone else about me, *fuck him?*

But something told me I had to try. I'd gone too far not to see this through.

I stood near the car, tucked away behind some carefully-manicured shrubbery, my overnight bag slung over my shoulder. A nuclear security guard hiding from resort security.

I heard her heels stomping toward me and stepped out, waving at her to quiet down. She threw the car keys at me with a smile. A bright white streetlight overhead made her teeth and bleached face look like a skull. She was, thankfully, carrying only one gym bag. This would've ended right then if she'd brought both bags with her, the money and the dope.

I unlocked the car door, my hands shaking, and got in, and nearly jumped out of my skin when she slammed her door shut. She slid across the seat and threw her arms around me, kissing me.

I fumbled with the keys.

"I love you," she said. "Now let's go find my dog."

I stopped.

"What?"

"We've got hours of dark left. So, we can find her in time."

"Mindy, we can't go back there."

She looked genuinely surprised.

"What if that dog has tags on her?" she asked.

"You don't know?" I snapped. "Where's the gun?"

"He has it on him. I couldn't get it."

"Mindy, my prints are on that gun," I said evenly. "A bullet from that gun is in some guy's head—-and you want to go back there?"

"Don't worry about it—-it's not like he would ever go to the cops for anything. Shit!"

She opened the gym bag and I could see the bundles of white powder inside. She used a fingernail, her one good one, to cut into the top bundle and scoop out some cocaine, snorting it. She'd left the money bag with Guy and my heart fell through the earth's crust.

Sniffling, she looked at me. "Don't worry. It's no big deal."

I put the key in the ignition and stopped.

"I forgot something," I said, the voice of a dead man.

"What?"

"In my room. I left my wallet on the nightstand and the keys to my car."

She said simply, "Shit. Well. Go get 'em."

"Okay."

She gave me a quick kiss and I slid out of the car, closing the big door as quietly as I could. I left my overnight bag with her but there was nothing in it to lead anyone to me.

I stopped at the entrance to the walkways and looked back at her. I saw her head lower into the gym bag. I knew this was going to be the last time I ever saw her alive. It was over. I was leaving her with all she ever really wanted.

As I quickly slipped through the walkways, keeping as far away from Guy's bungalow as I could, I checked the change left from the hundreds Guy threw at me for the rooms. I slipped into the lobby and asked the night person at the desk to call a cab for me. In minutes, the lime green cab pulled up outside and I rushed out, jumped in the back. A round-faced Mexican turned to me.

"I'll pay you two hundred and sixty dollars to take me to Phoenix right now," I told him, holding up the cash.

I never wanted to see her again because I could only imagine the two of us in shackles and orange coveralls, sitting forlornly in a courtroom if only for our arraignment. Guy would probably be hospitalized so we'd finally be rid of him. But Mindy and I would be together at last. At least until our sentences were read. If she wanted another Guy Reinhart, then she needed to find someone other than me. You chose the wrong bag, baby, I thought. You chose, and lost me.

I stared at the desert night crawling past outside the cab, a flowing darkness I still felt as a dust in my clothes and my nostrils as well as a grit in my teeth. Tall Saguaro cactus flashed by in the night like the ghosts of those who died doing something wrong in this desolate place.

I didn't want to see Mindy or Guy ever again, I didn't want to write their story anymore. I'd wanted to see the world to find something to write about and now that I had, I didn't want to write anymore. All the way back to Phoenix I tried to remember the girl I loved from that first night in the Stardust and I kept hearing a voice inside my head that said, *You should have just fucked her.*

17

(Your Name Here) Died a Rich Man

THE SUN WAS COMING UP. The dream inside my sleep dissipated as quickly as the dawn drained away the lights outside. As dazzling and surreal as Vegas was all night every night, the day breaks and the magic seeps back into the vanishing shadows to wait for the next sunset. The millions of lights cut out and you look outside at just another honking, cluttered city.

I dreamed I opened my eyes that last morning in the Stardust and she was sitting on the end of my bed.

Although it was a familiar pose, I'd never seen her from this angle before, facing away from me. I recognized the jet-black hair and the black leather jacket. Her legs crossed, she held her cigarette in front of her. She was looking at my Vegas shrine of Elvis postcards, the Coroner's Office T-shirt, and our Old West photo.

"Mindy, there's no smoking in these rooms anymore," I said and then I knew I was awake. She was gone.

I've never been the type to hang on to regrets, but I closed my eyes and watched the misty dream of Mindy sitting there the night I met her. Wanting so badly to grab her and pull her out of everything that was to come. But that didn't happen and it would be a lie for me to write it any other way.

Now you know as much about her as I did. Would you give a girl like her another chance? Can you understand why I did? Did I ever really know her? I know she never knew me. I've always wondered if you've fucked about fifty or a hundred-other people, your soul dries up and you have none of it left to give anyone. Maybe that was my Midwestern upbringing talking but I did question whether she was too damaged and spent to give anything anymore. I wasn't afraid to make Mindy the love of my life but I doubted if I could rise above the level of an episode of *The Flintstones* to her. I could only distract her from how much she'd lost of herself and hope for the best, which could be dumber and crazier than getting involved with her in the first place.

So, I ended up as the ultimate misguided nice guy. A fool too confidant in what little I had to offer her, a half-assed Prince Charming who couldn't tell the difference between a princess in distress and a dragon in denial. Angelique was both angel and devil by her street name, my Princess Dragon who rejected both rescue and love. At least my definition of them. Maybe she thought she was saving me.

In the fading dream, I called after her, *I'm so sorry.*

Awake and alone in my Stardust Hotel room, I just said to my empty bed, "Goodbye, baby."

———

GIL ROZELL, as far as I know, never did the hooker thing. Skoof wanted to, Cooper did, and others in our crew of nuclear defenders probably have.

I remember asking Rozell when the Los Arcos gang was returning to Phoenix, the day after I'd called the wrong girl up to our room, if he ever considered taking that route.

"Nah, I don't fuck with that," he quickly replied. "I wouldn't want to be that stupid asshole that actually fell in love with some whore. Statistically, it's gotta happen to some ignorant fuck and I don't want it to be me."

We laughed at such an absurdity.

I shook my head at that memory as I packed up my bags in the Stardust and headed downstairs. After throwing my luggage in the trunk, I walked back to registration to check out. Nearby was the car from the TV show called *Vegas*, a sharp little Thunderbird convertible, red and white. Next to it stood a Vegas showgirl, fishnet stockings on her legs and a big plume of red flowers over her head. To have so much costume, she showed an awful lot of skin. A flat belly, the curves of her breasts about to spill out, her long bare arms. No tattoos. She smiled at me as I waited to check out.

I tried to see through the costume and makeup. She had sharp, dark eyes, a cute nose, blonde hair slipping out the back of her headdress.

I grinned back at her, trying to look friendly and non-threatening.

I will fall for them every time. Despite all the pain and turmoil, the lost girl I identified at the coroner's office the day before and the divorce papers I still had to fill out, I can catch the eye of a beautiful girl and feel not only the desire but the need to submit myself to some fresh insanity. They drive us crazy at the mere sight of them, but we willingly jump into that madness every time.

Or maybe it's just lust after all.

I blew a kiss to the showgirl from where I stood and she smiled again at me.

———

DANNY, with earphones on, was drenched in sweat when I arrived at his house. I had decided to stay over in Vegas at his place for an extra night and visit with him since I'd been wandering around town alone, reliving my past, while he was solving murders. His wife was out shopping with the kids. Danny wanted to go out for a nice dinner to celebrate closing "our" cases.

"I'm sorry I'm a little late," I told him. "I noticed the chapel I got married in looked different, so I stopped in. They said the original chapel burned to the ground. Arson."

"Really?"

After a pause, I said, "I didn't do it."

He laughed.

I had married Allison in the same chapel where I'd married Mindy. Like everything else in my life, I took any chance to redo something and make it right. I never told anyone about the first wedding and, since three people can keep a secret if two of them are dead, no one ever had to know about that first one. Now I knew for sure they were dead.

Danny stopped his workout and we sat on the sofas in his living room while he told me about his latest case, a shooting that had happened before sunrise that morning in a strip club's parking lot. Drunken patrons walking in the middle of the road, a pickup truck with more drunken patrons inside pulling up and honking.

"I guess the guys in the road said F-you to the guys in the truck," he said. "So, the guys in the truck pulled a .357 Magnum and shot the guys in the road."

"Well, you can't let something like that go," I said.

"Oh, I know," he agreed, always able to pick up my sarcasm.

"Listen, I wanted to ask you about something."

"Sure," he said, not looking at me.

"If you don't find anybody for Mindy...I'd like to pay for any expenses for a funeral. Or whatever."

"They'll probably end up cremating her if we can't locate any surviving family members. I don't know if we will find anyone or not."

"Like I said, get a hold of me. I'll charge it if I have to."

"You might want to contact the coroner's office. They might ship her remains to you."

I thought about that.

"Well, she did want to end up with me. At least that's what she said."

He had on his straight working face, blank and professional with a touch of sympathy. God only knows the reactions he's seen from wives, families, loved ones.

I wanted to laugh. He was probably waiting for me to cry.

"There's something else I thought you should have," he said quietly.

He ran upstairs and quickly returned. He handed me a driver's license and I looked at it. It was Mindy's. A little haggard but with a thin smile. Late Eighties. Still enough to recognize her. The name was MELINDA S. BAILEY and my heart broke all over again.

"My name," I whispered.

How much did Danny know? Did he only find this ID or did he do some checking to find out more?

When Danny was my best man, he questioned why I chose that particular chapel when I married Allison. I didn't tell anyone the real reason why: because I'd been there before, because this time it wouldn't be a secret. The most stressful moment that day took place back at the bureau when we got a marriage license without setting off the bigamy alarm on the computer. The rest of the day had been a breeze.

"Destroy it, whatever," Danny said. "You don't need to be involved anymore."

What kind of risk did he take by swiping this evidence?

I wanted to tell him everything. Mindy had every right to use my name. I gave it to her.

"Thanks, man," was all I could say as I pocketed it.

Within five minutes, his cell phone rang and he snatched it up. I didn't pay too much attention to what he said, just how he said it. Curt and staccato, I could tell he was talking to Stephanie Killman and imagined her speaking the same way. Voices exchanging information. He hung up.

"She's gonna be pissed," he said.

"What?"

"That was Steph. The two suspects from that shooting are sitting in her office with the murder weapon and they want to give their side of the story...so I gotta go in."

"I heard you say five-thirty. Five-thirty in a half-hour?"

"Yeah. I won't be home 'til midnight. She's gonna be pissed."

"You just tied up three cases," I said. "Don't you get a break?"

"Yeah, when people stop killing each other."

"They should pass a law."

When he said that Homicide was putting a strain on his marriage, pulling him out of the house and away from his family, I decided I best be on my way. He wouldn't be home and I didn't want his wife to feel like she had to entertain me in his absence. He shook his head and said that maybe he could go back to patrol. Do shift work. People were just killing each other too fast for him to keep up with.

He told me to be careful driving back to Phoenix. We both left the house at the same time.

I felt like there was one thing I needed to do. There was one more person who had to be laid to rest.

———

"IS this your first time at a brothel?" she asked as we walked back through the Cherry Ranch.

There had still been a couple hours of daylight as I drove out to Pahrump, Nevada, just outside of Clark County. Where prostitution is legal. I'd read that it stays legal in Nevada as long as it remains in a "remote location." Away from the population. I drove the long desert road with the glum inevitability of someone taking a beloved pet out in the woods to shoot it, as well as the nervous anxiety of any child doing something really wrong. Appropriately, entire hillsides and large sections of desert were scorched black from fires started by careless cigarettes or random lightning strikes. I assumed they were random.

I glanced at every car I passed and wondered if they were heading this way for the same reason. Most had families in them, so I doubted it. A well-groomed, middle-aged couple in a Lexus followed me as far as the four-way stop at Homestead Road, but then I was on my own.

I pulled up at the parking space closest to the gate. Only one other car was parked outside. A Mexican worked on the yard inside the white picket fence. The façade that was supposed to look like a dude ranch looked about as convincing as a carnival midway depiction of one. It would've been fitting to see a big buckaroo painted over the entrance with a cartoon balloon that read: *HOWDY, PARDNER, HOPE YA BROUGHT YER BONER!*

I rang the bell twice before the gate buzzed open.

I had changed into my Clark County Coroner's Office souvenir T-shirt before making this drive. I decided that fucking and dying would now be bitterly entwined, that today they would be locked in a smothering embrace. It was time to take care of the last witness.

Before I could get up the steps and to the front door, a

figure appeared in the murky glass and opened the door. The Madam, a taller, thinner and much darker version of a Spice Girl, greeted me and led me into a long front room of dark paneling and deep leather sofas.

"Get comfortable and I'll get the girls and be right back," she smiled and strode out on her high heels.

I grabbed a mint and sat down. A brochure advertised full-feature bungalows that someone could check into for a night or however long they felt like staying. I couldn't believe I was here, doing this. But I had a reason, beyond just getting laid. It wasn't for material because I didn't do that anymore. There was now another mission.

Across the room, a thin curtain veiled what looked like a bar on the other side. I imagined that the girls lounged there on crowded days or nights while the Madam sat guys down and then opened the curtain for them, revealing the party and displaying the goods. But it was just me, so such theatrics weren't necessary.

I could hear the floor boards creaking behind me. The Madam appeared and stopped, allowing about a dozen girls to enter, all wearing lingerie and balancing on high heels. They stared at me, some trying harder to smile than others. I stood, but felt awkward about showing polite manners, since we all knew what I was there to do. Weird.

Ten were white, two were black. A couple were seriously overweight (you know somebody's had to have asked, "Do I get a discount if they're fat?"). I tried not to think too long about it since it felt more like I was rejecting eleven instead of picking one. The girl on the end was tall and had a good shape, so I picked her by pointing and said, "That one."

The Madam told me to follow that one, and we walked

into narrow hallways through what appeared to be a maze of trailers hooked together. She wore a black bra and thong under a see-through nightie. We passed an empty den of sofas where a TV played a newscast of firefighters battling a home ablaze. A half-completed needlepoint was dropped on one of the sofas. It had the cluttered look of having just been abandoned, so I figured the girls were here when I arrived.

The tall girl led me into a bedroom.

"I'm Felony Haze," she said. "What's your name?"

A part of me wanted to reply, *Steadman Shaft.*

"Jeff."

She sat down and handed me a menu. I sat down next to her.

"Just look this over and tell me what you want."

I read over the selection. Some had handwritten prices next to the selections. The cheapest choices were a bath and masturbation for four hundred dollars. A Straight Lay was eight hundred dollars. For almost twice as much, she would "act like a porn star." I noticed DVDs spread out on the counter of a dresser nearby, and her name was on all the covers.

I had been told on the phone when I'd called earlier that I could have a "pretty good party" for three to five hundred bucks. So here I was, cheap enough to squeeze out five dollars for prime rib with food poisoning but stupid enough to drop eight hundred dollars at the Cherry Ranch.

"I guess I'll have the Straight Lay."

"Okay."

She took the menu and said, "I'll need to check you out first, so if you could drop your pants."

She reached over to the dresser and turned on a bright desk lamp. I stood up as she got down on her knees in front of me. I obediently unbuckled, unzipped and pulled down my jeans and underwear as if submitting to a medical exam. She grinned and said, "Don't worry, this is the most embarrassing part, I promise."

She casually grabbed and checked and studied me.

"What are you looking for?" I asked.

"This is just to check for any warts or open sores."

"Not a problem," I said

It was a quick exam.

"Okay, good," she said and stood up. "Now I need a credit card and ID."

I also obediently handed over a credit card and driver's license.

"I'll be right back," she said, heading for the door. I could see a laminated sign hanging from the knob that said QUIET. "Would you like something to drink?"

"Uhm...Pepsi?"

"Coke?"

"Perfect."

The small bedroom window looked out at another trailer's outside wall. Across the room were a cluttered makeup table and a closed closet door. Then there was a bathroom. I could see discarded towels on the floor. So much of this was illusion: I knew it was a whorehouse but I didn't want to see evidence that anyone else had been here before me.

I read over the DVDs bearing her name. I would be with a porn actress.

She returned with my cards and a Coke. I put my cards and receipt away, and took the Coke, sipping it.

"Okay, I need you to take a shower," she said. "In there."

"Sure."

"Do you want to spend some time in the Jacuzzi?"

"Uhm. No. That's all right."

"You just want to get right to it?"

I nodded.

I showered, keeping an eye on my jeans (and wallet) in the reflection of the tile outside the closed shower curtain, and wondered how this charge would appear on my credit card bill.

I dried off and, with a towel around me, I stepped out to see her sitting naked on the bed, facing away from me. She patted the mattress.

"Hop up here," she said.

I dropped the towel and sat down next to her. She opened a condom with her teeth and said, "Okay, lie back here."

She was jerking me, pulling on a condom. She took me in her mouth.

"If I can ask, how old are you?" I asked.

"I'm twenty-one."

Between mouthfuls, she said she'd been at this for five years ("I know," she said, "Early start"), was bisexual, and had a little daughter who stayed with her parents. She'd just ended a long-term relationship with a creep who took all her furniture, so now she was buying a new house with nothing to put in it.

"What brings you here?" she asked.

I thought about that.

"I'm getting divorced, and this is my first act of defiance and independence."

She sat up, still pumping her arm, and grinned.

"That's the most intelligent way I've ever heard anyone put that here."

"Thank you."

She finished getting me ready when I asked, "Is it all right if I can just hold you for a few minutes?"

She thought about it for a second and said, "Sure."

She stretched out next to me and we gently embraced. I hadn't been with another woman except Allison for eight years. Two years of monogamy and six of marriage.

"You can't touch my face or my pussy," she said. "Believe me, that's for your safety as well as mine."

I rested my face in her breasts and thought about this. I couldn't kiss her? At either place?

I looked up at her, my lips at one of her nipples, and asked, "Can I kiss you here?"

"Yeah."

I cupped her ass with my hands and sucked and licked her nipples. Breaths pushed in and out of her nostrils. I could hear soft moans behind her closed mouth. They sounded like reluctant whimpers. Her closed eyes clenched. Her enjoyment wasn't part of the deal so she tried to keep me from seeing any.

"How long have you been here?" I asked.

"Two years in September."

"Do you like it?"

She shrugged and said, "The House gets half, so I'm only getting four hundred for this. I also have to pay rent and for the doctor exams every week."

"Wow. Doesn't sound like such a good deal. You're very beautiful," I said. "I'll bet you get picked a lot."

"Sometimes. You never know. I'm the only blonde working here now, so sometimes I get picked a lot."

"Oh. You are blonde. To be honest, I hadn't noticed."

She smiled. "Really?"

"No, I picked you because you were tall and pretty. Do you get along with the other girls?"

"It's a house full of girls. What do you think? You've got your cliques and stuff, and it's really bad when we're all menstruating."

"Okay, let's get you inside," she said and reached for another condom.

Twice she had to storm out of the room to tell the other girls to keep quiet in the TV room outside, once wearing a towel and then stomping out naked the second time. It didn't do any good since their joking and laughing continued. *House full of girls,* she'd said.

Afterward, I sat on the bed and stared out of her window as she checked text messages on her phone. Her view was another trailer right outside her window. A brothel of interconnected trailers that reminded me of a space station, a maze of hallways and bedrooms. There wasn't much time left on the clock when she rubbed her fingers on my back.

"You okay?"

"When I was kid, my first girlfriend lived in a trailer like that one," I said and gestured out the window. "She lived in a trailer park on the edge of town and she was my first little girlfriend in the fourth grade. She lived with her mom. No dad. She was so cute. Her name was Mary. My folks had split up by then so I was aware of the damage that's done to kids when that happens. I don't know that Mary ever had a father in her life. She was poor, she lived in a trailer, she didn't have a dad...by junior high, she'd fallen in with the stoners and hoods. I heard words from her that I never even knew existed. I saw her dancing at a Sadie Hawkins dance in junior high."

The prostitute looked confused and asked, "Who's Sadie Hawkins? I actually considered Sadie as a name."

"It was some dance where the girls picked the guys, if I remember right."

She nodded. "I like that."

"I never forgot watching her dance there because she was completely developed by then. Her boobs and her hips bumping and grinding for stoned thugs who'd been held back several grades. I'd heard she rode off with bikers before I graduated. I think she was the first one."

"Your first love?" she asked.

I turned to her and said, "No. The first one I wanted to save. That's been my whole life. If I could make her life better and make everything right...then whatever we'd been through would be worth it. It wouldn't hurt as much. It would mean something. But I've lost them all. I lost Mary. I've lost my wife...I just found out I lost someone else that I cared about. I couldn't save them."

I looked out at the trailer.

"They didn't want whatever I had," I added.

She patted me on my leg and I turned to her.

The young girl had a grin on her face as she shrugged, "What can I say? We're fucked up."

I reached over and gently put a hand to her cheek. If she asked me to wait outside until she got her belongings together to run off me, I would be sitting in my car with the motor running. But she didn't.

She just said, "You're a very sweet guy."

I thought: I am nothing.

———

SO, I did what I set out to do. The nice guy was dead too. The innocent romantic who meant well. The naïve and hopeful lover. The sexual redeemer. As dead and gone as everyone else now, but still among the living for some reason. I imagined Guy drawing a line through a check-mark in his ledger, which I'm sure he did when I left him with the bag of undetermined funds and Mindy with the bag of cocaine. A nice guy who turned into an asshole, a business partner gone wrong. No one left to keep the secrets.

I drove out of Las Vegas to legally fuck a pretty young girl and officially not feel a thing. I just wanted to get laid.

I didn't care anymore.

I was no better than anyone else.

Epilogue: "My Wife, God and Elvis"

November 2005

THE ELVIS-A-RAMA WILL CLOSE SOMETIME next year. The owner of the museum and the collection sold everything to the Elvis Presley estate, itself bought out by CKX Inc., an international company based in New York. There's talk of another museum opening in Hawaii and another turning up on the Strip somewhere.

Vegas wouldn't be Las Vegas without regular Elvis sightings. I don't know if there's an accurate count of the impersonators but I believe they should be granted protected status by the Nevada state legislature if they fall under a certain number. As reckless as that place could be with its past, burning through and blowing up its buildings and history and gods, I still expect to find a specter of the King somewhere in Las Vegas. It would be like a shopping mall in December without Santa Claus.

Sometime after I got back home to Phoenix, I bought a

new special edition DVD of Elvis' 1968 TV "Comeback Special." He never sounded better, unleashing that powerful voice to scorch away the years of lame Hollywood movies and hollow soundtracks. Prowling the tiny stage in that black leather outfit or standing reverently in the white suit before the enormous red letters of his name, he never looked better. As Rozell, another Elvis fan, used to drawl in a Southern accent, "Lookin' better than a man's gotta right to!"

I was five years old when the Comeback Special first aired. Since my father was an Elvis impersonator in Seventies Ohio, I'm sure we watched that show every time it aired, as we did anything Elvis. Even though I became a fan myself, I realized it had been a long time since I watched this special.

Late in the show, Elvis wanders through a big production number on a carnival midway set. He bumps into a huge fat man wearing a fedora. Elvis sings "Big Boss Man" as the cigar-chomping fat man circles him, striking menacing poses, shredding his denim jacket and breaking his guitar over his knee. I sat stunned, feeling like I was having a *Twilight Zone* moment. The Big Boss Man has a pretty woman with him, a kept vamp he clearly owns. She has black hair and she's wearing a shimmering outfit with a feather boa wrapped around her.

While using karate moves to dispatch the fat man and his goons, Elvis then sings the haunting song "It Hurts Me" to the vamp.

I know that he never will set you free
Because he's just that kind of guy
But if you ever tell him you're through

I'll be waiting for you

He finishes the song standing over a pile of bodies and the vamp turns up her nose and indifferently strides away, leaving him alone on the carnival midway. I paused the disc and sat up.

She didn't look anything like Mindy but she had black hair and the dress and the boa. The Big Boss Man had a beard and a sharp nose but he had the extra wide sports coat and the fedora, the loud caricature of a wanna-be mobster. I never put it together before. *Wait for me.*

Of all the crazy reasons and motivations I had for getting so mixed up with Vegas, I now had to wonder if a forgotten scene from an Elvis TV show triggered some of my interest in Mindy Spires and Guy Reinhart, just as waking up in college to a Joan Jett every morning programmed a lust for black hair and tough glares. What other dangerous situations might I jump into because I think something is "meant to be" but it ends up being a scene I saw on TV that I couldn't quite remember? I can at least appreciate what a great cosmic joke it was that my life, the son of an amateur Elvis impersonator, briefly turned into a big Elvis production number. If others had survived, I could've found this funny.

Had I looked up as a child at my father as he watched the show and saw his deep yearning to be the king of rock and roll? Did it imprint a meaning of true acceptance and legitimacy to my subconscious? Or was I just looking for someone else to blame my life on? No, I never looked for blame or excuses, only reasons and clues. Another sign I was getting older: I didn't just blurt out secrets anymore, I took all responsibility for them!

I wasn't alone in my Elvis moments. I recently read a news story online about a retired 62-year-old Elvis impersonator standing in line at a Vegas pharmacy when he was approached by a shady character. The shady character asked if he would be interested in buying jewelry, clothes and even a gold-plated revolver owned by Elvis. Remembering the March 2004 burglary of the Elvis-A-Rama, the impersonator set up a meeting and then called the police.

Three hundred thousand dollars' worth of memorabilia was recovered, everything that had been taken except for a $750 custom scarf. Online people commented that the thieves couldn't have been real fans since they stole diamonds and rubies worth tens of thousands of dollars but left Elvis' blue suede shoes, valued at one million dollars. They also blogged that the thieves would now be "dancin' to the jailhouse rock for real."

The retired impersonator had been struggling since his wife's death earlier in the year so his role in recovering the memorabilia gave him a peace to deal with his grief. He'd never headlined as Elvis in Vegas but now his picture was in the papers all over town. He told reporters, "I just believe my wife, God and Elvis have got their hands in this. They set me up to do the right thing."

It reassured me that complete weirdness still happens in Vegas—in a good way! I haven't been there since identifying Mindy but I think my next trip will be better. I know it'll be a swingin' time, and, somewhere, there's that Elvis engine still sitting back in some garage.

———

IT'S STILL THERE. It's always there. Right up the road, or just a short flight away. If you're lucky enough to drive or fly in at night, you can see the lights blazing, intensifying —morphing to suit your lusts and greed and every other exhilarating fault in your soul. The energy that tells you to make your worst your best. The perfect place to disappear as every cell of your being comes to life. What happens in Vegas, stays in Vegas. Viva Las Vegas.

I went to Vegas, met some people, and some serious shit happened.

But I still love you, Las Vegas.

———

MY DIVORCE CAME through in September.

Allison's already with someone else so I hope she can pull herself together and have a decent life. I hear her daughter is living with the tweaker boyfriend who supplied them but I'm out of that loop now. Not that I ever felt that I had been in it before.

My mother was more bitter than I was. Once everything was legally settled with the divorce, she told me how lucky I'd been that "the bitch" didn't go after my house and retirement. Since I kept the real reason for the divorce out of the proceedings, saying only that the marriage was irretrievably broken, I didn't think she'd try for more than half of my income tax return and a clean break.

Once the decree was stamped and signed, my mother grumbled her advice that still kept me grinning for years afterward: "Hookers are cheaper, Jeff." I'd ask her to embroider that on a pillow for me but I wasn't sure if she'd stab me with a knitting needle or not.

Tucson Homicide called and I told them what I could of the official story, the one where I *didn't* go with Guy and Mindy to the desert. The lie. My fuzzy recollections weren't enough for them to come to Phoenix for an interview but it helped. Detective DannyL Olsen had the files on the two shooters, the old man and the girl. Of course, I left out that I'd shot one of the drug runners in the face. Just as I believed it was Mindy who finished off Guy/Charles Blythe--how else did she get his gun? --I told Tucson detectives that I thought she was capable of shooting the Mexicans. But none of that really matters since all the drug runners got what they deserved, I guess.

Sometimes I remember that night as a bad-ass macho show where I'm standing in the whizzing bullets like Wyatt Earp and drawing to shoot like Dirty Harry, ridding the planet of another piece-of-shit dope dealer. Other times I'm more honest with myself and remember the paralyzing terror of a coward firing into the face of a mortally-wounded man, finishing off the life of another human being to save my own skin. However I remember it, it never goes away.

I contacted the Clark County Coroner's Office about arranging a funeral for Mindy but ended up requesting her remains. The Public Administration Office had to release her once it determined that her next of kin couldn't be found. I didn't think they would find anyone. After faxing all the paperwork, I arranged for a cremation and they sent her to me through the Postal Service. I was told, "Fed Ex and UPS won't handle human remains."

She arrived around the first of September, her ashes

packed inside a thick plastic bag in a solid cardboard box. To take my mind off my divorce hearing, I searched through Scottsdale shops until I found a bust of Nefertiti large enough and sealed her ashes inside. I also pushed the driver's license Danny gave me inside the bust, watching her photo and name sink into her ashes. Mrs. Melinda Spires Bailey. My mailman had handed her to me over the threshold, not in a wedding dress but in a box.

Nefertiti stands at the dining room window between two bookshelves. I stopped off at the house with a date recently and she asked, "That's Queen Nefertiti, isn't it?"

"No," I told her, "that's Mindy."

When she asked me over dinner what I'd meant, I only told her that I knew someone who claimed to have been the queen in a former life and left it at that. Any woman I date now eventually gets my one basic ground rule: no one here will fall in love. We can laugh, we can fuck, we can look like a great couple. Just don't ever expect me to care. I don't deserve to care.

I put the RADIOACTIVE WASTE binder back with my other journals, deciding against burning it. I added a few pages from my April trip, along with newspaper articles I downloaded off the Internet. Detective Olsen's case was closed and so was mine.

———

MY HOLLYWOOD AGENTS, the only people who would have loved to hear all about it, closed their office when the head of the agency retired to join Greenpeace in 1990. I still play at screenwriting like millions of others, still unrepresented and still outside of L.A. I read more than write anymore, losing myself in other people's stories during the night shifts at Los Arcos. I sit at my computer and try to write it all down, staring at the blank monitor only to remember the stupidity of my character and the blood on my hands. Sitting at my desk in my empty house, staring at the mute bust of Nefertiti in the window, I try to think of a better ending when I'm alone, but one never comes.

Guy had to settle for his sadistic butchering in a suburban home at the hands of the Mexican drug dealers he betrayed, suffering the ultimate indignity of getting finished off with his own gun. Not the Tony Montana blaze of cinematic fireworks he watched so many times, but I'm sure he wasn't thinking of movies in those last moments.

And Mindy ended up with me after all in my normal neighborhood with the normal life I had to offer. All that's left of her with all that's left of me.

So that's it. No one yelled "Cut" but the last scene is over. Plot points and character arcs that writhed and danced on the blinding sidewalks of Las Vegas like severed power lines drop lifelessly underfoot. The sets have been struck, blown up with dynamite, no less, while the final song is crooned by the coolest ghost in a long-gone lounge.

It's a wrap, The End, and I watch the credits roll up the screen like the last rites to a movie I didn't want to live anymore.

Also by John Kestner

Yesterday Rules

Thank You

Thank you for taking the time to read Vegas Working Girl. If you enjoyed it, please consider telling your friends or posting a short review. Word of mouth is an author's best friend and much appreciated.

Thank you.

John Kestner

About the Author

John Kestner was born and raised in Ohio, sometime after the War Between the States and before cable TV (there are areas still representing both eras). He attended Wright State University (Film/Partying) and Ohio University in Athens (Literature/Creative Writing/Partying) before heading west to Arizona.

A search for employment and a mild curiosity about the inner workings of a nuclear power plant led him to the Palo Verde Nuclear Generating Station, the world's largest nuclear plant (after Chernobyl blew up, of course). While "keeping the world safe for nuclear power," Kestner has written over 35 feature film screenplays, nearly three-quarters of them winning or placing in int'l and national screenwriting competitions.

John Kestner won Best Original Screenplay for Happy Camp at the 2017 London Independent Film Awards, was an Official Finalist (Comedy) for Little Red Pill at the 2017 Cannes Screenplay Contest, was also a two-time Platinum Award Winner for The Hard Moon Wolves and Magnum Eight at the Worldfest Houston Int'l Film Festival, and won the Golden Ace Award for Powerball at the 2010 Las Vegas Film Festival Screenplay Competition, as well as winning and placing in dozens of others.

His first novel, Vegas Working Girl, about some really

stupid behavior in Sin City in the 1980s, will be published in December 2017.

Find him online:
https://citylightspress.com/authors/john-kestner/
http://www.facebook.com/john.kestner
http://twitter.com/J_R_Kestner

www.ingramcontent.com/pod-product-compliance
Lightning Source LLC
Chambersburg PA
CBHW030635020726
47493CB00006B/1732